THE SILENT FRIEND

ALISON STOCKHAM

First published in Great Britain in 2023 by Boldwood Books Ltd.

Copyright © Alison Stockham, 2023

Cover Design: 12 Orchards Ltd.

Cover Photography: Pexels

The moral right of Alison Stockham to be identified as the author of this work has been asserted in accordance with the Copyright, Designs and Patents Act 1988.

All rights reserved. No part of this book may be reproduced in any form or by any electronic or mechanical means, including information storage and retrieval systems, without written permission from the author, except for the use of brief quotations in a book review.

This book is a work of fiction and, except in the case of historical fact, any resemblance to actual persons, living or dead, is purely coincidental.

Every effort has been made to obtain the necessary permissions with reference to copyright material, both illustrative and quoted. We apologise for any omissions in this respect and will be pleased to make the appropriate acknowledgements in any future edition.

A CIP catalogue record for this book is available from the British Library.

Paperback ISBN 978-1-80426-001-2

Large Print ISBN 978-1-80426-002-9

Hardback ISBN 978-1-80426-000-5

Ebook ISBN 978-1-80426-004-3

Kindle ISBN 978-1-80426-003-6

Audio CD ISBN 978-1-80415-995-8

MP3 CD ISBN 978-1-80415-996-5

Digital audio download ISBN 978-1-80415-997-2

Boldwood Books Ltd
23 Bowerdean Street
London SW6 3TN
www.boldwoodbooks.com

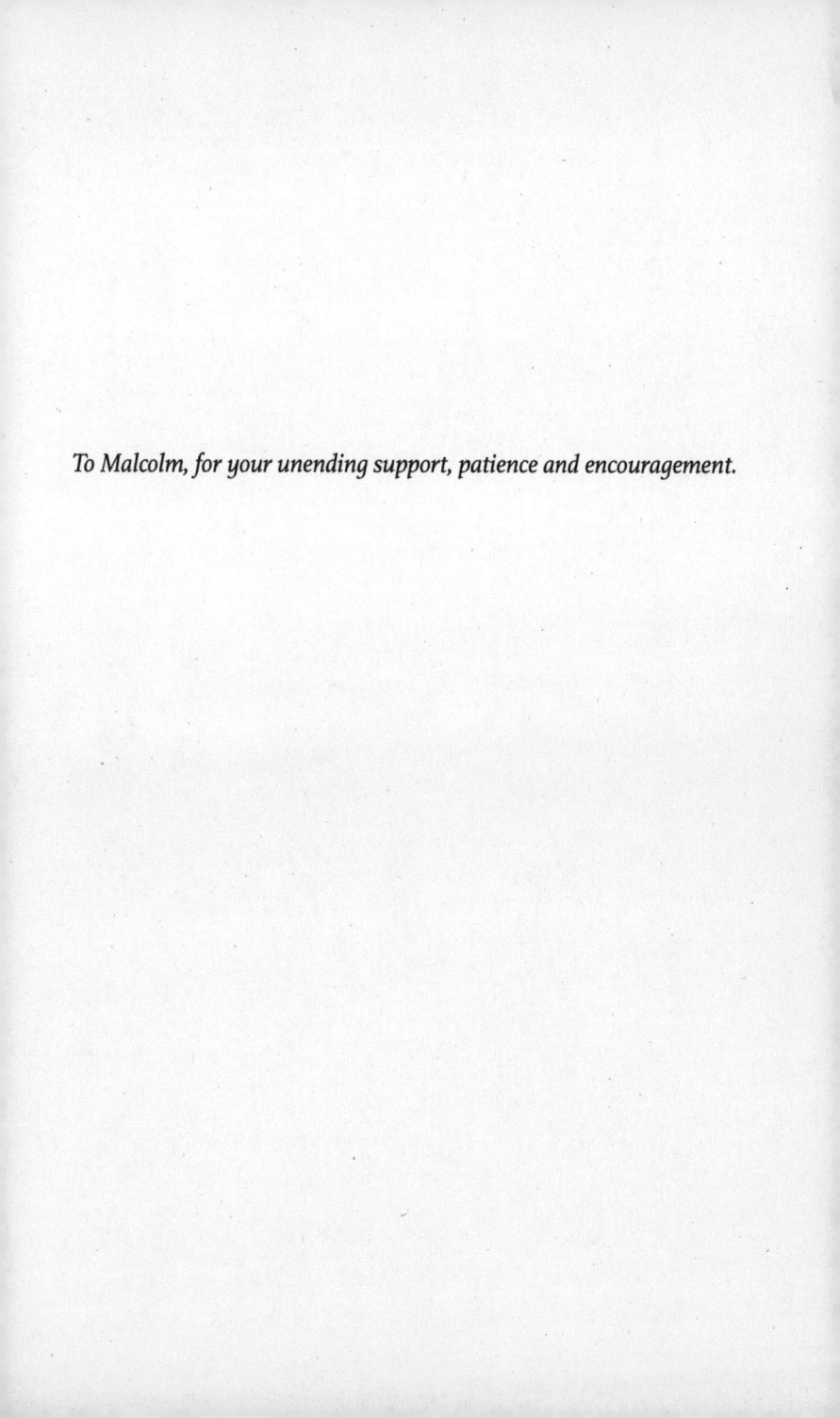

To Malcolm, for your unending support, patience and encouragement.

1

PRESENT DAY

She was alone. The water was warm and comforting as Louise lay in the bath. She adjusted position, shifting her weight to create ripples in its surface, moving its warmth over her skin in waves. She breathed in.

She listened.

Nothing.

The flat was silent. She breathed out and pushed herself completely under the surface. The sound of her own heartbeat pulsing in her ears reminded her that she was still alive. She might always be alone, but she was still here, albeit out of her depth. Suddenly a spark of terror flickered inside her without warning. She tried so hard to push the anxiety away – that constant creeping sense that something was about to go badly wrong; or had already done so but you have yet to learn exactly what. It was always there, but Louise tried to push it to the very edges of her thoughts.

Everything around you goes wrong, doesn't it?

She squeezed her closed eyes tighter and hummed to make the voice go away. No. She was not going to let it back in. Not today. Today was going to be a good day. She pushed herself further up until her face was above the water, bobbing around her jawline like a gentle lapping tide. She rested her toes on the still-warm bath tap and sighed. The pale blue shower curtain clung to the side of the bath like a chilled second skin. The whiteness of the tiles reflected the sunshine that was streaming in through the mottled window of the bathroom and the bright blue walls made Louise feel that she was somewhere in Greece – all whites, blues and sunshine. If she thought about it, it was sort of like she was on holiday. Not that she would know. She'd never been on one.

She repositioned herself in the water, moving the not-quite-dissolved bath salt grit away from her. Whoever had lived here before had left the rose-scented bath salts in the cupboard and Louise now wondered how long they'd been there. She lay back and closed her eyes, trying to empty her mind and enjoy the peace, when, at the edges of her hearing, Louise heard a commotion. Shouting. Raised voices – some angry, some strained – shattering her peace. Her eyes snapped open and she sat up, pushing herself out of the water. The coolness of the air hit her shoulders where it met the water droplets on her skin, making her shiver. She reached for the cup of tea she had left steaming on the windowsill, and as she did so, her eyes caught a glimpse of flashing blue lights and her breath stuttered as her pulse raced. Tea forgotten, she grabbed her towel, and quickly stepped out of the bath, trying not to slip on the now wet floor. Wrapping the towel around her, she rushed from the bathroom to the bedroom next door and carefully placed herself at an angle to the window where she could see but not be seen.

At a house just across the street was a police squad car, its lights still flashing despite it being stationary, the doors on the street-side flung wide open. Two uniformed officers stood on the pavement outside the house. Louise's heart rate settled a little as she watched the scene unfold across the road.

On the doorstep was a petite woman, with long blonde hair tied up in a bun. She was talking in an agitated manner to the policewoman, who was obviously trying to calm her down. The policewoman put her hand on the woman's shoulder only to have it shrugged away roughly. The woman looked behind her as a man, tall and muscular in that all-shoulders-and-no-neck way, was bundled out of the house by another officer, who looked as though he was struggling with this man's bulk. The man seemed calm, as though he was cooperating with the arresting officer and reassuring the distraught woman, and yet his feet also seemed glued to the ground, making it difficult to steer him towards the waiting car.

The blonde woman looked around her, her head flicking from side to side as if expecting someone to intervene but Louise saw the curtains move at the house next door and the outline of a person step back from the bay window. If this woman was expecting her neighbours to come to her aid, it was not looking likely. Whoever lived next door was clearly interested in what was happening but not interested in getting involved.

Suddenly aware that she had stepped closer towards her own window than she intended, Louise jumped backwards and the movement must have caught the woman's eye as her face snapped upwards and she looked what felt like directly at her. Louise froze momentarily and then stepped back into the relative darkness of the room.

Not wanting to risk being seen again, Louise walked back to the bathroom instead and surveyed the action through the frosted glass of the window there. It was just clear enough to be able to see the outline of the woman being briefly held by the outline of the man, before they were broken apart by the officers. They bundled the man into the car, placing a hand on his head to guide him into the rear seat, before closing the door, encasing him inside. The woman officer handed something, maybe paperwork or leaflets, to the woman left behind before joining her colleague in the car. They turned off the blue lights and drove away. There was a slight screech as the acceleration of the wheels grabbed at the tarmacked road and then they were gone.

Once the police had left, Louise opened the top window just enough to see better, hoping that in her distress the woman would not notice. Balancing precariously on the edge of the bath, so as to be able to get a good view but keep herself tucked out of sight, she watched as the woman stood, shocked into stillness, on her doorstep. She wrapped her arms around herself, looked up and down the street again but no one came. She looked up again at Louise's bedroom window but finding no one there, turned and went back into her house. The street fell silent again, only the faint sounds of traffic somewhere nearby, the odd bark of a dog and the tweeting of birds in the trees. It was as if the spectacle had not happened at all.

Louise had intended to try and keep a little distance; her new flat supposed to be a space where she could regroup. She needed to know where to go from here, what to do with her life.

But. What had just happened over the road?

Mind your own business, she told herself. But at the same time, she knew that she wouldn't. She couldn't. She had to know.

2

Telling herself that she should let the dust settle and keep away, it had been days since Louise had left the house and it showed. She'd done her unpacking, though there hadn't been much to unpack, and the flat was slowly beginning to look like someone lived there. It didn't matter though, no one else would see it. It had felt extravagant to buy a set of six matching cups as a house-warming gift to herself, she only needed one at a time. But now, being able to leave a cup wherever, and still have a fresh one ready for her next cuppa felt like freedom to her. She hadn't noticed the absence of such small things before.

When, unexpectedly, the doorbell rang, Louise, still in the jogging bottoms and T-shirt that she had slept in, hair scrunched into a messy ponytail and with as yet un-cleaned teeth, froze to the spot.

Who? she thought. *I don't know anyone. Or rather no one knows me.* Her mind flickered in panic as to who it could be before she realised that she had told no one where she was. The only person who knew was the letting agent and they had to give her notice if they were coming round. She felt her heart rate steady as she realised it'd likely be someone trying to sell her something she had no inclination to buy, whether that be windows or religion, and she could just ignore it until they went away. She turned to pick up last night's socks, which were still scrunched up on the sofa where she had taken them off while watching some terrible film, when the doorbell rang again. Realising that she'd have to shoo them away, Louise tried to pull herself together. She straightened out her T-shirt, redid her ponytail – hoping it would miraculously make it looked more washed than it was – and went to answer the door.

As she walked down the cheaply carpeted stairs, her feet making the hollow space beneath echo with the reverberations of her stride, she could see the outline of her visitor through the frosted glass of the half-glazed door. It was the woman from across the street. The one whose partner had been hauled off by the police the other day. Louise's throat went dry. Was she here to tear a strip off her for being nosy? Was she going to ask questions that Louise did not want to answer?

She was holding something that she was shifting in her hands. What was it? Aware that she'd been standing in clear sight of this woman and yet not opening the door, Louise stumbled forward and fumbled with the latch. She swung the door open too enthusiastically, its uPVC door weighing far less than her old home's heavy wooden one and the effect was as if she had said 'ta-da!' as she greeted her guest. The woman smiled a little at this and it put Louise immediately at ease. The smile on her face suggested that she was not here for a fight, and if she had been, her choice of what looked like a tin of biscuits suggested that she did not choose weapons well.

'Hi,' the woman said, smiling and holding her gift out to Louise. Despite the smile, you could see how tired and drained she was; her skin had a greyish tone to it. She was well groomed otherwise. You could tell that she took care over her appearance and that, in normal circumstances, she would be stunning. Louise reached out to take the present, not sure of what to do, of how she was supposed to react. As she took it, she noticed the slight curve to this woman's abdomen and Louise realised that she was pregnant.

'Hi... thank you,' Louise said before realising she needed to step up a gear. She was being weird. Something in her brain shifted and the little switch she turned on when she needed to be the other her clicked in her mind.

'Thank you! This is really kind of you. I'm Louise, I just moved in.' Why did she use her real name? That wasn't wise.

'I know,' the woman said, still smiling, 'I saw you the other day when...' A blush rose on her cheeks, editing out the grey and giving a glimpse of how beautiful she would normally be. 'Anyway, I'm Isabelle. Welcome. I like to welcome newcomers to the street, as it took me a while to meet our neighbours when we moved in.' Her mouth hardened into a line, which Louise took as resentment. She sniffed away tears that were clearly trying to spill out of her eyes.

Louise didn't know what she should say or do. She'd moved here intending to keep her head down for a while, but Isabelle was on the doorstep, pregnant and upset, and Louise was suddenly overcome with loneliness. She'd not spoken to another human being in... How long had it been? She realised she couldn't say and so she found herself opening her mouth and asking, 'Would you like to come in for a cup of tea?'

Before she could undo it or talk Isabelle out of it, the woman replied, 'I'd love to, thanks,' and stepped over the doorstep.

Louise skirted in front of her, making sure not to brush by too close. She wasn't sure if she smelled as bad as she feared she might and she suddenly realised that her embracing the freedom to slob had left her flat looking in an utter state and one that she did not want Isabelle to see. She raced to the top of the stairs and called back behind her, 'Just give me a minute? I wasn't expecting guests and it's a mess in here,' as she dashed into the living room and, grateful for not having got rid of all the cardboard boxes from moving, threw socks, unfolded clothes, old magazines, a half-empty pizza box and some empty wine bottles into one, then kicked it to one side of the room to appear as though she had not yet unpacked it. She then gathered all the mugs and glasses and dumped them into the sink and ran the tap on full, hiding them under a layer of bubbles from the dollop of washing-up liquid she drizzled over them.

She ran to the bathroom and rubbed toothpaste over her gums – where *was* her toothbrush? – sprayed deodorant all over herself, some dry shampoo into her hair then walked back into the hallway to invite Isabelle into the living room, hoping that the fug of scented aerosols that now surrounded her didn't make her gag. Pregnant women had an overly sensitive sense of smell, didn't they? She didn't want to make her first guest sick. Especially one as thoughtful as Isabelle, who had walked upstairs slowly enough to have given Louise the time to prepare.

'Come on in. Sorry about the mess, I am still unpacking,' Louise said, startled by how much she sounded like her mother, who had always been uncomfortable with strangers in the house.

'Sure, it's fine. We've not been here all that long either so I remember the chaos of moving house,' Isabelle said, though the smile that she had displayed when Louise had opened the door had dropped from her eyes and now her mouth was strained, the corners trying to pull themselves upwards but failing. She looked around her, unsure where to sit. Louise plumped up the cushions on the sofa, which had seen better days, and gestured Isabelle towards it.

'Tea? Coffee? No, wait, I haven't got coffee. Tea?' Louise stammered.

'Do you have any decaf?' Isabelle asked, in a voice that sounded as though she already knew the answer.

Louise shook her head. As a host she knew she was not making a good impression. She began reprimanding herself but then reminded herself that she didn't necessarily want to. She didn't want to make friends, she didn't need anyone checking up on her. She let the issue of a drink pass and a silence settled over the room. Louise was practised at silence. She knew how to handle it and how to use it as needed. She could make a silence feel comfortable, amiable, like nothing needed to be said, or she could make it uncomfortable, threatening, upsetting. It all depended on how you used your body language. Isabelle was twisting her wedding ring on her finger and looking around her but at a speed that suggested she wasn't actually looking.

What do I want? Louise asked herself. The answer came as it always did – information. Information gave you power and power was what Louise had grown up lacking, forever searching for it ever since. Power and control. And so she asked the one question that she knew Isabelle would not want to answer.

'So. What was going on with the police the other day? I saw them take... your husband away.' Louise's voice was light, innocent.

Isabelle swallowed and cleared her throat.

'You did see? I thought you did.' She looked at Louise a little accusingly, which Louise thought was unfair.

'Yes, I was just out of the bath. I didn't want to interfere.'

Isabelle straightened her back coolly but soon enough her eyes filled with tears, though she did not let them fall, she swallowed them down.

'Bit emotional, sorry. Carl always tells me to stop being so sensitive but I can't help it. It's even worse now I'm pregnant.' She patted her stomach, which made her smile, briefly.

'Carl...?'

'My husband. He's the man the police took away. It's all a mistake. I'm sure of that. He called his solicitor and she's sorting it all out for him.'

'So is he back home then?'

'Oh,' Isabelle said, her previous certainty deflating like a balloon with a leak. 'No. No, they've kept him for questioning.'

'Must be serious then?' She paused to allow Isabelle time to share what it was that Carl had been arrested for. She didn't. Louise let the question hang for as long as it took to make it clear that Isabelle wasn't going to provide more information without further questions. Louise wanted to know but she was going to have to ask.

'What have they accused him of?' Louise was keeping it as light as possible, as though Carl had been questioned for something minor, despite his still being held suggesting it was far from that.

'He... um... they said that he...' Isabelle choked and then burst into tears.

Louise looked around the flat in horror, wondering if she had any tissues anywhere. She jumped up from her chair and left the room, returning with a roll of toilet paper which she handed to Isabelle with an apologetic shrug.

'Sorry, all I have.'

Isabelle sniffed and took it, pulling a section from the roll, blowing her nose on it and tucking it away in a pocket. Louise noticed she was a pretty crier. Her face had flushed but in all the right places, not at all blotchy, more like someone had applied highlighter. Somehow her upset had made Isabelle more attractive. Is that why some women attract men who want to rescue them? Because at their most vulnerable they are also their most transcendent?

'They said he was involved in a robbery,' Isabelle said and then paused like she was waiting for Louise to look shocked. She was not rewarded. Louise had not had a sheltered life. 'They say he... they... that he...'

'You don't have to say if you don't want to,' Louise said. She was beginning to feel sorry both for Isabelle, who was looking more fragile the longer she stayed, and for herself, for getting mixed up in this. If it was as horrific as Isabelle seemed to be suggesting, it'd be all over the local rags anyway.

'They say he attacked a man. An elderly man. And now he's in hospital and they don't think he'll make it. But it's not true! Carl wouldn't do something like that! My Carl is a good man, a kind man. When I told him we were going to have a baby, he cried with happiness. He just wouldn't!'

'Why do they think it was him then? Could they have got him mixed up with someone else?'

'Apparently a delivery driver saw him running away and realised something was wrong. But the delivery driver must be mistaken. It wasn't him!'

Louise put her hand comfortingly on Isabelle's shoulder. Whatever the truth was, this was a pregnant woman, upset and in shock and Louise felt her heart go out to her. She seemed to have absolutely no idea what she might be mixed up in. Isabelle turned to Louise and started sobbing. Louise, unsure how best to respond, just held her while she cried.

After a while Isabelle's sobs subsided and she sat back up, blew her nose multiple times on the loo roll and then looked up at Louise.

'Sorry. You must think we're awful! Carl arrested and me in tears in your flat. It's just, we've been together forever. This is the first time I've been apart from him and it's all a bit much. It's like a bit of me is missing and I don't know when he's coming home. Or... or if he's coming home. Last week, my life was perfect and now? Now it's a car crash!' She burst into tears again but swallowed them quickly and regained her composure. Louise sat and listened.

'Sorry. I... sorry. I meant to come and welcome you and now you're probably wondering where the hell you've moved to! It's just no one... no one from the street has come to see how I am. I called my friends and they're "busy". We moved here from East London and it's like we've left the bloody country! It's '"too far" apparently, we've crossed the river and that's that. It's like everyone is assuming he's guilty and condemning me alongside him. It's not fair!' She pouted. 'And anyway, he's innocent.'

Louise nodded. 'People don't know what to do, so they just do nothing. Embarrassment, grief. It's all the same. They don't know what to do with their discomfort so they avoid it.'

I've never been comfortable so it'd be all the same to me, she thought.

'It's exactly that. But it hurts. They are supposed to be my neighbours, my community, and they're not here.'

Louise smiled supportively. Not knowing who Isabelle's neighbours were, she didn't want to comment. Speaking unwisely was often a bad idea, she knew that from experience. She knew she should let Isabelle go home, now that she had vented a little and Louise had found out a few things about her. Softly, softly, and all that. And yet. Yet Louise didn't want her to go.

'Sure you don't want that tea?'

'Oh, OK, why not? It's not like it's neat vodka, is it?!' Isabelle laughed and it lit up her face. Louise could see why Carl had chosen her. She seemed kind, genuine, open. Everything that Louise was not. Louise felt a flicker of jealousy. It was like school PE all over again, never being the one who got to hold the trophy. Or, in this case, be the trophy. Maybe Louise could learn from Isabelle what it was that made people choose her. Maybe if she got to know her, she'd work out the secret.

Louise went to her kitchen, sweeping empty packets and

crumbs into the bin. Nothing like the eyes of another to let you see your own filth. She'd only been in the flat a few days and it was a bombsite. She needed to lift her game else she would sink under the weight of her own inertia. She felt like she was in limbo, not knowing which direction to take. She'd moved to try and feel like she was in some sort of control over her own life, to try and feel connected to something, to anything. Now here she was, getting tangled up in a drama that wasn't strictly hers. Would she always have to be mixed up with something complicated or be utterly alone? Wasn't there something in the middle? Other people managed to have that. A normal life, boring some might say, but with friends, family. She'd never had that; she didn't know what it was like. But she knew she wanted to try it out. Just once.

She glanced back towards the living room as she waited for the kettle to boil. She could just about see Isabelle sat on the sofa, calmer now, glancing out of the window across the street to her own house. Maybe this flat was a refuge for her too. Maybe this was the place where everyone could take a step back from their own carnage and start again.

3

SEVEN YEARS AGO

Louise lay on her bed, still in her school uniform. The door to her bedroom, the box room of the house, was closed but she could still hear her parents fighting downstairs. Their dramatic voices, raised and emotional, were drifting through the floorboards. Their usual weekend argument had dragged through into the week and Louise was stuck in her room until they were done. Her stomach growled at her and she looked at the clock – 7.30 p.m. They'd been at it for hours now with no sign of letting up. They were going round and round and round, the threat levels rising.

'You're seeing her again, I know you are!'

'How many times, woman? I am not! It was ONE time and one time only! How long is it going to take you to get over it?!'

'You betrayed me! I don't think I'll ever get over it. I will DIE not being over it!'

'Shall I help? Or maybe I'll die first, just to get you to shut up!'

'You wouldn't dare.'

'Wouldn't I?'

'You're too weak to even try it.'

'Don't push me. You know how that goes. Anyway, you'd be a sad, single mother. Don't wish that on yourself.'

There was a pause. Whenever her dad reminded her mum of her parental responsibilities, her mother would either explode in a rage or dissolve into floods of tears, and eventually that sorrow or anger would make its way upstairs and she would take it out on Louise.

At the continued pause in the fighting downstairs, Louise sat up, pulling her knees up to her chest and pulling her school jumper down over them. It was her defensive position, as though she could pull her head down into the garment and disappear. Making herself as small as possible. Making herself not exist. It was what she believed her parents really wanted. She had ruined their glamorous, carefree existence by being born and they took no care whatsoever to hide this from her or to deny it. They were doing the bare minimum and waiting until she was old enough to leave home. She was fifteen. Not long now. Her mother would bemoan how long it was taking.

I'll be so old by the time you move out. I'll have more wrinkles and grey hairs than invitations at this rate.

Once I'm free, I'll have forgotten how to be.

You have no idea how much I have given up for you.

Louise had learned early on not to engage when her mother was in her maudlin frame of mind. It never went down well. How could it? When you have to justify your own existence to the one person who is supposed to love you unconditionally it's never going to work. They will always be able to scoop your soul from your bones and fold your heart up like an ordinance survey map until you are flattened and stored away.

It had always felt as though she was an imposter in her own home. A temporary tenant getting in the way of her parents' lives. They did not neglect her in the sense that she had enough food, clean clothes, her shoes always replaced as soon as they started to pinch. She had brushed hair and brushed teeth; dental check-ups and birthday presents. But it always felt like they lived their lives in a virtual departure lounge, killing time until Louise was old enough to board the plane and take off, leaving her parents to wander back home without her.

There was movement from downstairs. Low murmured voices and the sound of the front door opening and closing behind someone. It was closed firmly but not slammed. That meant it was her father who had gone out. Possibly to see the woman he had just denied existed. She existed. Her dad was not as smart or as discreet as he thought himself to be. He just gaslighted her mum into believing what she so desperately wanted to be true – that he was utterly faithful, she was just paranoid. But Louise knew the truth because she had followed him a few times. She had used her ability to make herself small to see where he went, who he met. He had a key to her house. Maybe he had a whole other family. Who knows? He didn't really want this one, would he really want another one?

Louise's house held a lot of secrets and sorrows and she took them all inside herself. She was the cause, wasn't she? She had ruined her parents' glamorous love affair by turning up and shifting the balance. Sometimes she wished she'd never been born at all. Living a life without love is hard. Even when you know you don't deserve it, when you can't actually put your finger on exactly what it is you are without, something at a very human level knows that it's missing. It's the smile at school pick up that you don't receive while your classmates do. It's the 'how was your day?' that never gets asked. It's the 'tell me your dreams' that isn't invited. It's knowing that nobody cares if you die. Not really, even yourself.

So when the door handle started to push down as her mum came into her room, Louise braced herself for another conversation where she had to try not to cry as her mum wished her existence away in order to comfort herself somehow. Louise took a deep breath and reminded herself that she could move away soon. It wouldn't be long.

'Lou? You here?' her mum asked gingerly.

'Yeah'

She walked into the room and sat on the edge of the bed. Her eyes were red and her make-up had smudged. Her thick black hair was pinned up but tendrils had escaped and draped around her face. She looked as though she had just returned from a big night out, worse for wear and ready for bed. She tried to smile but nothing reached her eyes.

'Hungry?'

'A bit.' Louise tried to sound unbothered but her stomach growled loudly at just the wrong moment.

There was a fleeting look of guilt that flashed across her mum's face as Louise realised she must have worked out that it had been hours since Louise had returned from school, found her parents at each other's throats and escaped to her room. It happened so often that Louise had taken to stashing spare food up here whenever she could. Once she managed to sneak a fiver from her dad's wallet, hoping he wouldn't notice, and had stocked up on the cheapest things she could find at the corner shop. Noodles that she sometimes rehydrated with lukewarm water from the bathroom tap, random cereal bars from brands she didn't recognise, crackers that were edible even if stale. Things to stave off the hunger until her parents remembered to feed her or stopped fighting for long enough to let her go downstairs to the kitchen to make something herself. Louise used to feel angry about it but then she realised that she was learning to be self-sufficient long before her friends would ever do. It was hard but it was making her strong.

'OK then. I'll go and make something.'

Her mum paused at the doorway, almost as though she was

going to apologise or say something to Louise. Something that might let Louise know she mattered to her, even just a little bit. Hope flickered in Louise's heart – a dangerous thing.

'Yes?' Louise asked, trying not to look as though she was asking for anything, anything at all.

'OK,' her mum repeated as she turned and walked away.

That flicker of hope withered and died. It turned in on itself and hardened inside Louise. She was alone in this world and she always would be. The sooner she accepted that wholly, the better it would be for everyone. She pulled her jumper over her head and tried beyond trying to stop the tears that now flowed down her face.

4
PRESENT DAY

'Did you want brights? Or pastels?'

'Um. Oh. I don't know. They're for someone I don't really know. I've not done this before,' Louise stuttered at the florist, who looked at her with a confused expression. But it was true. Louise really had never bought flowers for someone before. Or at least, not as a grown-up. She'd once persuaded her dad to help her pick flowers for her mum, but she'd apparently chosen badly as her mum barely registered them as she stuffed them in their packaging into some water. They had stayed forgotten in the vase until they'd withered and died and the water had turned to a murky brown that made the room smell of pond water and her mum had thrown them away. Louise had thought that flowers were a bad gift – *here have some dying plants* – for a long time after that. Until she'd realised it was her mother, not the gift that was wrong.

'Well, I could do you a seasonal bouquet with hints of brights in a more neutral collection, would that work do you think? Or tulips with some quieter foliage? Pretty but not in your face? A good compromise perhaps?'

The lady seemed to have clocked that Louise was nervous and

was being gentle with her. Louise was touched. Kindness was rare as far as she was concerned. Few people genuinely cared about total strangers and some didn't even care about those close to them. Most people were out for what they could get.

And yet, here she was, buying flowers for Isabelle. Stepping outside her own comfort zone for someone else. What was all that about?

After Isabelle had visited last week, and by accident, had stayed for a long time, Louise had spent the following days realising something. She missed her. She had enjoyed chatting about not a whole lot with her, and hearing about her and Carl, about their life together. It was like looking at the life she thought she wanted, like looking at the life she could have in this new part of town. She had assumed that she and Isabelle would not get on – they seemed too different – but had been proven wrong. They had talked for hours. Or, more truthfully, Isabelle had talked and Louise had mostly listened. Isabelle clearly didn't want to go home to an empty house and she only left as it had got to dinner time. Louise had felt too awkward to offer to cook for her so she could stay. She didn't want to seem needy.

The day after, the flat, which had seemed so cocooning, had suddenly seemed empty. She had spent the day unpacking and tidying in case Isabelle popped back over. She'd gone to the shops and got some things in. She could get away with it being a mess that first day and lacking the basics but if she came round again, then Isabelle would know that it was just how Louise lived. Existed. And somehow Louise didn't want her to think that, didn't want to see confusion, then understanding and then pity in Isabelle's eyes. She couldn't bear it. She wanted Isabelle to like her. This was new. Louise had only survived her childhood and school by not caring if anyone liked her or not.

As another day passed, it was clear that Isabelle would not

come round again without an invitation. It would be pushy, or rude or impolite, and Louise knew that Isabelle was none of those things. She was a class act.

So Louise realised if she was going to learn any more about her, if they were going to be friends even, Louise was going to have to go to her. She knew that she couldn't turn up uninvited and empty-handed. That would have felt even weirder than doing this in the first place. And so. Neutral with brights it was to be.

'There you go! That'll be £28.99 please,' the florist said with a flourish as she handed Louise a bouquet bigger than her face. Louise inwardly winced. Though these days she was fine for money, she hadn't yet lost that fear of not having enough... Spending nearly thirty quid on flowers felt obnoxious, unwise. What would she have to forgo to even it out? Her panic subsided when she realised that she wouldn't have to miss out. She could simply afford it. She rummaged in her jeans pocket and pulled out some crumpled notes and handed them over. The lady looked bemused again as she flattened them out on the surface of the counter before handing Louise her change.

'Hope they like them, whoever they're for!' she trilled, and moved to the next customer in line.

Louise took the flowers and headed out of the shop, suspecting that the jangle of the bell on the door as it opened and closed behind her was the signal for those left in the shop to gossip about what a strange woman she was. This was another reason that Louise didn't do things like this. She did not want to be noticed but to be no more than a flicker in anyone's memory. It was easier that way.

All her instincts were telling her to stop being ridiculous and go home with her overpriced flowers and keep on keeping herself to herself, but as she turned into her street, with the blossoming trees in front of the neat row of semi-detached houses on one side and her flat on the other, something in her shifted. She felt lighter somehow, almost at home. And so instead of scurrying back to her flat and spending the day barely watching terrible TV until it was time to sleep again, she turned right not left and stood outside Isabelle's house. Something in her stomach dropped when she remembered that she only knew which one was Isabelle's house from watching her husband being arrested. Would he be home? It had been longer than thirty-six hours or whatever timescale they could hold you without charge. Had they charged him? Perhaps she should go home? But her hand rose and knocked on the door all the same and Louise noticed how it was shaking as she did so. This was a clash of worlds.

'Oh, hi! I...' Isabelle said, surprised, as she opened the door. It was clear that she had not been expecting visitors. She was still in her pyjamas, even though it was early afternoon, and it looked as though she had not slept well, if at all. Her face was ashen, her hair pulled back and her eyes were red and puffy. Even a relative stranger like Louise could see that she was not in a good way.

'Oh, I'm sorry—' Louise smiled, working hard to keep the shock off her face '—is now a bad time? Are you not feeling so well?' Always give someone a respectable reason for their squalor, she reminded herself, no one likes feeling caught off guard and far from their best. Make yourself their confidante, not their judge.

Isabelle tried to smile back but the effort was clearly too much. She lifted her shoulders to shrug but that seemed like too much as well.

'Sorry, it's been... it's been...' and she started to cry.

At first Louise considered apologising and leaving Isabelle to her own sorrow but something stopped her. Being left was something Louise had too much experience in, and frankly, most of the time it had been the wrong thing. People needed people. People needed to be seen and they needed to be heard. It was as simple as that and Louise had learned well how much people are willing to give in order to get that. Her instincts kicked in and she took a step forward, crossing the threshold without being asked.

'Hey, hey, it's OK,' Louise said. She placed the flowers on the mirrored hallway table and gathered Isabelle into a hug. Isabelle did not resist and Louise felt her slump into her, as though she was now the only thing stopping her from collapsing into a heap on the hallway tiles.

The two women staggered, Isabelle still holding on, through to the living room. Louise looked around the room. Although there were echoes of the self-neglect that Isabelle had witnessed that first day at Louise's flat, the room itself was a totally different kettle of fish. The sofa was not a seventies brown corduroy hand-me-down that had seen better days but a plush light grey velvet with a soft mustard-coloured blanket draped over the side like that thick, soft icing you get on shop-bought birthday cakes.

'Here, sit down, catch your breath,' Louise said as she manoeuvred Isabelle onto the sofa. She felt odd man-handling her, an almost complete stranger, with an intimacy she was wholly unused to. Isabelle didn't seem to mind. She clearly had a totally different consideration when it came to personal space.

'Thanks. Sorry. I just... it's just been a horrible few days and I'm... I'm really tired and nauseous all the time from the baby. And my hormones and... Carl, well he usually looks after me and makes sure I have something to stave off the sickness but...'

Louise could see the tears starting to form in Isabelle's eyes and she yabbered at her to try to stop them. Normally, she could sit with someone's pain but here for some reason, she wanted to fix it instead.

'Don't worry. It's a lot, isn't it? Stuff has been going on that's for sure.'

She wanted to find out what had happened, where Carl was,

what the situation was, but she also didn't want to pry. She thought of how she got people talking, what usually made people open up to her.

'Let me go and pop the kettle on, eh? Everything feels better with a cup of tea, even if you don't drink it. Decaf, right?' She smiled encouragingly at Isabelle, who seemed resistant at first, probably feeling it should be her hosting. Louise saw the moment Isabelle relented and decided to let herself be looked after, even if it was by someone she barely knew.

Louise walked through the open-plan ground floor, the front and back rooms having been knocked together to form a long, open and airy living room that met a dining area before a doorway into the kitchen. It must have been extended because the kitchen was huge and went all the way across the width of the house. Louise looked around. The cupboards had glass fronts, displaying pastel-coloured plates and shiny glasses. There were quirky artworks on the brightly painted walls and a quote in neon pink next to the cooker about the kitchen being the heart of the home. The room had obviously been recently decorated by someone with a feminine touch and someone who believed in the importance of home. It was pristine. Isabelle had either used precious energy to clean relentlessly, or she had not fed herself properly in days.

'Where would I find the tea bags?' Louise called back to Isabelle. She'd already seen them by the kettle in clearly labelled jars but took the opportunity to open cupboards for a look, the noise of them being opened and closed covered by the innocent question. There wasn't much to learn – other than there were mostly branded items, no supermarket own labels. Whoever did the shopping did not worry about money. The food was very British, nothing too unrecognisable. She suspected that Carl was an HP and ketchup sort of man.

'Just by the kettle – in the blue jars,' Isabelle called back. She sounded calmer than before, the waver in her voice now gone, replaced by the voice of someone at home, someone relaxed.

'Oh yes, I see them!'

Louise made tea quickly, noting the lack of food in the fridge when she used the last of the milk. She carried the mugs back to the front room, where Isabelle had curled up on the sofa, tucking her legs underneath her and draping a blanket over herself. Louise placed the cup on the table to one side of the sofa and, cupping her own in her hands, lowered herself into the high-backed grey tweed chair across the room.

'This place is like a hotel or something!' Louise said admiringly. It was glossy, curated, like nowhere she'd ever lived.

Isabelle blushed. 'Thanks. It was a real fixer-upper when we moved in. A "family home in the making" the estate agent said.' She smiled as she hugged her burgeoning bump. 'It was my project to oversee the work. Carl didn't want me to do any heavy lifting, but he let me design it however I wanted. Said it was my gift, being able to see things as they could be. Like when I first met him he said. I see potential. I love interior design, I read all the magazines for tips. I think a home should be as nice as you can make it, don't you? Oh...' She trailed off as she realised her faux pas, considering the faded beige-ness of Louise's flat.

Louise shook her head kindly.

'No, it's OK. I've literally just moved in. No time for blankets or nice lampshades yet and as I'm renting I won't get to paint it. I don't know if I'll be there long to be honest.'

'Oh?' Isabelle looked genuinely saddened by this and Louise's heart lifted. She wanted her to stay. She wasn't an uninvited guest; she was an unexpected guest. Those were two very different things. Louise wasn't sure what to share of herself with Isabelle, she wasn't used to sharing much at all but she wanted to get Isabelle talking.

'Yes, I don't tend to stick around most places long. I get...' She struggled for the right word, one that didn't give much away. 'I get restless. I like to move around. It's why I don't have too much stuff that's mine. Too difficult to pack up and go.' Louise nodded, liking this positive framing of the life she had stumbled into. It made her sound nomadic, free, like a bohemian spirit who went where the wind took her. Isabelle didn't need to know that she'd never lived more than fifty miles from where she grew up and she'd only got that far because she got tired of living in fear of bumping into her parents and having to cope with them not begging her to come home to them.

'How about you? How long have you and...'

'Carl.'

'Oh yes, Carl.' Louise said casually, like she'd forgotten his name. 'How long have you two lived here?'

Isabelle sat up straighter, a flicker of happiness crossing her face as she thought back.

'Just over a year. I had just finished my job. I'd hated it and we knew we were going to try for a baby, so Carl suggested that I quit and renovate the house while we waited to get pregnant. We moved out here for the space and the green. Better for the kids.'

'Kids?'

Isabelle laughed. 'We're aiming for a football team! I've always wanted children, it's the only thing I've ever wanted to do really, be a mum. Carl gets that, never pushed me to find anything else. He's happy to come home and I'm here and the house is nice and dinner is ready. Quite traditional really.'

'Must be nice to have someone to look after and someone who looks after you,' Louise said, a wistful expression on her face.

'It is. And now I'm finally pregnant.' She patted her stomach, her face glowing with happiness suddenly. And then her expression changed, her voice faltered and it was as though the sun had gone behind clouds that had suddenly draped the horizon in gloom. Isabelle sat, silent, deep in thought. When she looked up again, she jumped as though she had forgotten Louise was still there.

'You all right?' Louise asked, beginning to think she should leave. It was upsetting Isabelle her being there, asking questions. But she also wanted to know more about Carl and their situation and she had barely scratched the surface.

'Yeah. It's just really nice to talk with someone. We're a long way from our old home and I don't know many people here. I've been busy with the house. It's been hard to meet anyone. The house is ready for guests but no one's been visiting!' She laughed sadly, and looked at the floor.

Isabelle nodded and Louise took the opportunity to ask.

'So, how long have you and Carl been together?'

Louise was intrigued. Isabelle seemed so quiet and such a perfectionist that it surprised her that she would be with someone who had been arrested. He wasn't home, so she assumed he had either been charged or they were still questioning him. They don't do that for petty crime, it must be serious whatever it was they were accusing him of.

'Oh forever. We went to high school together.' She laughed, the sun reappearing on her face. She clearly loved him. 'It sounds silly, but he's my only ever boyfriend. Been together since I was fourteen, he was sixteen. I just knew. He's always had this tough exterior but he's so soft really. He's always looked after me and treated me like a princess. Nothing is too much for me. He wants me to be happy and he does everything he can do to make me happy. I've told him, just him is enough but he won't listen. He's so driven, he wants me to have the best of everything. It's the same with the baby. Ever since I got pregnant he's been working harder, so they won't ever not have what they want.'

This was the moment. Louise knew she had to ask. She couldn't ask exactly what she wanted to, but she could ask this and it just might tell her what she needed to know.

'What does he do?'

Isabelle half giggled, 'You'll think I'm such a ditz but the silly thing is I'm not entirely sure! He's an entrepreneur so he's always got several different projects on the go. He deals in antiques mostly though. He loved history and all that at school. He's self-employed, self-taught,' she said proudly. 'He's often brought home some really interesting old stuff, but he sells it on pretty quickly. As you can see, our own taste is quite modern. Light and uncluttered. Sort of Scandi.'

'It's nice, not dark like some old houses like this can be.' Louise nodded and they both fell silent. Both knew of the elephant in the room, but neither wanted to be the one to broach it first. Louise didn't want to seem like a gossip but she also needed to know what she may or may not be getting herself involved with here. Being dragged into a new drama was not her plan. But she liked Isabelle, something about her felt recognisable to her, though she couldn't put her finger on what.

'So...' Louise chewed her lip. It had to be done. 'Is Carl still...?' Louise stopped, she didn't need to say any more and she could see Isabelle's shutters come down. Her whole body language changed from open to shut, from light-hearted to cold.

'Yes. They've charged him and are keeping him in custody. Like he's a flight risk! It's ridiculous. He's not going to leave his pregnant wife and run off somewhere! Jane's trying to sort it all out. It's such a mess.'

Louise felt herself untense. She hadn't realised she had been tense until her muscles relaxed. She had clearly been worried that Carl was about to walk through the door and find her there. He wasn't someone to be on the wrong side of, however Isabelle tried to paint him as a loveable rogue. All the other evidence Louise had pointed to quite the opposite. At least now she knew he wasn't about to come home and kick off.

'He didn't do it. They've got the wrong man,' Isabelle continued. She crossed her arms in front of her looking almost petulant. 'His solicitor said they've got nothing solid on him, nothing but... conjecture. They've charged him with artificial burglary. No, no hang on... burglary artifice. And assault or something. Can you believe that? My Carl? He wouldn't hurt a fly!' She was raging now, her face flushed and her eyes sparking with fury. 'This delivery guy said he saw Carl running away from the "scene"—' she made quotation marks with her fingers '—and they've found Carl's DNA on some items of value in the house and suddenly he's a criminal?! I mean, yes, he is always late for everything, a ridiculous optimist when it comes to timing so he's always running everywhere cos he needs to be somewhere else ASAP and yes, his DNA would be on valuable items, he's an antiques dealer, he was there to see about buying some of this man's things. He isn't denying *being* there. Elderly people like to be able to release the money in their stuff so they can enjoy their retirement. Lots of Carl's customers are elderly.'

'He didn't do it then? Didn't attack the man?'

'No! Of course not! It's all just a huge misunderstanding and hopefully Jane, Carl's lawyer, will sort it all out soon.' Isabelle huffed, almost looking like the fourteen-year-old girl she had just told Louise about.

'And the man? The elderly man? How is he? Do you know?' Louise's voice cracked at this. The thought of someone's grandad being attacked, it made her so angry and so sad. Her own grandpa had been the best person in her life. He'd not been there for long, he died when she was still in primary school but he was the one person who she felt really saw her, actually loved her for her and she missed him every day. The memory of him was what got her up some days, what reminded her that she was worth the life she had been given, even when she felt herself that it couldn't possibly be true.

'Oh. Yes, sorry. You must think I'm so cruel. I'm not dismissive of him at all. I am so angry that he's been attacked. They haven't told me much, but from what I've been able to find out, he's holding on. That poor man. I wish I knew more. I could send some flowers or something, though Jane told me to stay out of it. Not to muddy the waters.'

Isabelle looked at the floor and picked at her fingernails. Louise could see that her cuticles were red. It was obviously what Isabelle did when she was nervous and she had clearly been nervous a great deal this week. They looked raw. Louise pulled her sleeves down over her own scars, tiny delicate white nicks on her skin. She was overcome with a desire to make it all better, and then she remembered the flowers she'd left in the hallway.

'Oh, your flowers!' Louise jumped up and went to the hall and returned with the bouquet. 'I hope you like them.' Louise felt suddenly embarrassed, as though her lack of taste or finesse was about to be laid bare.

'They're absolutely beautiful, thank you! I love them. I know just where they can go,' Isabelle said, brightening again as she stood up to take them. She placed them on the side table and got a vase from the cupboard. She looked distracted. 'Maybe I could call the hospital, ask how he is. They needn't know it was me after all?' she asked, as though Louise could give her permission.

'Why don't you let me?' Louise offered. 'I could pretend to be a journalist or something, checking facts.'

Isabelle frowned and dipped her head sideways. 'Sounds like you've done this before?' She laughed nervously.

Louise's heart rate flickered upwards. She was giving Isabelle the wrong impression of her. She was just trying to help.

'No! Not at all,' she said, trying to sound calmer than she felt. 'I've just watched too many TV shows, that's all.' She paused and then laughed, hoping to rebalance the chat.

Isabelle looked at her, with a confounded expression, as though she were trying to work her out and then she laughed too, a smaller, less sure laugh, but soon the sparkle returned to her eyes and she was genuinely smiling again.

'Exactly! That's exactly what it's like! It's some terrible daytime drama show and soon the whole misunderstanding will be cleared up and Carl will be home.' She absent-mindedly stroked her stomach and then stood up.

'Right, let me get these gorgeous flowers in some water. You've spoilt me, they're too beautiful!' She wandered into the kitchen, leaving Louise to look around the room.

Louise slumped back into her chair and let its soft warmth envelop her. She felt both totally at home and utterly out of place all at the same time. What was she doing here? What exactly did she want? She couldn't answer. Or at least not with one answer and her two answers utterly contradicted each other. She had got so used to ruthlessly controlling every situation in which she found herself that she couldn't stop. And yet, she couldn't control things here. She couldn't control how the situation would play out. She couldn't control what happened with Isabelle and Carl. She couldn't control how she wanted Isabelle to see her. She would have to let things unfold as they were going to. And that felt dangerous.

5

Bang! Bang bang!

Louise shifted in her bed, pulling her thin duvet closer around her chin as her asleep brain resisted the noise that was trying to force its way in and wake her up. Someone was banging on the front door but it wouldn't be for her, she didn't know anyone here. She curled her knees up towards her abdomen, bringing herself into the foetal position to keep her body warmth close to her. It was a chilly night and she didn't want to get up and out of her not-quite-warm-enough bed to find more covers. Then she'd have to start over warming up. No, she'd stay here.

Bang bang bang! The knocking on the door came again but then stopped. Something else caught in Louise's ear. A sob. Quiet at this distance but distinct. Whoever was knocking on the door was crying. Louise was suddenly hyper-awake. She reached an arm out of her bed nest and grabbed for her mobile phone that was lying on top of the upturned cardboard box she was using as a bedside table. She'd not got a bed frame and it was just about the right height for her mattress. She lifted the mattress up each morning, propping it against the wall to air it. It'd get mouldy underneath otherwise.

She'd learned that the hard way when she'd had to throw away her old one.

Bringing the phone close to her face, her eyes squinting in the dark against the screen's bright glow, she read the time: 03.15. Someone was crying on her doorstep at three in the morning. There were a couple of others living in the flats that shared the front door. It was the weekend so it could just be someone in full regret mode, too many tequilas making their way to their emotions and needing a friend to help them sober up. But, the flat below were away at the moment and the one across the hall seemed like they were too old to have friends like that. A what-if flashed into her mind. Isabelle. Reluctantly, Louise got out of bed and went to the window. She couldn't see her own doorway from here, as she was almost directly above it, the angle downwards was too steep. But she could see across the street. And the lights were on in Isabelle's house. A blaze of yellow in an otherwise darkened street. And the light was flooding out of the open front door.

She grabbed her hoodie, which had been slung on the floor, and threw it on as she ran out of her room and stumbled down the stairs. She didn't make any effort to be quiet, after all, if she'd heard the banging and the crying then the other flats would have too. A few heavy footsteps wouldn't make any difference and besides, she didn't know her neighbours anyway.

She could see the outline of someone doubled over outside, with one hand propping them up on the door frame. What on earth was the matter?

Louise fumbled with the door catch, finding that her hands were clammy and shaking. She threw the door wide open and found Isabelle, with tears running down her face, which was pale and terrified. She glanced up at Louise and whispered, 'I'm sorry. I know it's the middle of the night but I didn't know what to do. It's the baby. I'm... I'm bleeding and it hurts! I...' She gasped in pain and stepped forward, where Louise took her into a hug she had not initially intended to give.

'Hey, hey,' she whispered, trying to work out how best to comfort her. Was Isabelle having a miscarriage? She didn't want to ask but Louise felt that if she was going to be able to handle this well, then she needed to know.

'How bad is it? How much blood? And how pregnant are you?' Louise was very matter-of-fact. She needed to cut through both her tiredness and Isabelle's emotions to get to the nub of the matter.

'I... I'm eighteen weeks pregnant...'

Louise tried to turn that into months. She had no idea what eighteen weeks meant baby wise. Four months – ah, OK, so this could be bad.

'And, um, it's not so heavy I guess but it's red, it's fresh. And I'm cramping. It's not good I know that.'

Louise went into practical mode. She had seen this with her mother. She had been a teenager but had known even then what to do somehow. She'd never worked out if the fear she'd seen on her mother's face was in case the baby didn't make it, which it didn't, or if it did.

'Right, we need to get you to the hospital. Are you registered with them?'

Isabelle looked relieved. Someone who could look after her, make this all right, was there.

'Of course,' she said shakily, temporarily standing upright, before bending over again with the effort, 'St Thomas's. It's not far.'

'Right, well, it's Saturday night so no doubt A & E will be busy with drunk or fighting idiots but I guess we'd go to the maternity bit. Just let me grab my things and I'll call us a cab. Are you OK here for a second?'

'Yeah,' Isabelle whispered. She looked wrung out, frightened, in pain. A wave of fear swept through Louise. She wanted to be able to make it all better for her but she knew that it was out of both of their control. Even if they made it to the hospital, the news may not be good. She called a cab, urging them to be as quick as they could, then briefly closed her eyes and prayed, though to who, she didn't know, her grandpa maybe, to please just make it OK. Then she ran upstairs, grabbed her keys, phone, wallet, and at the last minute, a towel. She paused to glance in the mirror. She was wearing a T-shirt and joggers as PJs under her hoodie so she was fine. Respectable enough for a middle of the night hospital dash. Nondescript too, which was what she always aimed for. It'll be fine she told herself before sweeping a positive expression on her face and going back to Isabelle.

By some miracle, as Louise made it back downstairs, the cab drew up outside the flat. Perhaps her prayers had been answered already? Stepping into the cab Louise leaned forward to the driver. 'St Thomas's maternity hospital please, thanks, mate.'

The driver stopped and turned back, placing his arm across the seat beside him as he twisted his body to look. His expression shifted from one of joy to one of concern before settling on annoyance.

'Ah, I see. You bleedin'? Don't get it on my seats will ya? Costs a fortune and folk always ask questions about blood.' He turned back, no sympathy forthcoming.

'Just you worry about driving, OK?' Louise snapped back, pointing at the towel for his benefit before putting a comforting hand on Isabelle's shoulder. She whispered to her, 'Ignore him, he's probably had to deal with drunks all night. That'd put anyone in a bad mood. Just breathe and think positive, OK?'

Isabelle nodded mutely but she looked terrified.

* * *

The nurse pulled the curtain around the bed as she left Isabelle. She was pale and lying back on the starched green sheets of the hospital bed. She somehow looked simultaneously about twelve and a hundred years old. Fear has a way of doing that. Louise squeezed her hand.

'See? They think it's easing off. The bleeding. It might just be a scare.'

'It might not though. I mean, I have been under a lot of stress. And how could I tell Carl? It's what's keeping him going in there right now, he said so when he phoned me yesterday. Just me and the baby. It's all he has right now. I can't call him and tell him...' Her voice choked. 'I just can't!' She lay back and gravity pulled her tears down the side of her face and they pooled on the pillow by her ear. Louise felt helpless. It was not a feeling she was unused to but one that she had forgotten. It made her stomach feel hollow and her heart beat too fast. Whenever she felt hopeless before, she'd reminded herself what her grandpa had told her. *There's always enough hope for a story, my treasure. Always. They allow us to look for the happy-ever-afters, wherever we find them.*

Louise hoped he was right. 'Let me tell you a story,' she said to Isabelle, and smiled. 'What do you want to know?'

Isabelle smiled back weakly and then said, 'Tell me about your childhood, some happy memory from when you were a girl.' She lay back on the bed, the waterproof sheet shifting noisily underneath her. She looked exhausted.

The hospital was quiet, calm, the lighting dimmed for those trying to sleep. In this prenatal ward there were no sounds of the pain of childbirth, no squawks of newborns demanding their mother's attention. It felt safe, a cocoon from the rest of the outside world with its worries and troubles, despite the patients being in here for medical complications. There are few places with that sort of feeling. Louise, despite being unreligious herself, always felt it in churches or cathedrals. A sense of the outside world slowing to a stop while you stepped inside. Perhaps that was why confession worked, Louise wondered, because you felt held by the atmosphere, you were free to unburden yourself.

That was how she felt now. She felt safe confessing a part of herself, one that she never revealed to anyone, to Isabelle.

She cleared her throat. She could do this.

'Well, my childhood wasn't so happy. There aren't a lot of moments to choose, but there is one I remember.'

Isabelle sat up and took Louise's hand and squeezed it.

'I'm sorry. I forget that not everyone gets that sunshine and rainbows childhood. You don't have to share if you don't want to.'

'No, I want to.' Louise smiled. 'It's making me happy to think of it. To think of him.'

'Who?'

'My grandpa. The best person in the whole world. In my whole world.' Tears shimmered in Louise's eyes as her smile reached them. Her whole face had lit up in a way that it rarely did.

'He loved music and he loved that I loved music and we used to sit around listening to old records and new records and drinking tea and him feeding me as many biscuits as I could possibly eat.'

'Typical grandparent there then!' Isabelle giggled.

Louise laughed too. 'Yes, I guess so. It felt like he was always trying to make up for what my parents didn't give me. They were, I guess you'd say, disinterested. I was more of a distraction than a main event to them.'

Isabelle's face saddened.

'Oh, it's OK. I'm used to it. They didn't want to be parents really. I think it was just what you did when you were married and of a certain age. I think now they'd be one of those cool couples who have a glamorous child-free life and travel the world.'

'Are they globetrotters then?'

'Oh, I don't know.' Louise waved her hand dismissively. 'I haven't seen them since I left home, years ago now. We're not in touch.'

'Oh.'

'Anyway, this story is meant to be happy!' Louise laughed. 'So it's not about them. It's about Gramps.'

A nurse popped her head back around the curtain and whispered, 'Would either of you like a cup of tea? The on-call consultant is a bit busy so I think you might be here a while.' She smiled apologetically.

'That'd be lovely. Thank you.' Isabelle said. 'Just white, no sugar please.'

'Same, thank you,'

'That was nice of her, they all seem busy tonight. Anyway, tell me about your gramps. He sounds lovely.'

'He was.' Louise nodded. 'So we'd sit and listen to music and often he'd buy records because he thought I'd like to listen to them. He was a regular at this little independent shop in town and he'd go and spend an hour or so talking to the shop assistants. He loved it because it made him feel young and kept him up to date. They loved it because not all their customers were as obsessive as they were. And, of course, Grandpa bought pretty much everything they recommended. He always used to say that you could learn just as much from music you didn't care for as from music you loved.'

The curtain twitched again and the nurse came through the gap holding two beige plastic cups with the nastiest looking cup of tea Louise thought she had ever seen. She was still beyond grateful for it. The adrenaline of the first part of the night was wearing off and it was still pitch-black outside and she was exhausted. She had to be awake for Isabelle and so bad tea was better than no tea.

'Here you go.'

'Thank you,' they said in unison.

The nurse took the opportunity to check Isabelle's temperature and pulse. All seeming fine, she said, 'We'll be able to set up a scan soon to check all is OK with baby, keep positive, eh?' she said as she went to check on her other patients.

'So your gramps bought you some music?'

'Yeah. He usually just played them and asked what I thought. I wasn't used to my opinion counting, so it was nice to be asked for it. But this time, he'd bought a CD especially for me. It wasn't my birthday so I was really surprised when he handed it to me, along with a CD player so I could listen at home. They weren't cheap so I was really touched.

'"Don' you worry, love. I got it off the pawnbrokers. Proper cheap. Some poor sod's had a bad day but it means I can treat m'granddaughter so it's worth it. I want you to 'ave a listen to this, proper good listen."

'And he put on the CD he bought. I can still remember now, the twinkly piano music starting. It made me think of snowfall, which is funny cos the first word of the song is snow.'

'That sounds lovely.'

'It was. The song always makes me cry. But in a good way now, mostly. It was all about a dad loving his daughter and asking her when she was going to love herself back. He was making a point. He could see I wasn't happy at home. He even apologised.'

'For what?'

'For my mum. His daughter. He said, "I'm sorry about yer mum. I love her but she's not cut out to be a mum is she? I know that, I see it. I wish sometimes you got a better one but then I don't cos... well, cos then you wouldn't be mine and you're the best thing I got."'

'Oh,' Isabelle said as tears started to well up in both their eyes.

Louise couldn't believe she was telling Isabelle this. She'd never told a soul about the chats she and her grandpa had had. Who would she tell anyway? No one ever wanted to know. Yet, she felt that Isabelle did care, did want to know. It all felt different. She had been brought suddenly and dramatically into Isabelle's inner circle and she felt that she needed to share something too. It felt good to talk about it, which surprised her.

'So you see, you care already so much. You're going to make a brilliant mum, I can tell. I just know it, even though I don't really know you. And everything is going to be fine.'

'You know me,' Isabelle said, quietly but firmly. She took Louise's hand and looked at her intensely. 'Sometimes it doesn't take time to know someone, you just see each other straight away. You see me and I like to think that I see you.' She squeezed Louise's hand affectionately.

Louise's heart swelled. Maybe Isabelle was right. Maybe they did know each other after only just meeting. They obviously didn't know everything about each other, but that could come. Maybe she needed to open up, she'd been closed for so long that she'd accidently built her own prison.

'You know,' Louise whispered, something on the tip of her tongue that she wanted to say but didn't know if she could admit it out loud.

'What?'

'Sometimes... sometimes I've wished Grandpa hadn't loved me. Which feels, you know, shitty.'

'What? Why ever not?'

'Well, cos then I knew what I was missing with my mum and dad.' Louise looked at her shoes as her heart broke again. When would it ever stop doing that? 'I knew how they didn't love me. Or at least not how they were supposed to. And somehow, well, I think almost, if I'd not had love from anywhere, it might have made it easier to bear. I'd not have really known what I was missing. But I knew.' She nodded, chewing her lip to stop herself from crying. 'I knew.'

'Oh Louise...' Isabelle gingerly pushed herself up on the rails on one side of the bed and swung her legs over. She stood up and went to Louise and wrapped her arms around her. Louise, unused to such close touch, flinched at first but then she relented and for the first time since she was a child, she let herself be held. At that moment she asked the universe again for the baby to be OK and then she made a promise to herself – she would do everything in her power to keep Isabelle and the baby safe.

Whatever it took.

6

Louise fluffed up the sofa cushions and helped Isabelle to sit down.

'I'm OK – you don't need to do this,' Isabelle said, smiling. 'The scan showed that she's OK.' A huge smile broke out on her face. 'She. I didn't know what we were having! I was a little annoyed at first when the sonographer said she, but I guess a middle of the night shift emergency scan isn't the best time for being picky. I'm having a girl! Carl is going to be so happy. Another little princess for him to look after. Though, I think he'd have loved a boy to follow in his footsteps.'

'I'm sure he'll be happy whatever, you're safe, the baby is safe. The doctor said you need to make sure you don't overdo it and try not to get stressed. So. Feet up, I'll get you some water. It was a long night; you need to rest. Actually, should you go to bed? Or do you want to sleep here? Shall I go home? Or do you want me to stay?'

Louise was aware she was blabbering, which was not her usual self. Something had shifted and far from wanting to keep herself distant, she found herself wanting to be as involved as she could be. She could sort everything that way. Though, should she tell Isabelle everything? No, she reminded herself, the doctor said Isabelle needed to be as stress-free as possible. Everything could wait. It didn't matter now.

'Stop!' Isabelle giggled. 'I'm fine. I do need to go to bed and so do you. If I look anything like you do right now, then I must look shattered!'

'Oi!'

'Ha! It's alright. But I ought to call my mum first. I left her a message before I came over to yours. She's awful for turning her phone off or letting it charge somewhere and forgetting about it. I should have called the landline but she doesn't always answer in case it's a cold caller. But I don't want her to worry, so I'll just let her know. Could you bring me my bag maybe? My phone is in there.'

Louise looked around and located Isabelle's bright red leather bag. It looked expensive enough that it would pay her rent for a month. Did Isabelle really think that antique selling did that well? *Stop it!* she told herself. *Stop analysing, it's just a bag.* She handed it to Isabelle.

'Can I use your bathroom? Didn't want to leave you at the hospital and now all those cups of awful tea...'

'Of course, it's at the top of the stairs. The downstairs loo is full of Carl's work stuff. I keep telling him that just because it used to be a storage cupboard, doesn't mean it still is!'

Isabelle turned to her phone, scrolling away various notifications with an expression of irritation causing her forehead to wrinkle in the middle. Then, as though she checked herself, she straightened her face out and pushed the wrinkle away with her forefinger, before returning it to the phone screen.

Louise left her to it and walked quietly upstairs. It felt odd being unaccompanied in a house that was not hers. That feeling never left her. She used the bathroom and noted the expensive bottled soap in a colour that matched both the hand towel and the wall. The room was immaculate, like in the hotels that Louise had seen on

TV. The windowsill had a large plant in a matching colour plant pot and there was a row of glass jars, like the old-fashioned sweet jars from when sweet shops were a thing, with cotton wool, cotton buds and a coordinating colour of bath salts, with a little wooden scoop in it. It was a different world to Louise's. Grown-up. She felt both intimidated and excited, like Isabelle was showing her a life she could have one day perhaps. But, then her heart dropped. She knew well enough by now that in order to get something, you had to give something up. The universe always demanded payment.

Leaving the bathroom, and hearing Isabelle still on the phone, she took the opportunity to have a little look upstairs. She told herself that she wasn't snooping, she was admiring Isabelle's interior design work at the same time as giving her privacy for the conversation with her mum. She was being polite, not rude. She snuck her head around the door to the room at the front of the house. It was the nursery. Painted in a calming yellow, with cute, framed animal cartoons on one wall and a jungle painted on the other. It was amazing. Baby was going to be one lucky child.

Next door was Isabelle and Carl's bedroom and Louise felt wrong being in there. The atmosphere felt off somehow and Louise's nerves ramped up. It was very feminine. Lots of floral prints and cushions on the bed in shades of purple from aubergine through to lilac. This room had no obvious trace whatsoever of belonging to Carl – not a hint of masculinity anywhere. The dressing table was clear and uncluttered. Wardrobe doors closed. No shoes, no clothes, nothing would suggest that he slept here. Perhaps the police had taken items for testing? Or perhaps like herself, Carl kept his possessions limited, his trace on a place minimal. Or perhaps he just adored Isabelle enough to let her do whatever she wanted with their house and she liked things perfect.

The other room was a spare room but was cluttered with lots of baby things that had been bought but not prepared yet, despite the front bedroom seemingly already ready for the baby. This room was full of toys and clothes and all sorts of things that Louise did not recognise. Her heart fluttered – if something were to go wrong with the baby, this room would be beyond painful for Isabelle.

Aware that she had now taken too long, Louise slowly and quietly came back downstairs. She didn't think Isabelle would be checking on her, she could hear her raising her voice from the front room, but she also didn't want to risk it. Also not wanting to risk wandering in on a private conversation, she busied herself sorting the flyers and post that had arrived. She could keep one ear on the conversation and yet make herself useful as she discarded lots of brightly coloured kebab house menus and double-glazing pamphlets.

Louise shook herself from her tired daze and realised that she could no longer hear Isabelle chatting. She listened out for sounds from the living room. Perhaps Isabella had paused while her mother dispensed some life advice or pregnancy care suggestions or just told Isabelle how loved she was, like mothers were supposed to do. Nothing. The only sound she could make out was sniffing. No, not sniffing, crying. Isabelle was crying.

Abandoning the post at first, and then going back for it in case she needed a prop, Louise walked back into the front room. The morning was bright and sunshine flooded into the room, touching everything with its brilliance and highlighting how completely spotless it was. Not a single speck of dust anywhere to be seen. Louise had a momentary flash of jealousy. This was how she wanted to live. But then, looking to Isabelle, crying on the sofa, she questioned that. Louise already knew we all live this life alone, whereas it seemed Isabelle was in the midst of learning that the hard way.

'What's wrong? What's the matter? Are you ok?' Louise said, gently sitting down next to Isabelle, picking up and offering a box of tissues from the coffee table. Isabelle took one and smiled gratefully, her pain clear to see on her face. It had crept into her eyes and settled in her strained expression.

'Yes... no. What I mean is...' She paused to blow her nose genteelly and to dab at her eyes, soaking up tears. Louise wondered if she ever looked bad.

'Your mum?'

'Yes. She, um, she... Well, she got my message this morning but didn't ring because she assumed I'd have let her know if something was wrong and she didn't want to wake me as I'd had a difficult night.'

'Maybe she was being thoughtful?'

'No. My mum likes to be involved. I know her. She was avoiding something, I could tell. So I pushed her on it. She didn't like that, kept saying she didn't want to make a fuss. Telling me I was tired and hormonal and should go to bed.'

'You must be exhausted...'

'No! Well, I am yes but...' Her voice trembled.

Louise could see Isabelle's hands were shaking too. Whatever had just happened between Isabelle and her mum, it had rattled her. Louise took the opportunity to get to the nub of things. Getting people to open up, to bare their souls to her, was one of Louise's talents.

'What did she say? It's clearly upset you whatever it was. You... you don't have to tell me, I know we barely know each other, you don't have to tell me anything.' Louise was treading carefully here. She wanted Isabelle to tell her but she knew that you can't force a confidence, you have to wait and let it come to you. 'It's just, well, you're obviously upset. Is there anything I can do?' She smiled and tipped her head to the side in a friendly manner. She had to let Isabelle make this next move.

'You won't believe it. What she said. She...' Isabelle suddenly switched from sad to angry, her face starting to go red as fury swept up inside her. 'She asked whether it might not be for the best. If this baby, if my baby, if our baby didn't make it! I mean! She's baby's granny! She's supposed to love her unconditionally!'

'Wow. That's, that's...' Louise considered her response carefully '...that's cold. Why would she say something like that?'

'Carl.' Isabelle's face wrinkled petulantly and Louise could see the cracks in this perfect lifestyle appear before her as clear as day. Isabelle's mother did not approve of Carl. Louise would have to tread very carefully here. Very gently. This was obviously going to be a very sore topic but one that could also provide a lot of information.

'What about him?'

'This whole mix-up with the police and the... what they say he's done. She thinks it's not a good time to bring a baby into the mix. And. She's never really liked him, despite all he's done since school to show her that he cares. That he loves me. She can't ever not see him as the boy he was at school – always in trouble. But that's cos he was bored, under-stretched. Look at him now! He's a success! I mean—' she gestured wildly around the room '—look! This house is beautiful and it's all due to him! Why can't she see that he's different, he's grown up?'

'I don't know. Some people think we can't change who we are, not really.'

'I think we can, we're all changing all the time. I know I can be really self-centred, I'm a spoilt only child but now I'm pregnant I know I don't come first. I've changed, why can't he have?'

Louise paused. What did she think? She wanted to change, she wanted to move on from the past but could she? Really? Even being here, now, was that change or more of the same? She was too tired to know.

'I think she's probably just trying to work out the best for you.

Sometimes those closest to us aren't able to do that. Too close makes it blurry, unfocused. I think the best thing is for you to get some sleep and talk to her again later. Or in a few days. Maybe the whole Carl thing will be settled by then.'

'Yes... maybe. I... I just thought...'

'What?'

'I thought, when it happened, when they took Carl and when his lawyers told me he'd been charged and had been denied bail, it was the worst thing that could happen. I'd be alone. But then I told myself I was being silly. I have family and lots of wonderful friends, even if they are not right here on my doorstep.'

Louise felt a pang of envy. She wanted all that. She had no one.

'But now? Do you know how many times my neighbours have called by to see how I am? How many of my close wonderful friends have called by to check in?' Furious now, Isabelle turned wild-eyed to Louise, demanding an answer from her.

'I don't know.'

'Well, I'll tell you. None. No one. A few lightweight, "It'll be OK, hon" messages, a couple of brief "I'd visit but the trains are a mess" calls from people who clearly think it's not worth the hassle. So I'm here, in my beautiful house, pregnant and alone! My family are an hour away across the city or out of the country, I've got no one here and now my own mother suggests it'd be better if I miscarried! It's all too much! I can't... I can't!' Her anger flooded back to sorrow and she burst into tears.

Louise said nothing but put her hand on Isabelle's shoulder as she sobbed. So, they were both alone in this world. Both the victims of the actions of others and both abandoned by those who were supposed to care. Perhaps they were soul mates, despite being so different on the surface. Louise let Isabelle's tears subside.

'I think the best thing for now, for you and for the baby, is rest.

My grandpa used to say everything looks better for a sleep. You get yourself upstairs and sleep. Everything else can wait.'

Isabelle looked at Louise and smiled weakly. 'You're right. I need rest. Maybe once I'm not shattered I can be more rational. I'm sure there's an explanation for it all.'

'Exactly. I can help you deal with all this later. I'm here.'

Louise followed Isabelle to the hallway, where she picked up her things as Isabelle headed upstairs. She could go home and sleep too. She could work out what she was going to do next, as she seemed to have got herself more tangled up in Isabelle and Carl's world than expected. This had not been her plan. She was supposed to be keeping things safe and uncomplicated; and yet, somehow, her heart felt lighter than it had done in years.

'Thank you, I'll call later. You're a true friend, you know that?' Isabelle said before disappearing into the bedroom.

True.

Louise wasn't so sure about that but she smiled at her in response all the same.

7

Walking down the road, Louise tried to block out the churning in her stomach as she had done so many times before. At school, her drama teacher had told the class to channel their nervous adrenaline into energy for the performance, relaxing into the fear. It was the one thing she learned at school that had really been useful in life. It usually worked, but today? Today Louise just felt sick.

On the overland train it had been easy enough to keep her distance from Isabelle, keeping hidden as she followed her. It was busy despite being in the middle of the day so it had been straightforward enough to be lost in the crowds. But here on the street, Louise felt exposed. She had only intended to follow Isabelle to try to bump into her, to try to strike up a conversation without it seeming engineered. She had not expected Isabelle to be going so far nor to be coming here. If she had, Louise would certainly not have followed her.

It had been days since she had seen Isabelle, despite Isabelle promising to call her once she had woken after her nap. Louise had spent almost all of that time completely stuck as to what to do. Should she go over? Should she phone? Was Isabelle OK? Had her friends finally stepped up and so she no longer needed Louise, a practical stranger to her, to hold her up as her life crumbled around her? Louise needed to know more but was paralysed into inaction. Had something happened to the baby? Louise winced at the thought. Having seen the little peanut-shaped outline on the sonography screen, its heartbeat flickering like a butterfly at its core, she had fallen a little in love with this person who did not yet fully exist in this world. All that potential, all that life currently curled up and growing, gaining strength to deal with the outside world. It must be such a shock to babies. It was still a shock to Louise some days. The brightness, the chaos, the noise and the silence. Must be nice to be safe, warm, secure.

Once they got off the train, it had been a few streets before Louise worked out the destination. HMS Wandsworth. Isabelle was going to see Carl. Louise had immediately decided to turn around and go back but something had stopped her. Morbid curiosity? Recklessness?

'Shit!' Louise dropped her head and swivelled around to face the other way. Isabelle had stopped suddenly and turned and nearly faced her full on. Louise had to be more careful. She was used to making herself small, unseen, unnoticed. So why was she doing such a bad job today? Louise took her phone and tilted her face down at the screen, as though looking something up. She held her breath and counted to twenty. Then she looked up. Isabelle had turned back towards her destination. Towards Carl.

Louise watched from a safe distance, taking cover behind the overgrown bushes in the front garden of one of the houses on the street a little way from the visitors' centre. The cream, brick-built houses were of the same style and age as the prison itself, but somehow, a brightly painted front door and an ivy creeping over the front of the house itself created a welcoming, desirable feel to the homes, unlike the striking, imposing facade of Wandsworth jail. Set back from the road, the main building seemed smaller than she had imagined. It looked like a medieval castle mixed with a Disney villain's country getaway. The whole area was nothing like Louise had thought it would be.

She watched as Isabelle went into the visitors' centre and disappeared from sight. She'd be an hour and then most likely take the same route back to the station, down one of the posh streets and across the common, avoiding the main roads. Louise knew that she couldn't lurk about where she was without arousing suspicion. It would be bad enough on a regular street but one so close to the nick seemed definitely unwise. So, with Isabelle inside, Louise decided to find somewhere along the route that she could wait. She had her story as to why she was over this way – old sports injury and a recommended sports therapist. She wouldn't specify and she was pretty sure Isabelle wouldn't pry. Good job, Louise had never done sports in her life.

Louise settled herself at a table outside one of the nondescript cafés that lined one edge of the common. Nondescript was always best. Nothing too memorable. She ordered exactly what the woman in front of her had ordered, for the same reason. Blend in, always.

Sitting down with her oat milk cortado, whatever on earth that was, Louise gingerly got out a pale blue folder from her bag, stuffed full of printouts and cuttings from newspapers and their websites. A few threads from some social media chats, though that was more to gauge what people felt, rather than the actual facts. Louise needed to know what she was dealing with. What had Carl done? What could Isabelle be walking into? Sure, she could have scrolled through the sites on her phone but somehow, being in black and white on a page made it more solid, more real. Plus, this could be dumped in a bin if needed whereas her phone search history could always be dug out.

Ignoring the sounds of the increasingly impatient toddler sat at the table next to her, Louise read the first article from a local newspaper. The story wasn't big enough to have made the nationals, a fact that she was grateful for, not only for the sake of the poor pensioner. Had his injuries been more severe, or worse, fatal, it no doubt would have at least made the *Evening Standard*.

> Local man arrested for Burglary and Assault, Elderly victim fighting for his life.
>
> Streatham resident, Carl White, 32, was arrested and charged last night for a callous attack on Dulwich pensioner, Edward Handshill, 92. Handshill was surprised at home by White, who is suspected of attempted burglary, and suffered multiple blows to his body and head, leaving him in critical condition. White was spotted running from the scene by Pete Lawson, 21, who said. 'He just looked dodgy, something wasn't right. I rang the bell but then saw him on the floor so I called the police.' There were no signs of forced entry, though some items have been declared as missing by Handshill's relatives. White is being held at HM Prison Wandsworth, awaiting trial. Bail has been refused. Local residents who wanted to remain anonymous say White is married and has a baby on the way.

Local residents, Louise huffed. So-called friends and neighbours, all the people who had abandoned Isabelle as soon as a hint of trouble arose. Even if Carl was guilty, Isabelle wasn't. She clearly had a very limited grasp on what he actually did day to day, so it was entirely plausible that he was guilty and she could have no idea. She took a sip of her coffee. It was quite nice actually, like making your coffee with porridge instead of milk, even if she had let it get too cold whilst reading. She started to relax and then tensed again almost immediately as she felt her shoulders unknot. She had to keep an eye out for Isabelle if they were going to bump into each other by accident. Louise wanted to support her. Isabelle was bound to be unnerved or upset by the prison visit and Louise could be the one who was there for her, to buoy her up as she talked about what was going on with Carl.

Refocusing on the job in hand, Louise got out her phone. She logged into her fake social media profile to look at the local neighbourhood thread about the attack. It was disappointing how quickly it had shifted from 'Do you think he did it?' to 'How could she not have known, she must have!' People so sure of their convictions issuing statements to strangers like 'I knew she couldn't afford all that stuff on what she said he did! It never made sense. Well now it does.' Or 'Always thought she was one above, queen of the street, like her home was her castle. Looking more prison like now, isn't it?' and 'They should lock him up and throw away the key. Never liked him.'

Not a single word of caution or support, not one person on the thread noting that, as of yet, Carl had not been found guilty, though it didn't look good. It was depressing how moments like this really showed you who your friends are and it seemed to her that Isabelle was finding out that she didn't really have friends at all.

Louise blew out her cheeks and closed her eyes for a moment. She could hear the distant hum of a lawnmower and the low rumble of passing traffic was almost hypnotic. She hadn't slept well. Her mind wouldn't stop racing between worries about what she was doing with her life and worries about Isabelle and this whole situation.

Keeping her eyes closed, Louise let the sunshine warm her face. It felt like someone had wrapped her in a blanket and she was momentarily grateful for the fact that the chair was horrifically uncomfortable, otherwise she may well have fallen asleep, strong coffee or not. She remembered her grandpa complaining about it: 'They make the chairs too damn uncomfortable to stop you dawdling. If the chair is hard and pokey, well then you don't stay and they have space to sell a drink to the next gullible sod who fancies an overpriced cuppa.'

The memory made her laugh and open her eyes. It was almost as if her grandpa had nudged her. Right in the middle of her viewpoint, walking gingerly along the path on the common that made its way to the pedestrian crossing, was Isabelle. Should she wait here and hope Isabelle would see her? That would certainly be best. How could she be following if Isabelle found her? But how could she ensure Isabelle saw her? Her heart rate rose as she realised she hadn't worked out the final bit of her plan. Louise looked around. She needed to make a noise, but a subtle one, one that would look spontaneous. She stole a look at the table behind her – the lady was holding an iced coffee. Before she had time to fully consider the consequences, Louise rammed her chair back, causing the lady to throw her drink all over the previously boisterous toddler, who burst into loud screams, making his mother turn to Louise and yell at her.

Perfect.

'Louise?' Isabelle said as she came over to the chaos. Louise noticed that she looked pale and drawn, cold, even though it was a sunny day.

'Isabelle!' Louise said, smiling widely before turning to the woman and toddler.

'I'm sorry, I didn't see you,' she said to the irate parent, who was trying to simultaneously yell at Louise and calm the sobbing toddler who was cold and sticky and wailing loudly.

'You should pay more bloody attention!'

'I'm so sorry, let me get you a new drink? Please?'

'Yeah... yeah OK. But to go as I've got to get this one home and changed... It's OK, lovey, this naughty lady is going to get Mummy a new drink... and one for you. And a cake. I'm sure she will do, lovey...' She turned and grimaced at Louise who had to work hard to keep the smile off her face. The kid would be fine, a drink and cake would placate the mother and she had managed to have Isabelle find her. A plan well executed.

'Just let me sort this? Are you staying? Can I get you something while I'm there, Is?'

'Oh, um, sure! Can I have one of their fruit teas? Don't mind which. Thanks.'

Isabelle sat where Louise had been. She looked exhausted.

Louise came out again a few moments later, carrying a brown plastic tray with a paper bag and cardboard cup holder with the two apology drinks in it. She handed them to the mother and child, who took them grudgingly and then went on their way. The child seemed far less bothered now about his stained clothes and was playing with his toys from the comfort of his pushchair. No harm done.

Louise then laid the tray down on the table by Isabelle and passed her a fruit tea and a plate with a Danish pastry on it.

'Thought you might be hungry. You can take it away for later if you're not. You just looked a bit tired, thought you might appreciate a pick-me-up.'

Isabelle smiled gratefully. 'Thanks. I'm ravenous actually, I hadn't realised until you gave me this.' She took a big bite and chewed before speaking again, holding her hand over her mouth to avoid talking bits of pastry over Louise. 'I was too nervous this morning to eat, even with the pregnancy nausea. I know it means a good strong pregnancy but oh, I am sick of, well, of feeling sick.'

Trying her best to be breezy, Louise asked, 'Why? What were you doing this morning? Hospital appointment? Check-up?'

'No, though the midwife said she would see me again sooner than usual due to the bleeding. No, I... this morning I—' she leaned over conspiratorially, quietly, as though if others heard her it would be the end of the world '—I went to visit Carl. He's here, Wandsworth.' Her chin jutted upwards, defensively, her jaw clenching.

'Oh! Oh, I hadn't realised! No, I can see why you'd be nervous. First time visiting?'

Isabelle's jaw unclenched. Her face relaxed.

'Yes. I'd never been inside a prison before. Not that I did today either actually, they have a visitor centre. It's nice. Looks a bit like a café or a library. Not at all what I was expecting. I've watched too much crime drama, I think.'

Louise laughed, a touch, not too much. Supportive but not enthusiastically. She was treading a delicate line here. Isabelle was vulnerable but she wasn't an idiot.

'So, how'd it go?'

Isabelle took another bite of pastry and washed it down with a big gulp of the tea. Louise wondered if it tasted the same as its colour. She found that all fruit teas looked pretty enough, smelled lovely but tasted of almost nothing. She preferred builders' tea. She waited, allowing the silence to sit between them. She would let Isabelle speak when she was ready and say what she was ready to say.

'It was fine. Strange. He was not himself, on edge. I mean, I get why. It felt structured, like we were in a play, saying our lines as we were supposed to but not getting into anything more. He kept saying over and over what a massive mix-up it had been and how he'd be out soon and how I wasn't to worry.'

Louise's words tried to form in her mouth but her tongue tied itself in knots and she couldn't speak. Isabelle clearly believed him. She wasn't so sure.

'There was one odd thing though.' Isabelle's brow furrowed.

'Yes?' Louise managed to say, despite the increasing sense of dread growing in the pit of her stomach. 'What was it?'

'Well...' She stopped to sip more tea, and as she did so, she glanced out over the common, where a group of dogs were greeting each other happily, bouncing about in the sunshine, barking and wagging their tails.

Louise almost didn't want to know, but also, she felt it was vital that she knew the deal here.

'Go on...'

'Well, it's just that he seemed happy enough for the guard to hear whatever it was we were talking about, but when he caught the guard moving away a touch, looking bored or something, he immediately leaned in and told me "The money is sorted. I will make sure it keeps coming." Why was that so important? I mean, he's going to be out soon and we have savings.'

Louise was struck by Isabelle's naivety. She had told Louise that she'd never lived alone and had basically gone from her parents' house to Carl's. She'd never had to worry about rent or paying bills or choosing between food or heat. She had clearly never counted out pennies to try to get dinner that evening or have a bank card declined due to insufficient funds. And now, now that her husband, the sole breadwinner was in jail, it hadn't occurred to her to worry that the money might run out. It literally hadn't crossed her mind. He was innocent, he would be home soon, it would all be all right. No questions.

Did she want to be the one to shatter that illusion? Should she? What would it gain? Louise felt angry at Isabelle suddenly, angry at her life being so damn easy, so straightforward. But then she immediately felt bad. It wasn't Isabelle's fault. Just like her own life being hard wasn't Louise's fault either. Sometimes life just is. Her anger waned, to be replaced by pity. Isabelle was about to find out how hard life could be.

'Isabelle?'

'Yes?'

'Do you believe him?'

'What do you mean?'

'I mean... that he's going to be out soon. They've refused bail. That's... not good. That he had to tell you about money covertly. Have they frozen your assets? Your bank account? Have you checked? Do you have your own or is it a joint one? Has anyone said anything to you about it? His solicitor? And how can the money keep coming? He's self-employed isn't he? How can he keep it coming in if he's not working? It just... just doesn't all fit, that's all.'

'Are you trying to say something?' Isabelle was going pink as her defensiveness rose. Louise wasn't worried. She could see the doubt creeping in at the corners. She could see that Isabelle was beginning to ask questions that she'd never asked before. And that she wasn't finding any answers that she liked.

Louise would have to be careful but she could help Isabelle free herself from this tangle of half-truths and dependency. Louise could help her accept the truth.

But would that be a good idea? Or a very bad one?

8

TWO WEEKS AGO

She poured some tea from the woollen cosy-covered teapot and then placed it back on the tray that sat on the table between them. There was no noise apart from the gentle tick of the clock on the mantlepiece – it was so quiet you could practically hear the dust settling as it shimmered in the sunlight that streamed through the windows.

'Do you take sugar?' she asked.

'Ooh, yes, please. At my age you need all the sweetness you can get! I should be hosting you though, you are my guest after all,' the elderly man said, pulling his hand-knitted cardigan around him to keep out the chill.

She looked around. The room was covered in knitted items. A blanket by the chair beside the TV, arm covers on the sofa, even some of the plant pots filled with African violets that sat in the window bay had a knitted colourful cover on them. They seemed too feminine to be his own work. Someone close to him was a crafter. She wondered who. A wife? But where was she? A daughter or granddaughter perhaps? Someone not close by who sent their love through the post in yarn form? Who was it that she needed to be aware of?

'I love the tea cosy! It's so colourful! Did you make it?' she asked, her voice light and cheery, belying the interrogation she wanted to start.

'Ha ha! Me? No. I'm as clumsy as a drunkard on a Saturday night,' he chuckled mischievously. 'No. My wife made them.'

'Oh?' she said, looking around demonstrably. 'Do we need another cup?'

His smile dropped, just a touch, as grief, hiding just under the surface, made it into his eyes, which shimmered with tears.

'I'm afraid not. She died earlier this year. I keep all her things nearby to keep her close.'

'I'm sorry, I didn't mean to pry,'

'No, it's all right, dear. You weren't to know.' His quivering hands picked up a delicate bone china cup and he took a sip. 'I miss her. It's dreadfully lonely without her here and I keep her things to talk to. It's all as though she has just popped out to the shops and I like it that way.' He looked over the room and a flicker of a smile raised itself on his lips. 'I can convince myself on good days that she's not gone. And on bad days, I know that she's only just around the corner really. I just can't see where she is yet.' He took a biscuit, a custard cream, from a matching floral plate and took a delicate bite. He was elegant; refined in his sorrow. 'Though I'm ninety-two so I don't expect it'll be too long.'

'She sounds lovely,' she said, offering some platitude to keep him talking. She wanted him to talk. She was here to listen.

'Oh, she was! She'd be ever so annoyed with me if I got rid of her knitting. She did this tea cosy and I can still remember the swearing!' He chuckled and bent his pale, knotted fingers around it. 'It's a difficult shape, see? Or rather it was once her hands got bad. Arthritis. Oh, enjoy being young, my dear! It's so hard when things stop working as they once did. I'm so much more forgetful than I was and you get ever so frustrated with yourself.'

They sat peacefully while they drank. Or at least he did. She pretended to do so. It was important that she didn't need to use the bathroom or leave him at any stage. She also didn't want to leave any more of a trace of herself than she had to. She wanted to be nothing more than a vague memory in his befuddled mind.

'It's so nice to chat. I find myself talking to the television these days. But of course, they don't talk back. They'd probably tell me to stop chattering on even if they could!' He laughed wryly. 'Tell me about yourself, my dear, did you say it was St Matthew's you were from?'

Her eyelid twitched, just a fraction of a second while her brain got up to speed. Which version had she told him? Which version had got her over the threshold and into his inner sanctum with refreshments all laid out? She had several, starting with the least complex, and if that failed, working up to a story that had so many pieces to it, it was as though she were an author of some tangled whodunnit. It seemed that the simplest one had hit the mark here. It almost saddened her how often that was the case. So many people, particularly the elderly, were so chronically lonely that they wanted to believe anything for some company. She recognised that loneliness and she knew how best to manipulate it.

In her own mind she wasn't doing anything wrong. She was giving these people what they wanted, what they needed. What their own friends and relatives were failing to provide. So if she were to provide it and take as her payment a small fraction of the final inheritance of that neglectful circle, well, that was fair wasn't it? The universe allocating things as they should be allocated. That, and frankly, she had received nothing in her relatively short life so far. No love, no support, no finances. So she had to find it, make it herself or take it for herself. That's what she was doing. Quid pro quo.

'Yes, that's the one. We're just around the corner and we're reaching out to local parishioners who might appreciate a little company. We can do visits, help with shopping or light housework or cooking. Whatever you need really.' She shared a broad helpful smile.

And to be truthful, she was happy to do any of those things. It's just that it came at a price. If the local church community really cared, they would already be doing this. It wasn't her fault people fell through the net. She was just there to catch them.

He smiled back and said, 'Just a chat now and again would be lovely. I'm OK for the rest of the things at the moment. I like to try to keep independent.'

Just then, through the comfortable silence that they sat in, was a noise. A clatter of several items falling to the floor in the next room. She froze, hoping that the aged ears of her companion had not registered it. She plastered an innocent smile on her face. But it was clear from the additional wrinkles that joined the permanent ones on his face, that he had heard and he was perturbed.

'Did you hear that?'

'Hear what?' More innocent smiling, despite her palms becoming damp with sweat and her heart rate starting to rise; her body telling her to get out, to leave and to leave now.

'Someone else is here. Are they with you?' He turned to her, angry now, his sudden realisation that this charitable act was likely a scam. 'Who are you?! Really? What do you want with me?' He stood up, as fast as his frail body would let him and he reached for his walking stick. She considered stretching out her leg and kicking it out of his way but by the time she'd processed this option, he had his hand on it and she couldn't guarantee it wouldn't take him to the floor with it. She didn't want that. She didn't want to cause him any harm. That was not the idea. No harm done was the deal she agreed.

'I don't know what you mean, I'm sure it's nothing. Here, have another biscuit.'

'I don't want another biscuit! Who's there?! Who is it? What do you want?!' he called out into the hallway.

'There's NO ONE THERE!' she yelled, hoping that it would give him time, time to grab whatever it was he had found and go. The old man was slow, there would be time. This could all still be fine. Rescuable.

He walked from the room, intent on finding out what she would not tell him. She found herself suddenly frozen. Immobile, statue-still at the tea table, like some marble Alice in Wonderland or Mad Hatter. If he goes and finds an empty room, then I can talk my way out of this and offer to leave for his peace of mind and all will be well. We can just take this property off the list and move on like we've done before.

Just as she was convincing herself all was well; that all would be fine, she heard it. The howl. A cry of pain and then the repeated whumps of flesh hitting flesh. She leaped up and ran to the kitchen taking care not to touch anything as she did so. This was bad. This was going to be bad. She had to get things back under control.

As she turned into the room she saw him.

The man, on the floor, his head cracked on the stone tiles, blood leaching from his ears and Carl in a trance, kicking him over and over and over again.

'STOP IT! STOP! CARL!!! STOP! NOW!'

The sound of his name brought Carl to his senses as he stopped kicking and whipped his head up to face her.

'Don't use my name, stupid bitch!'

She ignored him.

'What the hell are you doing?! No harm done! No violence. We agreed. So what the fuck is this?!!'

'He...' Carl stopped still, shocked suddenly. 'He found me and I...' He looked down.

The old man was conscious but only just. He was in a bad way. He was groaning, but it came out like a whisper, like an old door closing from a long way away.

This was so bad.

Louise had to think and she had to think fast. They needed to get out and get out now, but they couldn't leave him like this. If no one found him, he'd die for sure, and she knew no one would find him because they'd scouted him out. No one came, no one visited, no one checked. That's why they chose him. Expensive and regular deliveries of things but no people. Perfect. But perfect or not, leaving a mark for dead was never part of the plan. This was not who she was.

'We have go. You have to go. Now!' she shouted at him.

He looked at her, and for the first time, it was clear that she was in control. This whole racket had been Carl's thing, he was the one in control, but he'd lost it the moment he'd become an attacker instead of a thief. Getting his hands bloodied was not his role and it had clearly shaken him. He seemed unable to think.

Louise stepped up. She pulled herself to her full height, tried to feel strong, tried to feel calm and convince herself that this was all just part of a day's work.

'What did you touch? Wipe it down. Then, go out the back, remember, the latch is loose? Cover your hand with something, wiggle the handle until it gives and slowly, quietly, walk out.' She looked out towards the back door in the lean-to off the kitchen. 'There's some gardening tools. Take some. If anyone sees you, make yourself look like the gardener. When you're away, get rid of them.'

Carl nodded mutely. He looked around him, wiped down a few

surfaces with the cloth he took out of his coat pocket, looked back at the man, and then he left.

Louise heard the back latch go and Carl run. She caught the outline of him as he ran past the window on the side of the house, to the front. He should have taken the quiet route out of the back garden. She assumed he would have.

Shit.

She crouched down to check on the man, trying not to touch him or to get his blood on her hands. She'd have his blood on her hands as it was, it didn't need to be literal. He was in a bad way. She had to help him. Running from the room, she noticed a delivery van in the street. The driver was at a house opposite. He seemed to have several parcels and packets but she knew from their scoping out that he'd likely be calling here next. She didn't have much time.

Louise covered her shaking hands with her sweatshirt sleeve and picked up the phone. It was one of those really old-fashioned ones with the circular dial in the centre and the time it took between each number was painful.

Finally...

'Emergency services, which service do you require please?'

A gruff, deep voice came out of her. She sounded ridiculous but she didn't sound like herself at least.

'Ambulance...' She hesitated. 'And police. Think there's been a break-in.' The second the words were out she was cursing herself. Why? Why did she bring attention to the fact that they'd need to see if anything was taken? Had Carl taken anything?

She spoke out the address and then left the phone still connected, If they needed anything more they could trace it or whatever they did. She had things she needed to do.

First, keeping her hands covered, she turned the latch on the front door so if anyone pushed it, it would open without issue.

Next, she grabbed a cushion from the sofa and took it to the man. She had thoughts of placing his head on it to make him more comfortable but looking at him she thought better of it. A head injury, a neck injury perhaps. She didn't want to risk making it worse when trying to make it better. She'd fucked up enough, she didn't need to add to it, so she put it back.

And finally, she grabbed the entire tea tray, feeling guilty at what she was about to do, knowing the story of how it was a wedding gift, nearly sixty-five years previously. But now it was evidence, covered in her fingerprints. It was what could catch her and, as bad as she felt about it, she was not going to let that happen. She took it to the back door and noting a shed at the side of the garden, let herself out and dipped inside it. She found a dark corner and let the tray drop. Tea, biscuits and all. It smashed with a horrifying noise into many shattered fragments. Grabbing the broom, she swept the pieces into a corner, covering them with sacking that she found on a shelf. This place was covered in cobwebs. No one would be looking in here for a tea set they didn't know was missing. It would lie here unnoticed and forgotten by everyone.

Apart from her perhaps. This moment would define the rest of her life. It would be the day she rejected what she had become and walked away. Which is exactly what she did. Taking pause to check that she was unnoticed, that no one had heard the sound of breaking crockery and come to see, she let herself out of the shed. Slowly walking to the end of the garden, which was still beautifully kept with neatly shaped rose bushes and plants she didn't recognise, she climbed over the garden fence at the very back of the property. It led onto a tree-lined pathway running along the back of the whole road of houses, funnelling out onto the busy main road. She walked away; the sounds of sirens and birdsong ringing in her ears.

Louise hoped it was not too late. For him. For her. For everyone.
It had not to be too late.

9

PRESENT DAY

'Let me get that, you keep your feet up. Bump needs rest,' Louise said as she stood to go and answer the door.

'Bump needs another set of legs so I can swap mine out when I'm tired!' Isabelle laughed as she settled back down onto the sofa. She took a deep breath and rubbed the stretching curve of her stomach. 'Ooof!' she said, as another cramp came. The doctor had told her cramps at this stage were completely normal as the abdomen stretched and moved to make space, but Louise could see the flash of fear on Isabelle's face each time they came, still not convinced that the scare had been nothing more than that. Louise smiled reassuringly as she walked past into the hall.

When she came back she was followed by an elderly lady, slowly shuffling into the living room, one hand on a walking stick, one on the door frame to steady her. Louise walked ahead of her in order to help her to the high-backed chair opposite Isabelle. The lady was polite but resisted this help, glancing sideways at Louise with an expression that she could not read.

'Glynis! How lovely! Have a seat,' Isabelle said, her whole being brightening as she welcomed her guest. There had been precisely no visitors as far as Louise knew in the weeks since Carl had been arrested and taken into custody. Isabelle's stomach had grown, as had her understanding that this pregnancy was going to be something she undertook alone, and the parenting side of it likely to be similar once the baby was born. Isabelle had never done anything by herself and she had been understandably completely overwhelmed. Louise had done her best to assure her that she would be here, that she would help as much as Isabelle would let her. She had tried to reassure her that Carl might not be found guilty and could be home soon, but apparently his lawyers were not as optimistic and Carl had prepared Isabelle for the worst.

'Who's your friend?' Glynis asked, rather more sharply than Louise thought necessary. She didn't know her from Adam after all.

'I'm Louise, nice to meet you!' Louise said. She had won over more old women than she'd had hot dinners. The men were usually easier, a pretty young face helping to squash any questions that might have niggled at them. Women were harder, they wanted more information from you before letting their guard down. Women in general were a better judge of character, Louise believed. They had honed the skill by battling years of bullshit but they had also had years of knocks to their self-confidence. Years of being told they are less than. And this was the weakness that Louise was usually able to hook into and use. She didn't want this woman to give Isabelle any doubts about her. Isabelle was the only thing keeping Louise going. Louise's sole point of focus.

'This is Glynis – an old friend of my gran's,' Isabelle explained.

'Not so old, eh, thank you!' Glynis said a touch harshly.

'You take the weight off and sit down and I'll bring everyone some refreshments. You look worn out!' Louise smiled as she glided into the kitchen, keeping one ear on the chit-chat that was happening without her. She flung a few carefully chosen items on a tray. She'd make tea in a pot if she could find one. People of a certain generation didn't hold sway with tea bags in mugs, she knew that one. A lovely elderly lady, once won over, had taught Louise how to make what she had called 'proper tea'.

'Warm the pot first, else you'll shock the tea leaves. Always leaves, none of this dust you get in tea bags these days. A cup of tea is a thing worth doing properly in my opinion.' She'd gone on to explain the minutiae of the perfect brewing process before handing Louise a cup. She'd not been able to tell the difference to be honest but knew that sometimes the ritual was enough to make it feel special. Louise had felt particularly bad about doing her over, she'd been such a nice lady. But collateral damage came with the territory and you had to just block that out.

Louise rummaged in the cupboards until she found a teapot, dusty and clearly unused. Not a mark on it anywhere. She took it out, rinsed the dust off and boiled the kettle. She found a packet of biscuits in the cupboard, also untouched and laid them out on a plate. In a different sort of house she'd have looked for a doily to place underneath them but she knew that Isabelle wouldn't have any.

Walking back into the room, trying to feel a nonchalance that she didn't possess, Louise put the tea tray down on the coffee table. Why was it a coffee table and not tea? she thought as she put it down.

'Why are they called coffee tables and not tea?' Isabelle mused out loud. Louise chuckled. They really were meant to be friends; she just knew it.

'I was just thinking that!' she said and they both laughed.

'It's cos coffee got more popular and it stuck.' Glynis said, a little less stiffly as she surveyed the tray that Louise had prepared. She nodded at it. 'Glad to see that you know how to make a proper cuppa.'

'Whereas I didn't even know we had a teapot!' Isabelle laughed, trying to smooth out the tension that had somehow developed in the room.

'Somethings are worth doing properly aren't they, Glynis?' Louise said as she smiled the largest smile she could manage, despite something niggling at the pit of her stomach. The hairs on the back of her neck had risen, her body was trying to warn her of something but her brain could not settle on what that was. She shook her head. Glynis' lack of warmth was putting her off and she was out of practice.

Louise poured drinks for them all, handed them out and sat down on a chair to the edge of the room. Present but not inserting herself into a conversation that it seemed Glynis did not entirely want her in. She'd bide her time; she'd win her round. Softly, softly and all that.

'So really no one's been in? Bunch of judgemental sods the lot of 'em. It's not like you did anything, even if he is guilty!'

Louise flinched.

'Exactly, Glyn! But he isn't, he really isn't. He's told me all about it and even his solicitor said that he's been set up or something. He just wouldn't do something like that. It's horrible. The man is going to be OK, thank God, but he doesn't remember enough one way or the other.'

'How come, love?'

'Post-trauma dementia they say, but he wasn't all there before. So. He's just old.' Isabelle paused and then added, 'Sorry.'

'No offence taken, love. I know my memory isn't what it was. I know as much to know that I've forgotten and that's hard enough.'

Louise's heart rocketed into her throat as realisation dawned. She suddenly knew why Glynis' presence was putting her off, making her tense. She worked to keep her face neutral as terror unfolded inside her.

She knew her. She was one of them. One of the people she'd

worked on with Carl. The close call that they should have paid attention to but hadn't. They hadn't learned from it, or at least it seemed that Carl hadn't. He'd got too greedy, not paid enough attention to how the rest of it was unfolding.

It had been clear to Louise at the time that it wasn't going to work. Glynis was too sharp, if not 100 per cent, she had people looking out for her, and as Louise now knew, she was too close to home. A friend of Isabelle's. Their usual clients, as Carl called them, were confused and lonely. Easy to suggest things to, easy to make them believe what you'd just told them. Glynis answered back. She was not the placid old thing Carl had scouted her out to be. They'd abandoned things midway, Louise using the code they'd agreed beforehand. She asked to go to the toilet and had accidentally slammed the door shut and then shouted, 'Sorry, the draught caught the door!' out to the mark. It was Carl's sign to leave and leave immediately. Only he hadn't. He'd taken the chance to pocket the money that he'd found in an old biscuit tin. Louise had been furious with him. She recalled the argument.

'I said no. I used the code! She was far too curious and now she knows my face. Mine not yours. You should have left it!'

'It's fine, she won't notice. And even if she did, she won't think it was you. You'd not have had time to go from the bathroom to the kitchen and back. It's fine. Chillax!'

'What's the point of a code if you ignore it?!'

'Fuck's sake, Lou. Nothing went wrong. Leave it.'

'That's not the poi—'

'I said leave it!' he'd growled and she had known that she had to be quiet. She never knew exactly what Carl would do if she didn't drop things, but she knew very well that it was something that she didn't want to find out. There was a very cold, very angry thread running through him, wrapped around the charm that had drawn Louise into all this in the first place.

Back in the room with Glynis and Isabelle, Louise could feel her face getting hot. Glynis hadn't said anything yet but was still looking at her intently, questioningly.

Louise clenched her jaw tightly. She couldn't be recognised, not now. She was only just getting to know Isabelle, to get to know her situation, Carl's situation. She needed to know if she was off the hook, or what Carl might be saying inside. She needed far more information to decide what best to do. And besides, if she had to leave now, then Isabelle really would be alone and Louise didn't want that. If Louise could stay under the radar, well, that worked for everyone, didn't it? But if Glynis was about to drop her in it... Louise's mind was racing – how fast could she get gone if she needed to?

'Are you OK, Louise? You've gone all pale,' Isabelle said.

Louise swallowed hard and tried to speak. Glynis wasn't saying anything. Why?

'Fine. Just tired.'

'You've been looking after me and bump so well, we've neglected you. I'm sorry,' Isabelle said.

'It's fine, honestly. I'm fine.'

'So how's the baby doing anyway, love?' Glynis asked.

Isabelle's face switched immediately from concerned to glowing.

'Really well, thanks to Louise and her TLC. She's growing perfectly and all is fine. I'm fine too, feeling stronger every day, after all that early sickness. I'm nearly at the third trimester now.'

'The what, love?'

'The last three months. I'm nearly six months gone. It's going so fast! I'll need to get ready soon. I had hoped that Carl would be out by now. His trial hasn't been announced yet but his solicitor is doubtful it will be done and over by my due date.' She went quiet. 'He should be here. He's missing so much.' You could see the hurt and fear behind Isabelle's eyes and her not-quite fast enough masking of it. 'Luckily, I have Louise here to help me.' She then flashed such a warm and grateful smile at Louise that Louise felt her heart melt. They were actual, genuine friends. She'd not had that before. She would do anything to keep it. She'd never had anyone to fight for before, nor had someone in her corner, not for a long time. It was a good feeling. She liked it.

'That's nice, love. So...' Glynis said, turning back to look at Louise. 'How do you know each other? Have I seen you round here before? You look... familiar.' A look crossed her face, an inkling of recognition that made Louise feel immediately nauseous. 'Have we met?'

Louise's throat dried up. Her palms, still gripped into fists, were immediately clammy. She opened her mouth to speak but nothing came out but a whisper. She cleared her throat.

Get it under control, Louise. Calm. Confidence. Bluster it out. You can do this.

She cleared her throat again.

'Sorry, bit of dust or something caught the back of my throat. Ahem! Sorry!'

Suddenly a light bulb went off in Glynis.

'Ah, I've got it! You were that church girl, weren't you? Came round to chat to this old dear. Company for the elderly of the parish. That was it, wasn't it? You didn't stay long though! Rushed off after using the loo!' She cackled. 'I knew I recognised you. Been bugging me since I got here!'

Louise felt her heart stop as she watched her for signs of anything else, any anger, any fear. Anything that indicated that Glynis was aware of that her missing tea caddy money had anything to do with Louise's visit.

'You hear such horror stories, don't ya?' Glynis continued. 'Old folks being distracted by some nice young person coming to listen to the same old stories, come to give them the time of day that they don't normally get. And all the while some other sod is rifling through their things, taking what they can find. 'Ere... is that what they think Carl did?' She glanced at Louise before turning the question on Isabelle.

Louise's pulse was racing so hard she felt dizzy. She needed to think. Think. Was Glynis playing with her? Did she... did she know? Had she actually connected the dots and was biding her time before exposing her to Isabelle? Like a cat with a mouse, letting her run from paw to paw, batting her gently before pouncing in for the kill.

'I... no... I... I don't think so,' Isabelle stuttered, caught off guard. 'He didn't do it though, anyway. It wasn't him.' She asserted. 'But no, no one has mentioned anyone else.'

Glynis smiled.

Why was she here now? Louise wondered. What did she want? If it was to support Isabelle then this line of conversation wasn't working. Had she heard about Louise from someone? Though who? And what would they say? Or was she just an old gossip?

Louise was so tired of these complex levels of truth. There was always a hidden element, something said or unsaid that changed the meaning. It was exhausting. She'd had enough. She just wanted there to be one truth that everyone knew. What happened wasn't her fault. It wasn't the plan. It was never the plan. And even the plan wasn't her plan.

'What do you think? Eh? Louise? What's your opinion on it? People pretending to be churchy and then ripping folk off.'

'Come on, Glyn, don't be nasty. Carl didn't do anything of the sort and Louise isn't one of those people, are you, Louise? You've never said anything about a church.' Isabelle's face turned to Louise, kind, open and Louise felt herself calm. She would simply be who Isabelle thought she was and it would all be OK. She could do this.

'No, not me. I'm not that local, just moved here and I'm a stone-cold atheist, so although I think visiting the community is a lovely idea, it wouldn't have been me.' She smiled brightly and tried to sound confident in herself. 'I've just got that sort of face! Used to work in a bar and all the time people there were convinced they knew me. "No, mate, I just work here and you're in all the time!" Just too drunk to remember!' Louise laughed.

'See?' Isabelle laughed too, trying to smooth things over, 'She's got a recognisable face. You might have seen her around. She's been here since Carl... since... since he's been away. She was the only person who called round to see if I was OK. The only one.' Louise noted a slight pointedness from Isabelle towards Glynis, who had not visited until today. It had been weeks. If you knew what to look for, and Louise always did, you could see the slightest hint of shame cross Glynis' face, at the embarrassment that she'd not looked out for one of her own.

'Ha!' Glynis cackled. 'Drunken fools, eh? I know a few o' them! Fair enough, fair play to you, I just thought I recognised you, but must be mistaken. No shakes, no harm.' She smiled at Louise for the first time since she'd arrived and Louise felt the knot in her stomach loosen. She didn't know her, not for sure. But it was close and Louise could have ruined things for Carl by being here. He'd be furious. Or would he be pleased with what she was doing? Befriending Isabelle, helping with the baby. Or was she storing up trouble for herself?

Was it time to walk away? She didn't want to. She really didn't want to. But was this a warning sign? A warning that she ought to listen to.

10

THREE YEARS AGO

The late afternoon sunlight flooded in through dirty windows. The light was musty and distorted and the pub was dark. A traditional pub. The heat of the day had warmed the room up and it was sweltering inside. The smell was palpable. A mix of stale beer, old cigarette smoke that the carpet had absorbed over the years, and the sweat of the customers who lingered too long at the bar. Louise had to shower after every shift to eradicate it from her hair, from her skin, where it remained long after she had gone home, draping itself over her like a shadow, catching in her nose as she moved.

It had been a quiet afternoon. Most people didn't want to be indoors on such a glorious afternoon, or they'd been in for a quick drink after work and then gone on to a more glamorous location than this beat-up old boozer on the corner of a busy road. It wasn't most people's ideal place to work either but it suited Louise. The owner, Steve, didn't ask too many questions and paid in cash. When Louise had turned up looking for work, it suited them both. Steve could barely keep the pub going, being rather too fond of his own products, and on her first shift he had left her to it and gone upstairs to sleep off a hangover, leaving a total stranger in complete control of the cash register and the stockroom. It had occurred to her that she could clear him out and leg it, and he'd have no idea where to find her. He'd asked her nothing, not even her last name.

Louise had no interest in ripping him off. She just wanted a regular job where she could earn money and use the time to decide what she wanted to do from there. The pay was pitiful but without having to pay tax on it, it was enough to rent a room somewhere nearby to live. To be honest, somewhere to live was an exaggeration. It was somewhere she could keep her meagre things and exist, safely. A room with a lock on it, with shared bathroom and kitchen. She'd left home after a huge row with her parents and hadn't finished college. Or rather she had finished – she'd done her exams – but hadn't stuck around long enough to find out what her grades were. It didn't matter. She wasn't ever going to university. Not for the likes of me, she thought, echoing what her mother had said when Louise had raised the matter. Too much money without a guarantee of a job. Not worth the risk. But merely going through the motions towards adulthood hadn't given Louise time to work out what she wanted to do with her life. Until now, all she wanted to do was what she had to do. Survive. She had no one and nothing. It was lonely.

'Eh! Get us a pint would you, love?' Steve shouted from the little office room at the back of the bar. He was struggling with his accounts, and no wonder, when half the produce wasn't legit and no one other than himself was legally employed at the pub. According to his accounts, Steve managed and ran the place solo – doing the orders, pulling the pints, cleaning the toilets. In reality there was a team of people, passing through, paid cash in hand and never stopping long. The most loyal people were the customers, some of who spent more time there than in their own homes.

Louise drew Steve a pint of his favourite, a super strong ale from the brewery down the road. It sold well because they did a good deal and Steve could sell it at a favourable price. You could get 'lashed for less' he'd said, but Louise didn't see that in the customers. They just got more drunk than they might have done. The kebab shop opposite did well out of it though, as punters staggered out of the pub at closing time and weaved as straight a line as they could to buy chips and meat of questionable quality covered in garlic sauce. Louise retched when she imagined what they must smell like the following morning.

She was just back from delivering the drink to Steve, who was swearing at his spreadsheet that was 25 per cent legitimate, 25 per cent exaggerated and 50 per cent total fiction, when the door opened. The light outside was so bright compared to the dullness of the interior that Louise was blinded by it initially but then, above the old tobacco and beer she caught the note of expensive cologne and she knew it was him. Her heart skipped a little and she felt giddy. She swallowed hard to control the butterflies fluttering in her stomach that always appeared whenever he did.

'All right, Carl?' she said as she tried to sashay back to prime position behind the bar, nonchalantly tidying the paraphernalia there, straightening beer mats and adjusting the jar of dusty straws and swizzle sticks for the soft drinks and cocktails that no one ever bought.

'All right, Louise darlin', looking stunning as always! You're too good for this place. I know it every time I walk through the door into this godforsaken dive and see your pretty face!' He smirked at her, throwing a bunch of keys and a wad of paperwork onto the bar, as though he'd just reached his own office.

Louise blushed hard, though she tried not to. He had such an effect on her, she couldn't help it. Something about his voice, part East London but somehow part Westminster too, made her stomach turn in excited knots. Maybe it was the hint of a promise that perhaps he'd show you a new world, something nobody else could, if you were lucky enough to be in his orbit. She didn't know exactly what he did, but it was something glamorous enough to pay for his expensively cut suit and handmade shoes, but down to earth enough that this was still his local.

'What can I get you?' Louise tried to stand tall but her knees were shaking. He excited her but he scared her too. Amazing cheekbones didn't mean you should trust someone. She learned pretty quickly who to trust and who to give a wide berth, but with Carl she didn't know which way to turn.

'Ah, it's Friday, go on then, I'll have a quick pint, since you offered.'

She slowly poured the drink, trying to make it perfect. Not too much head, despite the additional bubbles. She wanted him to think that she was the best barmaid ever, not a barely out of college girl, out of her depth and floundering. As though she were a wife, welcoming him home after a hard day's work, Louise placed the drink in front of him. She wouldn't charge him. Steve wouldn't notice, or care. She'd seen that Steve was intimidated by Carl and would probably agree to a free watered-down beer to keep him on side. She could add it to the 50 per cent fiction stock check.

'Cheers,' he said as she placed it on the bar. If he noticed her shaking hands, he didn't say anything. He picked it up, wiped the base on the nearest bar mat and took a quick sip. His face betrayed his dislike of it but only for a millisecond. Louise caught it, she always did. It was how she was able to keep the regulars happy and the drunks under control. She could see emotions and feelings and thoughts almost as soon as their owners registered them themselves, and being sober to their less than sober, was faster to react.

'Good day?' she asked casually.

'Yeah. Yeah, pretty good actually.' He smiled, his bright white teeth gleaming at her. 'In fact, that's one thing I'm here for. Got a proposition for ya. If you'd be interested. A little deal I could use your help with.'

Her heart fluttered and her voice caught in her throat as she went to answer. She cleared it with a cough and then said, 'Yeah. Sure. What were you thinking?'

Carl looked around, checking the pub for anyone who might be listening. The old guy who was always here was asleep in the corner. Louise thought he was maybe homeless as he was here from the moment they opened until they kicked him out at night. Some nights Steve even let him kip on the sofa in the bar. A couple had just taken their drinks and headed out to the excuse of a beer garden, with its atmosphere of exhaust fumes from the A road it was adjacent to. Other than that, it was Carl and Louise. Just the two of them. Almost a date.

'Let me get you a drink and we can talk it through. Make it a double if you like.' He smiled generously at her, his blue eyes twinkling as he did so. Louise would rather not drink at work. She didn't like being vulnerable when she knew she had zero backup but the bar was empty and Carl was here, to deal with any hassle the customers might have felt like dishing out. She relaxed a little.

'OK, I'll have a rum and Coke then,' and she went to the optics and made one. Lots of ice, slice of lemon – like a little taste of some Caribbean island she knew she'd never likely see. A holiday in a glass. She took a sip and appreciated why Steve drank so often. It was an escape, and God knows, she knew how attractive an escape route could be. She was looking for one, just not one found at the bottom of a bottle.

'C'mon here...' he said, walking towards the dusty-looking banquette at the dark end of the pub. They sat down and a small puff of dust rose into the air when their weight hit the neglected fake velvet cover with more beer stains than should have been visible in the dim light. The specks floated in front of them, dancing in the streak of light that cut across the gloom. Louise coughed and they danced away from her back into the murk.

'Steve could do with a cleaner. This place is grim back here!' Carl laughed.

'He has one, but he never checks up on them and pays them badly so they cut all the corners they feel entitled to cut. I get their point, the pay here isn't great.' Louise chuckled nervously.

'It isn't fair, is it?'

'What isn't?'

'Inequality. The balance of wealth. The balance of power. It's off.'

'I... I guess.'

'I know. Did you know that in London, the richest 10 per cent own nearly half the wealth? And the poorest 10 per cent own nothing. Nothing!'

'Wow. How is that possible?'

'Cos some people have less than nothing. Debts, shonky landlords, rip-off prepaid meters swallowing their cash. And it spirals. You ever spiralled? There's no stop button is there? No "I wanna get off the ride" button. You just get poorer and poorer till you're done. And then you die.'

Louise wrinkled her forehead in confusion. Was Carl a socialist? Was he trying to convert her to something? She had had no idea what the conversation was going to be about but she hadn't thought it would be political.

'I guess. Yes, it's hard,' she agreed, trying to work out what she thought, and more importantly, what Carl wanted. Why was he here having this talk with her?

'It is hard. You're right. Heh!' He laughed, suddenly less intense again, taking a sip of his drink. 'Makes you want to believe in Robin Hood, doesn't it?'

Louise smiled. She loved Robin Hood. A story about him was

her favourite childhood book, which her grandpa read to her. She loved how an outsider could find their tribe and go about setting right the wrongs and making everyone happy, apart from the evil greedy Prince John and his sheriff of Nottingham, who got their just deserts. The memory of those bedtime stories, full of love and kindness, painted a smile across her face.

'Heh. You like it, I can see. Setting things right. Adjusting the balance. Could see it from how you are in here. You're quiet, but I've seen you.'

Louise blushed. He'd been watching her? She took a large sip of her drink, blanching a little at how strong it was. She could feel her stomach tying itself in knots, the acidity of the alcohol rushing into her bloodstream, making her feel light-headed and woozy.

'You have?'

''Course! Steve hires a gorgeous new barmaid, I want to know who she is, what she's like. Can I trust her? Can he trust her? You've seen how he is. He's ripe for being done over in his state and he's an old friend. Can't and won't let that happen. Got to look out for your own, haven't you?'

'I wouldn't know,' Louise said quietly before she'd even realised she'd spoken. She slipped her hand up to her mouth, her pale long fingers covering her lips to stop any more truths slipping out unguarded.

'How'd you mean?' Carl said, suddenly serious. His warmth towards her, his genuine interest in her well-being made her want to cry. No one really cared how she was. No one. Her heart went cold and her muscles tightened. The seam of granite that had been growing, slowly spreading, her whole life, hardening her from the inside, grew a little more. Took more of her softness and enveloped it, squashed it, like the earth squashes carbon. Only it didn't make a diamond, it just made coal. Dark. Black. Ready to burn.

'Just that you have to look out for yourself, don't you? My

parents were too wrapped up in themselves to really look after me. I was in their way. An accident. A surprise they didn't want but couldn't do anything about once they got me.'

She took a large gulp of her drink to try to numb her pain. The harshness of the rum stung the back of her throat and the sweetness of the Coke made her feel a bit sick. She wished she'd chosen something else, something more sophisticated. Something to make Carl see who she could be, who she wanted to be. Who even was that?

'You can really only rely on yourself.' Her mouth settled into a thin line.

'Yes,' Carl nodded sagely. 'That's true. Which is why I wanted to talk. I have a proposition for you.'

Intrigued, Louise leaned forward across the sticky varnished tabletop. 'Go on...'

He spoke at length, in detail. He'd clearly worked it all out. Louise was shocked. She sat back, saying nothing at first, letting it all sink in. Working out the implications of what he was suggesting. Working out how she felt about it all. She lifted her glass to her lips only to find it was empty. The double rum was working its way through her bloodstream, into her mind, making things fuzzy. Or was it making things clearer; moving aside all the usual junk, usual worries, usual filters, to get to the crux of her thoughts?

'So. You want me to be your... business partner?'

'Yeah, you could call it that. My last associate moved on,' he said matter-of-factly, 'I need a new one.'

'You'd size up who we, who we...' Louise was trying to come up with a nice way of saying it but she couldn't and decided that honesty was the best policy, to be completely clear about things '... who we target. I knock on the door and keep them talking, either on the doorstep or inside if they'll let me in and while I'm doing that, you...'

'Go in the back way and take what's worth having. Yeah. Sell it on, split the proceeds fifty-fifty. Stuff they'll barely miss, stuff that's just cluttering up their houses. No harm done. Practically a good deed. House clearance costs a fortune these days. Daylight robbery!'

Louise waited for him to laugh at his joke before understanding that he didn't realise he had made one.

'But we'd be robbing them,' Louise said, pointing out the absolute truth.

'Well... yes,' Carl said, 'but... not like that! Look, we're really careful about how we do it. We pick only certain clients. Those who have all the stuff, all the money, but have no people. No one to talk to, no one to look out for them, no one to leave all the stuff to. So we give them that. You give them that. You make friends with them. We don't necessarily take stuff on the first visit. Depends on the person. You offer them a listening ear, someone to chat to, something to look forward to. You give them companionship, someone who gives a shit.'

'But we'd be taking from them?'

Carl threw his head back and laughed. A deep, hoarse and throaty laugh, in which you could hear every cigarette he'd ever smoked and every glass of whisky he'd ever drunk. It made something stir in the pit of Louise's stomach. Attraction? Fear?

'Well, yes, but doesn't everyone take from everyone else all the time? I mean, if they left all their money to their family, isn't that just as give and take?? If they'd left it to the local cats' home, isn't that a sort of contract too?'

Louise thought a while on this.

'I suppose so.'

'And some folk, well, they're just born with their transactions already lined up for them, already laid out. Inheritance, child support, allowances. And some of us, like you and me, well, we have to find our transactions. Just cos we ain't got them all ready and waiting, doesn't mean we have to go for the lowest of the low, does it now? Just cos we were born poor doesn't mean we have to work all the hours God sends for sod all, does it? No. How is it any different to those working in the City, eh? They spend all day selling fake money for fake money, using other people's wealth to get rich themselves. Sometimes their clients get more money back, sometimes they lose it and that's all legal, isn't it? This? Well, our clients at least get a little face-to-face interaction, a chit-chat that makes their day, someone to actually listen to them properly. They don't really lose anything. And neither do we.'

He sat back, satisfied that he'd said his piece and waited to see what Louise's reaction would be. She watched him, trying to read his face. She sat back herself, let the idea sink in. Modern-day Robin Hoods. Taking from those who didn't need it for those who had nothing. Like her. And once she had it herself, she could redistribute it if she wanted. Once she'd got enough for herself, somewhere to live where the mould didn't threaten to overtake the walls, somewhere she didn't have to put a chair behind the door when she slept as the lock was as unreliable as her unknown housemates. Once she had a safe place to stay and enough food, well then, she could help out others, couldn't she? She could drop money into collection boxes and not look the other way when charity muggers tried to stop her in the street. Right now, literally every penny she earned from her hours in the pub went on paying for the dump she rented and had to be eked out in the supermarket's reduced section at the end of the day, when the red stickers were brought out, so she could pick up the damaged cans and going-out-of-date fresh food. It was the only way she could eat. And it was barely enough even then.

She was tired of barely enough. She'd spent her whole life with barely enough. Barely enough food, barely enough thought given to her well-being, barely enough love. She wanted more. She deserved more and she'd take more. These clients deserved more too. She hated the thought of someone like her grandpa sitting, deteriorating in their own home, alone, with no one to chat through their day with, just waiting out the silent, lonely hours until death. It wasn't good enough. None of it was good enough. She found a strength to her voice as she outlined her non-negotiables.

'Nobody gets hurt. No one gets harmed. We don't take anything of obvious sentimental value. If it's looking like a bad choice once we're there, we get out asap, we touch nothing. We're giving them time and attention in return for cash or things to be sold on. Right?'

Carl smiled, nodding slowly as he watched his newest member of staff fall into line.

'Exactly. Do no harm, nice chat, cuppa and a biscuit while I do a little tidying, a little decluttering. Me or whoever you're working with. It'll sometimes be me, sometimes one of the other guys. We're a crew, we move about. Keeps things unpredictable.'

There was a flicker of doubt in Louise's mind, a brief second where she knew what she was agreeing to was wrong, but she stamped it out. *Enough. I'm tired of surviving. I want to live.*

'We don't take from anyone who can't afford it?'

'Nope.'

'And you move the stuff on after? My face is the risk upfront, your face is the risk after the fact?'

'Precisely. Like I said, fifty-fifty. Equal partnership.'

Louise chewed her lip. It was time to put herself first. If she couldn't have love, then she could at least have money. What was the saying? *Money wouldn't make you happy but you'd have a better class of misery.* Louise wasn't sure that was right. Money could fix a lot of her misery.

'I'm in. When do we start?'

'That's my girl. I'll be in touch.'

Louise's breath flickered in her throat as adrenaline shot through her, she was part of something now. A team. She wasn't alone and she had been given the power to take some of what life had denied her. She just had not to think too hard about what she would pay for it.

11

PRESENT DAY

It was late. Louise and Isabelle were both curled up, at opposite ends of the sofa, watching some mindless reality show. Louise wasn't really paying attention, not really knowing or caring who these overly tanned people by the pool were, but Isabelle seemed to know the who, what, where, of it all.

'And she is so into him but he isn't into her but he's not going to let her know that yet cos it doesn't work for his plan,' Isabelle was saying.

Louise nodded, not really following, but noticing that Isabelle was rubbing her stomach more often than usual at this time of night. In the four and a bit months that Louise had known Isabelle, she knew that baby was usually quieter until later in the evening when she would go nuts and the two of them often watched as discernible outlines of feet or elbows poked a shape out in Isabelle's skin. It was both beautiful and horrifying and Isabelle would usually squeal and then laugh at herself.

'You OK?' Louise asked, nodding towards Isabelle's bump.

'Hmm? Oh this? Yeah, it's fine. The Braxton Hicks are just ramping up tonight. Sure it'll settle down.' She picked up the bowl of spicy snacks to her side and ate a few more. 'These probably aren't helping either!' She laughed before almost immediately segueing into a gasp of pain.

Louise's face furrowed into a concerned frown. She'd been keeping watch on the timing of Isabelle's discomfort and it seemed to be settling into a definite pattern. Around every fifteen minutes or so if she was right, not too out of sync with the commercials on the show they were watching and each episode was getting longer. She'd not read a lot about pregnancy and birth. It seemed a bit invasive somehow, despite them being friends, but what she had learned suggested that Braxton Hicks, practice contractions, were far more random and shorter than this.

'When are you due again?' Louise asked. She knew the answer, but wanted to put the suggestion to Isabelle that it may be time, but in a gentle way, less likely to freak her out. It had been hard, the past few weeks, the slowly dawning realisation that Carl was not going to be home in time for the birth. Isabelle's mother had needed persuading to be her replacement birth partner, needing to travel back from her home in Spain in time, and Isabelle wasn't feeling secure about how it was all going to go as her mother was of a different generation with different views about childbirth and babies. All matter of fact and not a lot of empathy as far as Louise could see. Families it seemed, even the ones that looked good on the surface, had a lot of complexity that outsiders didn't necessarily see.

'Four weeks. Though it could be up to six, so it might not happen soon!' Isabelle beamed, but then again winced as her abdomen tightened. 'This baby won't stop kicking my bladder!' She laughed and hauled herself out of the chair with some difficulty. She was petite, the bump was sitting way up front and gravity kept trying to make her sit back down.

'Here, do you want a hand?' Louise said, hopping to her feet, as light as a gazelle in comparison.

'Oof. Please. I'm such a lump! I am looking forward to getting my body back, I know that. Pregnancy is so sneaky. The "get this done with" starts to overtake the "I'm too scared to do this".'

As Isabelle stood up, she held onto Louise and then it happened. First there was a trickle and Isabelle froze, looking mortified.

'Oh. My. God. I am so sorry. I am beyond embarrassed.'

'What? Oh.' Louise looked down to see the trickle running down Isabelle's legs.

'I think I just wet myself. I am horrified. Please, please let's never mention this, ever.'

Louise took Isabelle's arm and smiled. 'It's OK, it's nothing.'

And then it wasn't nothing. It was very much not nothing at all when Isabelle moved towards the hallway and her waters broke. It wasn't like the movies. It wasn't like an epic flood but an unmistakable puddle that was growing at her feet.

'Shiiiiiiiit. Shit. Shit!' Isabelle turned to Louise, looking panic stricken. 'What do I do?'

Louise tried to stay calm. She needed to be to keep Isabelle calm. How hard could it be? This happens every day, all over the world.

'OK, so I think those Braxton Hicks were contractions. You were having them about every ten to fifteen minutes or so. I think you're in labour?' She tried to be reassuring without being overbearing. She didn't know a whole lot, but Isabelle needed to realise that perhaps this was it. It was time.

'It's happening? Now?! But, but she's early! We're never early! We're a family of latecomers, late for everything, all the time!' Isabelle stammered.

'Yeah, I don't think anyone told her that!' Louise laughed and pointed to Isabelle's bump.

Isabelle laughed weakly, 'Yeah. Could you get a towel? They're in the cupboard on the upstairs landing. I'm not moving, I don't want to ruin any more of the flooring. God, Carl will be furious, this hardwood cost a fortune to put down. He wanted laminate! He should be here!' she said, starting to cry.

Louise said nothing. Carl would be losing his head like some decapitated chicken, she knew that. After all, she'd seen how well he coped in unexpected situations and it wasn't good. It wasn't good at all. He wasn't someone you wanted with you in a crisis. You wanted someone composed and deliberate. You wanted Louise.

She went upstairs, got the towel and the hospital bag she knew Isabelle had packed just last week, despite saying it was too early to be so organised. Louise took a moment to regroup at the top of the stairs. She was worried, selfishly, because things had settled into a good place. Carl was out of the picture for the time being, his trial not for a few weeks yet. It didn't seem that the police were looking for anyone else in connection to the robbery and assault. She had a new home, enough money for the time being and she and Isabelle were becoming fast friends. A new life was stretching out in front of her and she liked the look of it. A baby would change all that. Isabelle's mum was supposed to be coming to stay and who knows which family members might come to help, which friends might feel remorse for abandoning Isabelle and creep back, arms full of gifts and mouths full of apologies? Isabelle would have someone else to focus on, another person to care about and Louise wouldn't be her first port of call any more. She got an inkling of how new fathers might feel, suddenly shunted down the pecking order in the affections of their partners. Before, she'd never have said it was possible to be jealous of a baby, but this one wasn't even born yet and Louise wasn't wholly sure how she felt about it. Her. Not it, her.

The Silent Friend

Back in the living room, Isabelle was hanging up the phone. She'd shuffled back towards the sofa but hadn't sat down. That upholstery would be hard to clean, Louise knew she'd be thinking. Louise wondered how she'd cope with sticky toddler handprints.

'I don't believe it!' Isabelle cried, a definite wobble in her voice.

'What?'

'Mum. I can't get hold of her. No answer on the landline or the mobile. She's not online to message either. I don't know where she is. I told her that she needed to be available in case the baby came. That she might have to jump on the next available flight to London. I knew she should have come over sooner. She's my birth partner! It's bad enough that Carl isn't going to be here and now neither is my mum!'

'I mean, it might be a false labour yet. And don't they say first births can take a while? She might be able to get here in time. It could be days, couldn't it?'

'What do I do?'

'Call your midwife? She'll say whether to stay here or go into hospital, won't she?'

'Yes. Yes, I'll do that.'

'Here.' Louise handed her the towel and Isabelle shuffled to the cheaper chair and sat down, getting out her mobile again and with shaking hands, selecting the number.

'Hi, yes, my waters broke. Yes, just now. Thirty-six weeks. Isabelle White. OK, yes, OK. I don't know.' She covered the mobile with her hand and whispered to Louise, 'What colour is it?'

'Is what?'

'The... fluid.' Isabelle indicated the puddle, embarrassed.

'Oh. Oh! Um.' Louise went to check. 'Sort of clear? No real colour.'

'Clear. No, no greens or other colours. No. No show. Contractions...'

'Ten to fifteen minutes apart, about thirty to forty seconds long,' Louise said, grateful that the TV programme had been as dull as it had been. She'd only been paying attention because of that.

Isabelle looked grateful and mouthed 'thank you' at her. Louise smiled. They were in this together.

'Oh. OK. Yes, yes, we can do that. Yes, I've got all my things. Yes, OK. Thank you, bye.'

Isabelle hung up and was silent. She looked in shock. Pale and flushed at the same time somehow. She sat for a moment, her face impassive. She wrung her hands together and took a deep breath before letting it out, nodding slowly. 'OK,' she said to herself. 'OK.'

'OK?' Louise asked, dipping her head down to try to catch Isabelle's eye.

'Yes. OK.' Isabelle looked up, her expression now one of stoicism. 'The midwife said I sound like I am in early labour and if I want I can stay at home while it progresses. But she also said that the maternity hospital is getting busy. At the moment they have space for me. But she also said that if nothing progresses in the next fifteen hours...'

'Fifteen?'

'Fifteen hours, I'd need to come in to speed things up and she doesn't know if they will still have space then, or where I'll end up. She said if I want to, I could come in now. They've space on the antenatal ward and would move me into the delivery unit when I need to. But I have to go now.'

'OK... so what do you want me to do? Wait here? Call your mum again? See if I can let... let Carl know somehow?'

'No. No.' Isabelle shook her head vehemently. 'I don't want him to know. He'll only worry and what can he do? It'd be torturing him, knowing it's happening without him. Once she's here and safe, I can let him know the good news and he'll be too happy to be sad about missing it. I know him, he'll get angry and frustrated and that's not good for his case, is it?'

'Fair point.'

Louise had seen Carl not get his own way and Isabelle was right, it wasn't pretty.

'Will you come with me?' Isabelle said quietly.

'What?'

'Will you come with me? To the hospital? I don't know if Mum will make it and I don't want to do this by myself. I... I can't, I know I can't. Will you be my birthing partner?'

Louise was momentarily shocked. It was such an intimate role to be asked to play and yet she had to think about it for barely a second. She wasn't sure how she felt about the baby, she had conflicted feelings, but she knew she wanted to help Isabelle.

'I'd be honoured. If you want me there.'

'I do. I know we've not known each other long, but, I don't know, it feels longer. Like we're cousins or sisters or something. Do you know what I mean?' Isabelle blushed, like she was asking Louise on a date or something.

'I do.' Louise nodded as something inside her shifted. That niggle at the back of her mind telling her to be careful, to stay distant, was dismissed. She was choosing to step closer, despite what that might bring.

'Right. Wow. This is it. She's really coming. She's really going to be here soon!' Isabelle beamed, ecstatic despite her nerves. She was showing a strength that had been growing in her ever since Carl's arrest. She was already a different person to the woman he left on the doorstep that morning months ago. Louise had seen it, seen her question her own decisions less and less, seen her stand up for herself and her future family more, advocating for herself in a way Louise felt like she had not been given space to do before. She wondered what sort of shock Carl was in for when he finally got home.

'I'll just pop home and grab a few things. Then, shall I get a cab?'

Isabelle nodded as she bent to hold onto the sofa and breathe her way through another contraction.

Clocking that the intensity of the contractions seemed to have increased, Louise said,

'I'll be back as soon as I can.'

Across the road in her own flat, it was dark and cold. She'd barely been back there in days. She'd been staying over at Isabelle's, keeping her company. It was easy in Isabelle's house to forget the bigger picture somehow. Carl was in jail, but for how long? Would they find him guilty? Did Louise need somehow to talk with him about all this? Isabelle didn't know who Louise really was, but how long could Louise keep up that lie? Was it possible to just become someone else and leave your past behind, like that last bag on the baggage carousel at the airport, abandoned as it goes round and round unclaimed, its owner having left it behind and moved on?

A new life was on its way, ready to meet her loving parents. Were they loving? Was Carl? Isabelle adored Carl. But he was in prison charged with beating an old man nearly to death. Which one was he? A cruel, unpredictable violent man? Or a kind, supportive, loving one? Was it possible to be both or was one merely an act? Louise knew that people had layers, secrets. Was it fair to assume that Carl was any different? If he was only one thing, a bad person, then what did that make her?

Louise felt tangled up in a mess of who she was then, and who she was before and who she wanted to be now. That job, and all she'd experienced since, made her want to be better. Surely it'd be wiser to just up sticks and move, far away, out of London, where no one knew her and her past was unlikely to follow her. She could shed her skin, change her name and start a life again from the ground up.

She looked about her flat. She could take the things she was putting into a bag and add her money, more clothes and just go. Isabelle would eventually realise that she wasn't coming back and would get herself to hospital and would be fine. Louise's heart rate flickered and she felt her pulse pounding in her ears. She hadn't meant it to be but packing things into a bag had turned into one of those left or right moments.

When she was little, her grandpa used to take her on mystery tours. He couldn't walk very far and so he'd load them into the car with a bag of her favourite sweets and then at each junction, he would ask, 'So, which way? Left or right?'

'I don't know!'

'Doesn't matter, close your eyes and choose.'

'You too?'

'I'm driving! Can't close my eyes, luvvie. Besides, this is your adventure.'

It gave her such a thrill. She was in control of her own journey. She had a power that she didn't have in her normal life. She adored those trips – just her and Grandpa going wherever she felt like and with no idea as to the destination. Each junction offered different possibilities.

Which way now?

Louise put the remaining things in her bag and walked out of the door.

12

THREE YEARS AGO

'You did good kid.' Carl smiled at her as he leafed through the wads of banknotes he was counting. 'You kept her talking for ages and never even told her a thing about yourself. That takes skills. You listened, asked questions and paid attention as she rambled her life story at you. Hell, you even know what her late husband liked for breakfast! Gave me all the time I needed to weed out where she kept her valuables. I made a good choice in you.'

Louise's stomach fluttered at the compliment but then she immediately felt guilty. She had liked the client. She didn't want to think about how she would have felt once she noticed things were missing. She couldn't go there. She couldn't allow herself the luxury of empathy. She swallowed the guilt and smiled at Carl.

Things had gone to plan. She had knocked on the door of the woman who Carl had decided was a good 'hit'.

'The guys have had her under watch. Not many people come and go. She is independent and predictable in her routines. When she goes out she dolls herself up. Takes cabs, not the bus. She has cash.'

Louise had been greeted by a frail-looking glamorous lady

who'd opened the door carefully and peered out at the stranger standing on her doorstep. Louise's hands had felt clammy as she launched into the spiel she and Carl had practised.

'Hi, my name is Alana and I am from St Matthew's Church, just around the corner.' She turned back and indicated the general direction of a church that Carl's goons had assured him this lady did not attend. 'We're doing outreach in the local community to see if we can help with anything from light chores to just sitting and having a chat. Could I come in and see if you need anything?' Louise smiled, keeping her face as neutral, open and innocent looking as she could. She had chosen the most inoffensive look possible. She was wearing brown loafers, relaxed jeans and a striped T-shirt. She wanted to look like both everyone and no one.

'Oh. Oh, no I don't think I need anything, thank you.' She went to close the door.

'How was your morning?' Louise said, putting her hand on the door, outwardly looking casual but actually preventing it from closing. 'Mine was good. I'm studying at college and my latest assignment went really well!' she chirped, smiling broadly, belying the sick feeling that was coursing through her veins. What would her grandpa think of her now?

'Oh. Oh, that's nice, dear.'

Louise waited. The silence needed to be filled by someone other than her. Still smiling, still standing expectantly.

'What are you studying?' the lady asked finally. The English need for politeness over all other things winning out eventually.

Louise scanned the woman, behind her into the house too, for a subject that might keep her talking. She noted the put-together outfit, the earrings, the brooch, all very curated.

'The history of fashion. If you can believe it!' She laughed, indicating her outfit and acknowledging its blandness. 'The church suggested we dress plainly so as not to worry or concern our less forward-thinking friends. I can see you're not one of those though,'

A flicker of pride flashed across the woman's face. This was it. That was what Louise needed to hook onto.

'I can clearly see you know your way around fashion and haute couture. Who are you wearing?' she said, fanning her hands out to admire the outfit.

The lady blushed, showing a hint of the girl she would have been in her youth. She looked down, demurely, and then said, 'You can tell, I know! This is Prada. Oh, you must come in. I have so much I could show you!' And with that, she opened the door wide and welcomed in this complete stranger, one who had told nothing but lies from the moment she had knocked on the door.

Now, Louise was trying to work out how she felt, as Carl went on, crowing about how well they'd done and how pleased he was that he'd chosen her. He had managed to get a fair amount of cash, some jewellery that he suspected was real, and a few other items that were valuable enough to raise some funds, but not suspicion, and unlikely to be missed by their owner for some time yet.

'It'll be weeks before she goes to look for the jewels, and by then, well, they could be anywhere, couldn't they? She could have just misplaced them herself, couldn't she? Forgetful old bag.'

'Hmm,'

'Aren't you pleased? Look at how much you made?' His eyes narrowed. 'You're not feeling guilty, are you?' He almost laughed at her.

'A little. Yes. I mean, we didn't harm her and, like you said, she's got lots of money.'

'Found her bank statements, she's got plenty, don't worry about that. Not left her penniless, that's for sure. Just skimmed off the top from what her rich, dead husband probably evaded in tax.'

'I guess.'

'Look. She was lonely. Yes?'

Louise nodded.

'Did you give her an hour of your time?'

Louise nodded again.

'Did you listen to her stories about Paris in the sixties and seventies and listen to her going on about her parties and her holidays and all that guff? And was she happier when you left her than she was when you arrived?'

'Yes. Yes, she was floating on air when I left. Couldn't wait to ask me back.'

'Well, there you are then! You gave her far more than we took. Just cos she hadn't asked for it and she doesn't know what she paid for it, doesn't mean a fair transaction hasn't taken place. She'll miss you when you don't come back but then, hey, you can be another of her happy memories, can't you? And those are priceless!' He laughed and threw her envelope to her.

Louise laughed and picked it up. 'I suppose. I'd hate to think of my grandpa being lonely and I'd rather he had company than leave money to someone who didn't care enough to visit. If he were still here, obviously. Or if he'd had any money to leave.'

'Exactly. We're just spreading the inheritance to those who actually work for it. Now stop feeling bad and go buy yourself something nice!'

Louise shook away her bad feelings and reminded herself of how little she had. Carl was right. They weren't harming anyone. They were just making lonely people less lonely. And that was a good thing. Right?

13

PRESENT DAY

The room was unbearably hot and Louise had to keep taking swigs of ice water to keep cool. She could already feel a headache trying to creep in behind her eyes that she had to stop. She had to keep her energy up so that she could give it to Isabelle. And Isabelle needed it.

Labour had progressed quickly but then had stalled and it had been hours now with contractions coming and then stopping, before starting and still nothing much was happening. Isabelle was tiring and it was a challenge to keep the energy levels up but also keep the room calm, quiet, low lit and relaxing. There was an unwritten deadline that everyone was trying not to mention, which wasn't helping. The end of the midwife's shift was fast approaching and soon she would leave and someone new would replace her. Isabelle had told Louise she didn't want that.

'She's been great. She's my midwife. I'm too tired to make the effort to connect with someone else. I can't do that again with someone new. I need to have this baby while she's still here. I have to. I have to.'

'You can have this baby when this baby is ready, Iz. I'm here, I'm not going anywhere. We can do this together. I promise. And hey, your mum might make it here too.' She squeezed Isabelle's clammy hand to show her support and looked down at her. Her face was pale, her usually glamorous hair was lank against her face. She looked exhausted. Louise tried to force a bright smile onto her face but she was worried. She didn't know a lot about childbirth but Isabelle's waters had broken already and that set the clock ticking. The baby needed to be out within... Dammit, she couldn't remember. But there was a deadline. She knew that.

'I don't know... I'm tired.'

'Like, why does labour often kick off at night? I mean, you'd think there'd be some advantage to the mum not starting the whole process knackered to begin with, right?!' Louise laughed, trying to bring some levity from somewhere. Isabelle was starting to doubt herself.

'God, I haven't slept properly in forever anyway. I don't sleep properly without Carl there. And, well...' Isabelle's voiced wavered, her lips started to tremble and tears formed in her eyes.

'Iz...' Louise said, nodding her head.

He should be here, not her. Whatever complicated feelings Louise may have about him, she knew it was his place here that she was taking.

Louise wasn't sure who Carl really was. At first she had been flattered by his attention, his focus. He could make you feel like the only person in the world when he was talking to you, even though she knew, always, that Isabelle existed. In those early days, Louise let herself believe that there was a chance somehow. For her and Carl. But the more she got to know him, the more they 'worked' together, the less she admired him. The more she saw of his cruelty, his selfishness. Her belief in what they did dwindled, but by then she was stuck. He had all the information on her. She was the face that their clients knew. If she as much as raised an objection, he had all he needed to destroy her without ever implicating himself. She was tied to him. Only his failure to stick to the plan and his temper had given her the chance to escape. Yet she had chosen to stay close, to know more, to meet his wife. Why? She'd known what she was doing was unwise, but like a cradle-Catholic who can never quite shake that tie, she had found it hard to walk away. How bad was he really? And now, somehow, here she was, helping his wife give birth to his child. Louise knew she was being ridiculous. She knew she was playing with fire and yet she was still there.

'He should be here, Lou, he should. His child is being born. Albeit slowly! I just want him here! And why hasn't my mum called back? Can you check my phone again? Please?' Isabelle begged.

Louise had already checked several times and sent several messages to no avail.

'She'll call back. Maybe she's even on her way here right now and hasn't stopped to message you that, eh?'

'Just check? Please?'

'OK.'

Louise dug Isabelle's phone out of the bag on the floor and opened the screen. Isabelle had told her the password earlier and Louise just knew instinctively that it was also her pin code. Years of scamming people had given her a sense of who would be security savvy and those who assume it'd never happen to them. Isabelle, in her bubble of always getting what she wanted, was definitely in the latter camp. Louise could almost resent her and her easy, no-hurdles life. Except one, she genuinely wanted to be friends with her as Isabelle was kind and thoughtful, not precocious and entitled. And two, Louise thought that what she was experiencing now – Carl getting convicted and her friends abandoning her – was harder for Isabelle, because she'd never experienced hardship or heartbreak. She had been falling apart because she'd never had to be strong. Louise? She'd never had anyone but herself, Grandpa excepted, and because of it, it would take a lot to destroy her. She'd developed not just a thick skin, but a bulletproof skin. Nothing and no one got in. Until now.

Louise glanced at the message thread. Four messages. All had been read and a while ago. Unless, unbeknownst to Isabelle, her mum had left Spain and was on her way, she wasn't coming and she wasn't going to make it. Nor was she going to let her daughter know it. Anger rose in Louise's stomach. Why would you abandon your daughter now? Because of who she married and what he may have done? Whatever Carl had done, Isabelle hadn't. And surely now would be a good time to try to oust him? The thought flickered through Louise's mind before it was interrupted.

'Anything?'

'No, she's not seen them,' Louise lied, tucking the phone away again. 'Maybe she's not got signal, maybe we haven't, I can't tell. I'll go and call her in a bit, shall I?' Louise offered, hoping that it would be enough to calm Isabelle and get her mind refocused.

'Yes. Yes. OK.' Isabelle looked deflated. She looked like someone who needed her mum. Louise knew how that felt.

'I'm glad you're here.' Isabelle smiled at Louise.

'Me too. Though…'

Isabelle's face dropped. 'What?'

Louise smiled. 'I need the loo! I'll be back!' She laughed and Isabelle did too.

'Don't worry, don't think this baby's coming any time soon!'

When Louise got back, the atmosphere of the room had changed. The midwife and the consultant were both there, looking over the charts and the baby's heartbeat trace. Immediately, Louise could see something was wrong. The air was thick with concern and they were talking in low, hushed voices, huddled together conferring over something. Isabelle was lying back, eyes closed, looking completely exhausted. Louise went to her, reached out and stroked her hair. She was hot, too hot. She opened her eyes sleepily but they weren't really focusing on anything.

'You OK?' Louise asked, concerned.

'Hmm?' she said sleepily.

Louise turned to the midwife. 'I don't think she's OK?'

The midwife nodded something at the consultant and they turned to face them both. The consultant spoke first.

'No. Isabelle, you seem to have developed an infection somewhere, possibly due to your waters breaking early. Your cervix isn't doing what we'd like. It's not dilated enough for baby right now. Baby also seems unhappy, her heartbeat is slow. Looking at where we are, I think we're looking at an EMCS.'

'A what?' Louise asked.

'An emergency C-section,' the midwife translated, her face a little grimmer than Louise would like. It wasn't that bad, was it? Was it?!

'No, no. The plan wasn't for a section. I wanted a water birth...' Isabelle said, sounding more sleepy by the minute.

'I know, I know,' Louise said soothingly.

'Sometimes plans have to change, I'm afraid. The theatre is currently available, I suggest we go now. Here is the paperwork, have a look, sign and let me know. I'll be back. Claire is here if you have any questions,' the consultant said as she left the room.

Isabelle was quiet but she was crying.

'Do you have any questions?' Claire asked kindly.

'How necessary is the section?' Louise said, knowing how much Isabelle didn't want one.

Claire looked at her notes as if to double-check.

'We would say that it's necessary to give both mother and baby the best outcome here. Sometimes nature doesn't do what we want it to and we have to let medicine take over. Otherwise... well.'

'Are we talking life or death?' Louise said, suddenly shocked.

Claire paused, then answered simply, but gently, 'Yes. One or possibly both.'

'Oh. Right. OK,' Louise said, taking it in. 'OK, let me talk to her.'

Minutes later, the consultant returned with a porter in tow. By this time Isabelle was sobbing but she understood. She had woken up a bit so it meant that she was capable of signing the forms. Louise was glad, both because it meant Isabelle was aware of what she was doing, but also, Louise didn't exist, not really, and she didn't want to pop up on any official forms. She was not here. She was never truly anywhere, not if she could help it. It was a difficult habit to break.

The porter took the bed and moved it through the doorway.

'Follow me,' the consultant said.

The rest was a blur. Louise couldn't have told you where they went (there was a lift, so she knew it was a different floor), or who she spoke to or what they said. All of a sudden she was in scrubs, in an operating theatre, holding the hand of a very scared Isabelle, who was lying on a metal bed, with a curtain up by her waist, beyond which the obstetrician was pulling the baby out of her.

'It will probably feel like I'm washing up in your abdomen, but if you have any pain, let me know?'

Isabelle said nothing but stared blankly at the strip-lit ceiling, eyes barely blinking. When they did, they pushed fat tears down her cheeks, pooling by her neck. It was as if she was barely present and Louise felt a cold jolt of fear. Fear for Isabelle, fear for the baby. What if the worst happened? What if baby had one parent gone and one in jail? What sort of start in life was that? Louise found herself getting angry on behalf of this not-yet-born child. One she had previously resented. This baby deserved more.

The anger was pushed away by more fear. Fear for herself. Louise had not truly admitted this to herself until now, but she wanted to be part of something. She was tired of being alone, showing her real self to no one. No single person on this earth really knew her. Isabelle was the closest she had to that now and she didn't want to let it go, despite the crazy complications she knew that created with Carl. Both of them could tell Isabelle their version of the truth and destroy the other in Isabelle's eyes. Louise had to keep him on side, keep Isabelle in the dark, for now. Louise could take care of things while Carl was... away. Isabelle would be none the wiser and Louise, well, she'd have them both. And the baby. A family, though a rather strange one, but didn't they say that all families are strange if you look properly?

Louise turned to Isabelle. She wiped a tear from Isabelle's face and whispered to her.

'It'll be OK. I know nothing is how you wanted, nothing is how you thought it would be but... she's nearly here, you'll both be safe. I'll look after you and her, and it'll be OK. I promise.'

Isabelle blinked, and slowly turned to look at Louise, a depth of sorrow in her eyes.

'Promise?'

'I promise.'

Then everything was sealed by that sound. The best sound in the world. The baby cried.

'It's a girl. A healthy girl,' Claire said. 'Well done, Isabelle. Well done.'

She handed the baby to Isabelle who gazed adoringly at her newborn daughter.

'Hello, you,' she said before kissing the top of her head, all exhaustion, worry, stress, gone. For now, nothing else mattered but this moment.

Louise felt her heart swell. She felt elated, a joy she'd never experienced before. Then, she suddenly felt alone. She was surrounded by so many people but she was totally separate. These were not her colleagues. This was not her family. Isabelle had wanted Carl, then her mum. She was third choice.

'Louise... Louise!'

'Oh, sorry, what? Sorry, I'm tired. Not like you obviously but...'

'You've been amazing, thank you. You must be exhausted too. Do you want to?'

Louise looked confused.

'Do I want to what?'

Isabelle laughed kindly. 'Do you want to hold her?' She nodded down as best she could still lying down, oblivious to the stitching up the doctors were doing the other side of the green sheet.

'Really? I mean she's so tiny...'

'Here. You'll have to take her, I can't really move...'

'Oh right, yes. Sorry.' Louise was suddenly conscious of her limbs. She didn't want to drop the baby. She took her in her arms and was struck by how tiny she was but by the weight of her too. Like a small bag of shopping, only warm.

'Hiya,' she said, at first self-conscious of talking to someone who she knew would not reply. This tiny human looked up at her, her big blue eyes in her small face unfocused and blinking, her tuft of brown hair sticking up, looking like she'd just had quite the time of it. 'Bet this is all a bit much, isn't it? I know I feel it and I'm a grown-up!' She laughed.

'You're good with her,' Isabelle said. 'I was going to let Carl name her but I can't wait. What do you think about Charlotte, Lottie for short?'

Louise looked at her. 'Lottie,' she said. 'I like it.'

'Lottie it is then. Carl'll like it. It was his granny's name.' Isabelle looked pained and Louise couldn't tell if it was physical pain, post birth, or if it was speaking Carl's name when he should have been here himself. Louise felt a flicker of sympathy. He'd missed the birth of his first child. But then, the Carl she knew might not have cared. That was all 'women's stuff' and he'd probably have preferred to wait for news from the local pub.

Louise didn't want to miss a thing. She held on tightly to Lottie and suddenly all of her worries and anxieties fell away and an absolute certainty came to her. This was the point. This was what she was here for. This was what all the rubbish that had been thrown her way was bringing her towards. Lottie. And Isabelle. And now.

She knew then that she would do whatever it took to look after her. To keep her safe and for her to know the love that she herself never had. She looked at Lottie and said, 'I promise.'

Lottie wriggled and grabbed hold of Louise's finger. Louise took this as an understanding.

Promise.

14

'I can't do this,' Isabelle said tearfully, as she shifted her position to try and find a way to feed Lottie that didn't make her wince. 'Everything hurts, I'm sore, I'm exhausted and she won't latch. She won't do it and I don't know how to make her.'

It had been a few days since they'd left the hospital and it wasn't going well. Carl was allowed to phone, but somehow Isabelle had decided that he would be allowed out to visit the baby, which wasn't the case and it had utterly deflated her when she realised that he would never meet his first child as a new-born. She wasn't in a position to visit him. She could barely get dressed. She was depressed, anxious and the baby could tell. Lottie wouldn't be put down, wouldn't sleep anywhere but on her mother. If anyone else tried to hold her, to give Isabelle a break, time to shower, eat, breathe, Lottie would wail and wail, turning puce until Isabelle broke down and took her back.

'You've not done it before. It's gonna take time to learn, isn't it? It'll be ok.' Louise said, unsure what to suggest. She had no idea what she was doing either. Isabelle's mum had yet to arrive, despite sending messages and flowers after Lottie was born. Isabelle didn't understand why her mum was staying away having promised to be there and the upset from that wasn't helping things either.

'Will it??' Isabelle replied, half angry, half hopeful, desperate for assurance that she wasn't getting it wrong. 'She's not gaining any weight, the midwife said so yesterday.'

'She also said it's normal for babies to drop weight after their birth while everyone recovers and works out what's what. Remember? You grew Lottie to a good weight,' Louise said, feeling like she was talking about someone's prized pumpkin. 'She's got wiggle room.' Louise was grateful she'd been listening when the midwife visited yesterday, even if explaining who she was had felt odd, like she shouldn't have been there. 'A friend,' sounded so vague, she almost wished she'd lied and said they were sisters. It felt like they were. Louise hated seeing Isabelle struggling but not being able to do anything about it.

'That's true,' Isabelle said, shifting again, wincing as the wound from her C-section pulled. 'God, I feel like I've been beaten up. Ah! Ow! No, no, it's OK, Lottie, that's it,' she said as Lottie finally latched on. The contented little swallowing sounds she was making assured both of them that something was working. 'Thank God, I thought my boobs were about to explode!' Isabelle laughed, the tension temporarily broken.

'See? You can do this. Let me get you a drink and something to eat. They said you need more calories and water so you've enough energy and don't get dehydrated.' Louise smiled as she headed to fix a snack for Isabelle. She felt proud to be the one looking after her but angry at Isabelle's family for abandoning her. It's not like they were leaving her and Carl in their little bubble. As far as they knew, she was alone. They didn't know Louise was there. Who leaves a new mother, post-C-section, alone with their baby? The hospital didn't even want to let her out; it was only because Louise promised to move in while Isabelle recovered that she wasn't still in the hospital, unable to sleep due to the noise and constant movement. Isabelle had been desperate to get home. It had been too much.

'I can't stand it, Louise! I have seen more fathers and happy couples and doting families in the past twenty-four hours than I ever want to see. I'm glad for them, I really am, but each one is like a slap in the face. That should be me and it isn't me. Do you know what I mean?'

Louise had nodded. She did know. It was like all the school performances, when afterwards, everyone's parents rushed to tell their children how well they did, how proud they were of them and she had to stand, watching, at first hoping and then knowing that she would not have the same. That her parents weren't there and weren't coming. They never did.

'Isabelle?' Louise could hear crying from the other room. She hurried back to find Isabelle sitting on the floor, Lottie cradled in her arms, and Isabelle was sobbing. Huge ugly sobs, gasping for breath. Louise went to her, crouched down and took Lottie, shushing her complaints.

'You OK? What happened? Did you fall? Are you hurt?'

Isabelle said nothing but continued to cry, loudly, without the usual self-consciousness that she had, not caring or even registering that Louise was there. Her eyes were cloudy, red-rimmed and overflowing with tears. Louise wondered whether it was the moment that the enormity of it all had hit her. Or if the baby blues had kicked in like that website she'd read had warned about.

'I... It's...' Isabelle hiccupped. 'He's, he's not coming home. Not for a long time, is he? He's going to miss all of this. I'm going to have to do it all alone. My mum's not here, Carl's in... in prison and I don't know for how long. I... I have no one.'

That stung, but Louise knew what she meant. She was new to the party and Isabelle didn't know if Louise would walk away too. If her own mother could then surely Louise could and Louise felt guilty, because she had considered it.. She looked at Isabelle, sobbing on the floor. She had realised all her foundations were unstable, all her walls had come crashing down and she was exposed, not knowing which way was up. And she had a baby to look after, one who wasn't feeding easily.

'I don't know where the money that keeps coming in comes from. I don't know if we own this house, if we own it together, if he owns it or someone else does. I don't know whether he's guilty or not. I don't *think* he is. He says he isn't but I don't *know*. I don't know anything! I'm so stupid!'

'You're not stupid. You're not,' Louise said, squatting to sit next to Isabelle, hoping that Lottie would take proximity to her mother as good enough. She seemed to; post-feed she seemed sleepy and calmer now Isabelle's cries were diminishing.

'I feel like an idiot, Louise. I believed everything he told me. And what if it's not true? Is that why my friends won't come and visit? Is that why my mum isn't here? Does she not believe him and does she think I'm in on it? Does she think her daughter is in some sort of horrific criminal gang? Who does she think I am?'

Louise's stomach contracted. It *was* horrific, what she and Carl had done, what he had done time and time again even before Louise had met him. Surely, if Isabelle found out the truth, she could never forgive Louise for being part of it? Carl? Maybe she would forgive him for their shared past and their new family. But Louise would just be a criminal who snuck her way in and lied through her teeth at a time when Isabelle was at her lowest and most vulnerable. Louise felt sick. What sort of a person was she? Was she actually just repeating her duplicitous behaviour over and over, under the guise of a new leaf? If Isabelle ever found out the truth about her, then this friendship would surely be over. Even the briefest thought of that made Louise's blood run cold. This was all she had. Sitting on the floor, holding Lottie, who had miraculously gone to sleep draped near the top of her shoulder, next to Isabelle. This was all Louise had ever wanted. She couldn't let Carl ruin it as he had ruined her chance at starting again when he pulled her into his sordid set-up. There was only one thing Louise could do to keep it all. She and Carl would need to come to a mutual understanding. A pact of silence, neither admitting their guilt to Isabelle, protecting each other by doing so. She was going to have to go and see Carl somehow and sell this set-up to him, like he'd sold his set-up to her. Make him see how she could keep everything ticking over for him, if he would let her. Still... colleagues of sorts. Isabelle would never have to know.

Louise could do that, couldn't she?

'Let me call,' Louise said, gently nudging Isabelle.

'What?' Isabelle sniffed, all energy for crying being spent. The glamorous woman Louise had first met was wrung out, exhausted and hadn't showered properly in days. Louise couldn't persuade her to leave Lottie for long enough.

'Let me call your mum.'

Louise could find out through her what was known about Carl and his case. She'd been in a bubble with Isabelle and it wasn't safe to be that clueless. Louise needed information and Isabelle needed her mum. This way Louise might be able to kill two birds with one stone.

'I...' Isabelle looked up at Louise. She could have been ten years old, not the heading towards thirty that she was. You never stop needing your mum, even when your mum was the one who let you down. That's the sucker punch. Even if you try to let go, there is always a hold. It's a bond, even if it's one that threatens to strangle you.

'Yes. Yes, call her. I want my mum. I need her here.' Isabelle sniffed, then indicated the still-sleeping Lottie on Louise. 'See? She likes you. Thank God! I need a shower!' She laughed. The first real laugh Louise had heard since the birth. She smiled. She would be here for Isabelle even if everyone else couldn't or wouldn't.

But first, if this whole scenario was going out to work out, she needed information.

15

It had taken a lengthy phone call, with lots of tears and an early-morning flight from Spain, before the cab drew up outside Isabelle's house with her mum inside it, ready to meet her grandchild.

Isabelle had slept fitfully but then had a long bath, washed and dried her hair, was wearing clothes that she hadn't slept in and Louise had tidied up. The house looked almost as before, if you discounted the piles of baby paraphernalia that had made its way down from the spare room. Most of the stuff in there had been left unused. They'd barely left the front room, let alone the house, with Isabelle unable to move more than at a slow shuffle, one hand on her scar for fear of the stitches splitting. Louise couldn't understand how, if you'd had major surgery for something else, a stomach issue or similar, you'd be sent home with instructions for weeks of bed rest and crazy painkillers, but they cut you open for a baby and you were discharged with nothing more than a suggestion to get paracetamol on your way home.

The doorbell rang and set Lottie off crying. She didn't like sudden noises. She didn't like silence. She seemed happiest when there was steady background noise. Louise had done a lot of hoovering, which at least meant that the floors were spotless. From her place on the sofa, Isabelle patted Lottie on the bottom and shuffled about, attempting to at least create some kind of swaying movement that seemed to settle her down. Once the scene in the living room had calmed, Isabelle indicated to Louise to get the door.

'Now?' Louise asked, not wanting to act as hostess in a home that she was aware wasn't hers.

'Now.' Isabelle nodded, looking as though she needed to steel herself for a fight despite also looking in need of a hug.

In the hallway, Louise felt her nerves jangle. What was Isabelle's mum like? On the phone to her, Louise had tried her best to be charming and persuasive but she'd got very little back. Perfunctory yes and no answers, like someone was holding her hostage and only allowing certain responses with absolutely no chit-chat. Maybe it was nerves. Or embarrassment at being chased to visit her new granddaughter. Or maybe she was angry, though with who, Louise didn't yet know. She could feel her brain click into the mode it did when she was working with Carl. Welcoming, friendly, scanning for clues, happy, light, underhanded. She was both grateful for these skills but felt dirty using them here, using them on Isabelle's family. But they were her family too now, weren't they, in a way? She had the right to use her talents to protect them. To protect them all. She just wasn't sure what or who she was protecting them from.

Louise swung the door open and stepped back to let Sandra, Isabelle's mum, in. She couldn't see her at first as she was hidden behind a bouquet of balloons and a ridiculously oversized teddy bear. All she could see were her legs and feet clad in a pair of zebra print pumps.

'Sandra? Um, come in?'

The balloons started moving forward, propelled by the zebra feet and as she passed her, Louise saw a petite, shorter version of

Isabelle, with a smart cropped pixie cut and a tailored jacket with a nod to Chanel, pass her. Sandra looked Louise up and down as she passed, heading into the living room. She looked back at Louise, confused. She did not look happy.

'Who's that? Is that who called me?' Louise heard her say to Isabelle as she closed the front door. She hovered in the hallway, waiting for Isabelle to reply but before she could, Sandra continued.

'Aww, there's my baby girl, and her baby girl! Come to Nana poppet! Come here...'

'Mum,' Isabelle said, stony voiced, 'she doesn't know who you are. Give her a minute, eh?'

'I'm her nana!' Sandra retorted, 'she'll be fine with me. Hand her here, eh?'

'No,' Isabelle said. 'She's nervous around people. She doesn't know you. She would if you'd been there. Where were you? You didn't answer my calls, you didn't call back. It's been five days!' Louise could hear the hurt in Isabelle's voice. It was cracking as anger jostled with hurt.

'Now, come on, love, that's not fair...' Sandra was talking to Isabelle as though she were a child, and even from the hallway, Louise could sense the rage building in Isabelle. She couldn't see her but she knew Isabelle well enough now to know that the muscle to the side of her eye would be jumping, part tiredness, part anger at her mother's patronising tone.

'No. No! Don't "not fair" me!' Isabelle yelled as Lottie burst into wails, picking up on her mother's stress.

Louise moved quietly into the back of the room, hovering in case she was needed. It was clear she would be able to hear everything from the hallway anyway, and it's not like she could go out to give them privacy. Isabelle needed her. She needed someone on her side.

'Now look what you've done. You need to think of your baby first...'

'Like you did with me, you mean?' Isabelle retorted. 'Can you take her please, Lou?' she said, holding up Lottie to Louise, who gently tiptoed around Sandra to take her. She was aware that this would not please Sandra and she knew that she needed to de-escalate things here. It was getting too aggressive for her liking.

Patting the baby's back gently, which settled her, Louise moved back to the edges of the room.

'I'm sorry, but who are you?!' Sandra asked.

Louise coughed but stood tall. She did not need to justify herself to Sandra but she also didn't want to make things worse. 'I'm Louise, a friend. It was me who called you. Nice to meet you.' She held out one hand in greeting, the other keeping a tight hold on Lottie, who was now gurgling happily. The two of them were bonding and Louise loved being the next best thing to Isabelle, but knew that Sandra would feel Louise was overstepping her mark.

'I don't know you,' Sandra said, her lips pursed into an angry line.

'No,' Louise breathed out. She felt relieved. Carl had always been very good at keeping the two parts of his world very separate, but Louise felt a brief shock of fear that perhaps Sandra knew the truth, that Isabelle was just in denial about Carl's business. But... no, she couldn't see anything flickering underneath Sandra's words. How Carl would feel about Louise bringing his worlds together quite so dramatically, she didn't know. She'd have to work that out. No sense in worrying about it now.

'No, I'm new. Look,' she said, trying to defuse things. 'Everyone's tired, why don't I go and fix everyone an early lunch and you two can chat? You must be hungry after such an early flight.' She adjusted Lottie so the little bundle was tightly held and she took her with her into the kitchen. The room was immaculate, despite being one of the three spaces they spent all their time in. Louise knew now that mess made Isabelle stressed. So this was one of the rooms Louise cleaned while Isabelle rested. Properly cleaned too, not just chucked-stuff-out-of-sight clean like she did in her own flat. Even the tea and coffee jars were adjusted so they sat in an Insta-worthy row.

'It's the only thing I can control, Lou,' Isabelle had said and Louise knew what she meant. Everything else had spiralled out of her control the day that Carl was arrested.

Louise opened the fridge and cupboards, getting out a picnic-style lunch that could be eaten one-handed. They'd learned quickly that it was the only way they got to eat at the same time. Otherwise it had to be in shifts with the other holding Lottie. Gently swaying to keep Lottie calm, Louise put everything on a small tray that she could carry one-handed too – a skill picked up from some passing waitressing job which was coming in useful now. Louise walked, slowly and carefully, back into the living room. The air was so thick with tension you'd have needed a butcher's knife to slice it. Louise's stomach knotted. She felt responsible somehow. If only she'd been able to stop things sooner, if she'd been faster to pull the plug on that job then Carl wouldn't have seen the old man at all, he'd have been long gone, the man would be fine and they could have regrouped and changed tactic. But maybe she'd taken too long to decide something was off. Maybe this whole mess was her fault? She had to do everything she could to fix it. And try not to make it worse.

'Are you serious? Are you actually serious, Mum?'

Sandra was stony silent as Louise entered the room and carefully placed the tray down on the side table.

'Yes,' Sandra finally said. 'I am. I think you should ask him for a divorce.'

'I... I can't believe... Why?! Why would you say that?!'

'He's in jail. For a horrible, horrible crime. Do you want someone like that around her?' Sandra gestured towards Lottie. 'She deserves better! So do you. I've always said it. Ever since you met him at school. He was trouble. I could see it then and look where we are now.' She sniffed and shook her shoulders, like she was trying to shake off bad memories.

'I...' Isabelle faltered. She lifted her tear-stained face to look at Louise, dropping her eyes to rest on her tiny daughter, barely a few days old and yet already at the centre of a storm. A father in jail awaiting trial, a grandmother who stayed away, a mother unsure that she could do this. Louise could see it in Isabelle's face. The fear that she was failing Lottie, not even a week into this world, already.

Sandra saw this too and continued her attack.

'You remember your father? On your wedding day? He asked you if you were sure?'

'Doesn't everyone get asked that? You know, a joke? He was looking out for me.'

Louise knew that Isabelle's dad was a sore spot. One late-night chat, a few weeks ago now, Isabelle had told her that her father had died a few years before. She had been a real daddy's girl, had almost passed from him to Carl without having to stand on her own two feet. She missed him every day. She said that he was the only man she'd ever been able to rely on 100 per cent. Louise wanted to ask 'what about Carl', but hadn't want to speak his name.

Bringing Isabelle's dad into this was a cruel move by Sandra but one also likely to be effective. She was a mother too, after all, trying to protect her child from what she saw as danger.

'No, love. No. He was giving you an out and was hoping that you'd take it. We supported you because you loved him and we wanted you to be happy but he'd always been a worry to me, to us. Come back, love.'

'I never left! What do you mean?!'

'You say that but you have. All those family events that you couldn't make cos you and Carl had plans, or he didn't feel like it, so you didn't come either.'

'He's shy, he finds big events difficult.'

'Shy? No, love. He likes his own way. And he likes you to follow.'

'I... I guess. But we were a team. Together.'

'Is that why none of your friends are here either, love? Where are they, eh? Apart from this new one.' She nodded her head at Louise. 'They were all petrified of Carl before, but now? Now they know for sure what he's like, you're too dangerous to be friends with! Did you know that? My friend Stella said her daughter...'

'Oh, nice. You're all gossiping about me, are you? Who needs friends like that!' Isabelle spat back, but Louise could see the pain register on her face as the reality of her friends abandoning her hit. 'Carl is my best friend, my family. He won't leave me like they all have!'

'Is that still the case now he's inside?'

'He...'

'Well, what kind of a father is that? Do you think Lottie deserves better?'

'He's innocent!'

Louise was stuck to the spot. What could she do? She knew Carl was guilty, she knew how ruthless and cruel he could be, that Lottie did deserve more. She wrung her hand by her side, feeling the shake in it. Maybe this was it, the time to tell her the truth and let Isabelle make her decisions with all the information at her fingertips, rather than have her blundering around in the half-dark. But. If she did that then Isabelle would know about her too. She would know how sordid a life Louise had been living. She would know how everyone else in her life had rejected her and she might decide they had been right to do so and Louise didn't want that.

But keeping Isabelle meant also keeping Carl. Louise knew that she couldn't work with him again, not like before. She was done with that. If he was found guilty, he'd be looking at least six years, more if the judge decided the violence was premeditated. He'd have done at least seven months by the time he was sentenced. If he kept his head down, he could be out in four years? If he handed over any associates, would he get less? If he dropped a few of his gang into the police's hands, would they reduce his time? Would he sell *her* out to get home faster? He didn't know that she was here, in his home, with his family. Or did he? He had people everywhere. Maybe they were watching the house for him, keeping an eye on them both, reporting back.

No. The only way for Louise to keep Isabelle was for both of them to keep Carl and to keep Carl happy. Louise would go and see him. It would be risky, yes. She would need to be both blatant and underhand for it to work but she had to explain to Carl what she was doing. That she was on his side still, by Isabelle's side, for him. For them both. To convince him that this was the right plan – safest all round.

There was no other option she could think of. Maybe jail would have softened him, shown him that a new path was needed. Maybe Lottie would be what he needed to start again. Be better. And they could keep each other's secrets. Put them in the past and leave them there.

'I think she deserves a father. And he deserves the chance to be a father,' Louise said, quietly but firmly.

Sandra whipped round towards Louise, with a mind-your-own-business look on her face. 'I think he lost his chance for that when he beat an old man so badly he's still in hospital! If he ever gets out in anything other than a body bag!'

This was clearly one move too far for Isabelle, who was still clinging to the idea of Carl's innocence like a raft in the carnage of her former life.

'He's innocent! And he's her father! I'm not keeping him away from her for anything. And as for what she deserves – she deserves a nana who actually bothers to come and meet her! Not wait practically a week and then trash talk her daddy!'

'I waited for a reason, if you must know.'

'And what reason is that?'

'To make my point. Parenthood is hard. It's relentless. You have to be ready to do it whether you feel like it or not. You've been lucky, you've never had to struggle. You've been looked after your whole life but now it's time to do the looking after. You can't do this by yourself, love. Carl is a liability and one who may not be out of jail before Lottie starts secondary school! That's a long time to struggle alone. Come home. Let me help you. Just, you have to leave him, lovie. You have to.'

Isabelle was shocked for a minute. She looked as though she had been slapped.

'You... you left me alone, from giving birth, for the first week of looking after my baby, to make a point?! You let me struggle, in pain, without you so that I would do what you tell me? So you could show me that you're right and I'm wrong and I should scuttle on home?'

Sandra paled.

'No, no it's not like that. I wanted you to know what I meant. No one can explain how hard it is to look after a baby. Not really. They can tell you that you'll be tired, but you have to experience it to know just how tired. I thought then, you might understand what I'm saying.'

'It sounds like you wanted to torture me so I'd do as you say.'

'That's not true. I didn't come here for you to insult me, Isabelle.'

'What did you come for? To help? Cos you're not helping!'

Isabelle struggled to her feet to face her mother. 'To tell me I'd got it wrong? Again? Like you always do!'

'I do not always tell you...'

'You do! You always think your way is better and that you're right! You hate it when I'm not perfect. When you can't show me off, your little princess. That's why you don't like Carl, because I listen to him. Because he wants the best for me and that doesn't necessarily fit your plans! Well. I'm my own person. With my own plans. And my plan right now is to show you the door!'

Wow. Louise had never seen this side of Isabelle before. She was showing a strength of character that she didn't know she had. Louise thought that Sandra was right, that Isabelle did do what Carl wanted. Everyone did what Carl wanted, that was how he operated. But, if battle lines were being drawn, then Louise knew from experience that you had to pick a side. And she was tired of being on the losing side. Siding with Isabelle, and therefore Carl, was most likely to give her what she needed. A place to belong. A future that she actually wanted. And so she handed Lottie to a visibly shaking Isabelle and indicated to the hallway.

'I think it's probably best if you go now, Sandra, don't you?' Louise said, as kindly as possible. She could see the shock and hurt on Sandra's face. Her baby, albeit grown up, had rejected her. She clearly thought that she would be able to regain the daughter she felt she'd lost when she chose Carl. And now, she'd lost her even more. Families can be like that, Louise thought. It's a huge game of chess, moving pieces from position to position. Sometimes you're in a position of strength, and sometimes, one wrong move sees you out of the whole game.

'Izzy, let's not fall out...'

'Go, Mum. Just go. We'll talk another day. I'm too tired now.'

'Iz, I'm sorry, I didn't mean...'

'No.' She turned her focus entirely to Lottie, shutting out the world around her. The conversation was over.

Sandra's face was a picture of grief when she turned to look at Louise. Louise's heart broke. Her own mother hadn't cared enough to be upset at the idea of losing her. She probably barely even noticed when Louise had upped and left that day. She hadn't seen her since.

'This is your doing, it must be,' Sandra spat at Louise as she walked past her in the hallway. 'My daughter would never throw me out. Never.'

'Sandra, this doesn't make me happy either. But she's exhausted, she's lonely and she's terrified. We need to support her, not tell her what to do, tell her what she's been getting wrong, tell her what she is or isn't. Look, I'll talk with her. I'm sure once she's calmed down this'll blow over. But I wouldn't set it up as you against Carl. Cos I don't think you'll win.' Nobody won against Carl. This jail term was a blip, Louise was sure.

'I don't trust him. And I don't trust you either. I will be back.'

'I'm sure you will. And I'll be here,' Louise said, staking her claim, standing territorially in the doorway as she closed the door on Sandra. She watched the shocked outline of Isabelle's mother stand still for a moment before walking away. Louise needed Sandra at arm's length. She needed Isabelle to need her. She needed Carl not to feel threatened. She needed to keep her awful truth from Isabelle if she were going to keep her as a friend. She couldn't lose sight of that, even if it meant keeping mother and daughter apart. She felt awful as she looked at Isabelle and her daughter, as she went back into the living room, but then the fear of losing them took over, and she put that in a different part of her mind, and locked that door.

16

It was a rare morning these days when Louise woke up in her own flat. She'd practically moved in with Isabelle and Lottie and was loving being part of their world. Isabelle was getting used to being a mother now the first few weeks had passed. She was taking to it well and Lottie had started to settle into a routine which was making things easier. Louise had wanted to show that she wasn't overstaying her welcome by offering to go home and Isabelle, not wanting to seem clingy, had agreed. Neither of them were happy about it, but they still danced around each other at times, not wholly letting the other one in.

Louise had felt odd at first and coming back to the cold, dark flat felt like a rejection, like an indicator of what it would be like if Isabelle ever found out the truth. There were no happy voices in the background, no offers of help given or received. She was alone. She had thought that she'd never be able to sleep. But the build-up of tiredness from many broken nights had taken care of that and she'd been asleep barely minutes after her head hit the pillow and had woken up, with a start, eight hours later. Daylight was streaming in through the curtains that she had left open to keep an eye on Isabelle's house across the street.

Today was a big day. They were taking Lottie to officially register her birth. Isabelle had left it as late as possible under some false optimism that Carl's trial would be thrown out almost as soon as it had started and he would be able to come with her. It was under way and it was not looking good. Isabelle couldn't bring herself to go and watch. It made it all too real, she said. She had visited Carl a mere handful of times since he had been arrested and not at all since Lottie had been born. She hated it every time, preferring the romanticised version of pining for him from the comfort of her own home. Prison was hard, grey and cold. Isabelle was none of those things.

At first, Louise was groggy. Her brain not fully woken from what was a deep and much-needed sleep. But as she lay there, her duvet pulled up to her neck, there was an unmistakable feeling of dread in her stomach. She couldn't put her finger on what it was. She said to herself that it must be the remnants of a dream, still playing at the very edge of her consciousness. She often had bad dreams and this felt similar. A sense that something was very much not right. But what? Maybe she was just missing Isabelle and Lottie. She'd get up, have a quick cup of tea to wake up and then shower and head over. The bathroom was nicer at theirs, but it felt weird to turn up, all sleep dishevelled rather than clean up in what was, on paper at least, her own home.

It was after making her tea, black as she'd no milk in the flat, that she saw it. Coming back into her bedroom to find a towel for the shower, it was as clear as day. A mark on the rug at the foot of the bed. A footprint.

It wasn't hers. The rug was a gift from Isabelle, to hide the worn, threadbare carpet underneath and it was new, still plush and fluffy. The bright yellow wool contrasting with the rest of the beige interiors. And clearly, in the centre there it was –the distinct shape of a muddy footprint. A boot. Much bigger than her own. Much bigger than Isabelle's. And it hadn't been there the last time she'd been here; Louise was sure of that. Or at least she thought she was sure. Had it been there before she went to bed last night? Or had whoever made it been standing over her, watching her sleep? She threw up a little of the tea she had drunk into her mouth, where it pooled, bitter and warm. She spat it out into the cup, which she held in her shaking hands. She looked back towards the door, and now, in the murky threads of the carpet she could see other, smaller marks leading from the entrance. She thanked Isabelle for her love of colour pops. A darker rug could have concealed the evidence. Would that have been better? Louise wasn't sure.

She found herself suddenly sweaty, beads of perspiration gathering at the back of her neck. She could smell her own fear. She smelled like a piece of meat, an animal waiting for its execution. Someone had been here. If not last night, then recently. And they were tall and heavy. A man.

It couldn't have been Carl, obviously. Even he couldn't break out of jail and get back without being noticed. And, if Carl had escaped then the police would have been straight round to Isabelle's and she would have called her immediately. Putting her mug down on the floor, Louise made a grab for her phone. No missed calls. No messages. Checking online, she could see that Isabelle hadn't checked her phone since 4 a.m., Lottie's early morning feed. Everything was fine.

But someone had definitely been here. Was it random, a break-in where they found that there was nothing worth taking? But no signs of a forced entry and the footprint, which suggested someone didn't mind leaving traces of their visit, indicated not. A thief would get in and get out. Louise knew that first-hand. She stood in the same spot and looked towards the window. From there, even a taller person than her would not have been able to see into Isabelle's house. The room was too big, the window at too tight an angle. So if it wasn't for Isabelle then it must have been for her? Who knew she was here? Did someone want to check up on her? Only one person might want to know her whereabouts.

Carl.

She didn't matter to anyone else. If he knew that she was living here, then he more than likely knew by now that she'd befriended Isabelle. It was obvious that's what she would have done. How did that change things? Did it change things? Would he be pleased? She was helping Isabelle after all, keeping an eye on her and keeping her own mouth shut at the same time. Or did he think she was digging for dirt, looking for information that she could use on him, which if she was honest, was a major reason for coming here in the first place. She had needed to know everything there was to know in order to protect herself. Was Carl now just doing the same? Keep your friends close but your enemies closer? Which did Carl now consider her? She didn't know and that made her uneasy.

Louise went through the motions of getting ready. She showered and forced herself to eat a couple of old crackers that she still had in the cupboard. If she could stop feeling sick, she'd be able to concentrate more, to think more clearly. This felt like another moment when she could run. Isabelle would be too caught up with Lottie to be able to chase her. Maybe Sandra would come round again before she went back to Spain and, finding Louise gone, they'd be able to find a resolution between the two of them. Carl might get out soon enough and then they could go back to how they were before, barely a blip in their life together. Louise was the blip. Inconsequential. Maybe she should just go. Maybe she should have gone already.

But. Louise cared now. Lottie was here, an actual baby rather than an abstract, a not-yet-here human. She was tangible. Louise had held her, soothed her, changed her nappies and helped feed her when Isabelle was exhausted. She had looked after Isabelle. They were a team, however strange a team it might be. That made things harder. It was harder to walk away from her part in it because she felt it. Love. She was loved. Lottie loved her. Isabelle loved her and she loved them. She had had so little of it in her life that she felt the enormity of it now that it was in her hands. She didn't know if she had the strength to walk away from it. What if she never found it again? She didn't want to live that life. She wanted to live this one.

She threw the box of old, stale crackers in the bin. She would. She would live this one. Carl would just have to deal with that. She'd go and see him somehow and assure him of things. She wasn't doing anything to harm him; she wasn't doing anything to give him away to his wife. In fact, she could be said to be doing him a favour, keeping all those who were bad-mouthing him away from Isabelle, keeping her in her bubble of innocence where she really still believed he was a good man. Louise's stomach knotted. He wasn't a bad man as such. She was sure he'd never hurt Isabelle or Lottie. That wasn't him, was it? She'd met some of his acquaintances who were quick with their fists and harsh with their words, whoever was in front of them – loved one or enemy, adult or child. He wasn't one of them. It could work. She would make it work. She wasn't going to lose Isabelle and Lottie now. They needed her and she needed them. She was a new person with them. They were what made getting out of bed in the morning something Louise felt she could do, that she wanted to do.

Still, it was worth knowing what had been going on here and letting whoever it was know that she knew they'd been here if they were to come back. So she grabbed the bag of flour that her predecessor had left in the cupboard and sprinkled it liberally over the doormat and smoothed out the surface. Whoever came in next time would make marks in it and even if they smoothed it back, they would be unlikely to be able to tidy up the spattered flour. They'd not be able to hoover – the vacuum didn't work. She'd know they'd been back and they'd know she was aware that she was being watched. Not quite the usual welcome mat but a message on the threshold all the same.

Stepping carefully over the stoop, Louise closed and locked the door to her flat, went downstairs, out the front door and, checking carefully for traffic, crossed the road.

'Morning, you two!' Louise said cheerfully as she opened the door to Isabelle's. 'How was the night?' She was all prepared to find an exhausted and bedraggled-looking pair but as she stepped into the living room, she found a clean and tidy space with a showered and made-up Isabelle looking Instagram glamorous. Lottie was lying on her play mat, staring intently at something at the edge of her vision.

'Wow, you two look great! How did you sleep?' Louise asked, a little put out at how well they'd done without her.

'I feel great! Lottie slept in three batches, fed and went straight back to sleep. I feel like a new woman!' Isabelle said, running her hand through her brushed and styled hair. 'And we're going out! Out of the house! I feel like I'm on holiday! Maybe we could go for lunch afterwards?'

'Um, yeah, sure! Why not?' Louise smiled. It was lovely to see Isabelle so cheerful. *If I am being watched, they'll see I'm looking after her. That I'm not a threat*, she thought and then her stomach lurched at how odd a thought that was. She knew her relationship to Carl was fucked-up. She just sometimes realised quite how much.

'And this came this morning too!' Isabelle trilled, still seemingly on top of the world. She handed an official-looking letter to Louise to read. Louise caught sight of the Her Majesty's Prison Service logo on the page and her breath quickened. She took the letter, trying to conceal her shaking hands. Isabelle was happy, she needed to look happy too. She glanced at the letter and looked up to see Isabelle beaming at her.

'Lottie's finally been added to Carl's visitor list! I have no idea what the delay was, his solicitor wouldn't say. But now we can book a visit. Finally! For Lottie and me once we get her birth certificate today!

He can meet her! I'm so excited!'

Would it always feel this awful? When the good things in her life met with the bad? She forced a smile on her face.

'That's great! Do you, do you feel that you're ready to take her? Do you think you'd be able to cope?' Louise needed to see him *first*, she needed to buy everyone some time.

Louise saw Isabelle's face fall, as though it had dropped off a cliff edge.

'No, no, I don't mean I don't think you can!' She backtracked, 'No, it's just you were worried about it, weren't you? And how Lottie would be. That's all.'

Isabelle straightened, bouncing back fairly quickly from the knock to her confidence. Louise noticed and was relieved. She couldn't undermine Isabelle for her own ends. That wasn't who she wanted to be any more but old habits die hard.

'Well. Yes, I am nervous. But I thought if today went well, it's not that different, is it? Leaving the house, a specific time for an official appointment? A bureaucratic building, all grey chairs and sturdy carpet. And the prison visiting room isn't scary or loud. And you'd be there to help.'

Louise couldn't help it. Her eyes widened and she said 'What?' a little too sharply.

Isabelle's face fell again. Sometimes Louise felt it was like dealing with a child – all black and white, never any grey. She felt disloyal for thinking it but it was the truth. Isabelle had been cosseted by her parents and then cosseted by Carl. She had almost always got her own way, up until his arrest. She'd grown a lot since then but still, the slightly petulant child popped out now and again, and this was one of those times.

'Well, I sort of, well...' Isabelle stuttered, perhaps realising how presumptuous she was being. 'You can't come in, obviously, the visit is for the two of us and he doesn't know you.'

Louise swallowed hard and hoped to God that Isabelle didn't pick up on how her nerves were jangling, how every fibre of her was vibrating with the adrenaline now coursing through her veins. At some point her two worlds were going to have to meet if this was ever going to work, but for that to happen right in front of the prison where her former partner in crime was doing time... She'd never be able to keep her cool, surely the officers would recognise a criminal at large when they saw her. It'd be written all over her face. She had to visit him but alone, so she could be the old Louise. Not with Isabelle – it was all too complicated.

'I thought that you'd help. You could wait, in that café I bumped into you at? Is that... is that my asking too much? I just want Lottie to meet her daddy. And him to meet her. He must be so excited, I know I am. She's going to be Daddy's little princess I can just tell.'

Isabelle was glowing, like this had been what her whole purpose was for. To give Carl what he couldn't just take. Isabelle had given him a legacy. Louise couldn't steal away the joy that was radiating from Isabelle. They'd work something out. Goodness knows what, but they would.

'Sure. Sorry, I was just surprised that's all. Sure. I can come.'

'Oooooh, thank you!' Isabelle squealed as she hugged Louise tightly. 'What would I do without you? No, I don't want to know!'

'Same,' Louise said, calmly. It was as close to 'I love you' as she had ever got to saying.

17

Louise held the heavy dark wood door open as a still glowing Isabelle pushed the pram with a snoozing Lottie inside it back out through the doorway.

'There you go, my princess,' Isabelle cooed into the pram, 'you officially exist. Charlotte Cassandra Louise White.' She turned and smiled up at Louise.

Louise beamed back at her.

'I still can't believe it. You didn't have to, you know. I'm glad that you did but you didn't have to.'

'I know,' Isabelle trilled as she leaned forward and stroked the downy hair of her sleeping daughter. 'But I want her to know how important you are to us and how I don't think we could have done these weeks without you. Everyone else, everyone, abandoned us. You didn't. You knew the situation with Carl, right from the start, and you stepped up, not stepped back and that means something. I want to tell her why she has your name. And hopefully the Cassandra will please my mum and she will calm down and come round to things. How could she not? I couldn't go full Sandra, can't lumber a baby with a middle-aged lady's name! But her nana is there.'

'Will Carl mind?' Louise asked fearfully. When he found out his daughter was named after both his wrathful mother-in-law and his former accomplice, he surely wouldn't be pleased.

'Oh no, he doesn't believe in middle names. Thinks they're for posh people or religious ones and we're neither. But I like them and we discussed a first name so the rest is up to me.'

They walked in companionable silence for a while, Louise wondering what she had done to get so lucky. Isabelle was an open, trusting person and here she was, welcoming Louise into her family. Would she be so welcoming if she knew the truth? She thought her mum was being judgemental but would she think differently if she knew her mum was right?

'How about there?' Isabelle indicated a small café just a little way up the road. It was busy but in a buzzy way rather than crowded. The smell of whatever food they were serving drifted down the road and hit Louise. Her stomach growled so loudly that Isabelle heard it.

'Heh! I'll take that as a yes then! Didn't you have breakfast? You're always on at me to make sure I eat properly but one night away and you're neglecting yourself!'

Louise nodded, realising that the two stale, half-eaten crackers were all that had passed her lips in over twelve hours and that probably wasn't helping the low-level anxiety that was bubbling away in the core of her. Her stomach acid was swishing about with nothing to do but gnaw away at her own insides, making sharp pains jab at her when she least expected it. Stress pains. She'd not had those in a while, something she was only realising now. They'd been part of her life for so long that she'd stopped noticing them. Meeting Isabelle had made her happy. And being happy stopped her pain.

They took their seats at a table outside the café and Isabelle chattered away, a happier parent now she was out and about.

'Aw, she's so beautiful, how old is she?' the waitress cooed at the sleeping Lottie in her pram as she came to take their order.

'Thanks,' Isabelle said, glowing in the reflected praise, 'she's just six weeks today! We've just been to register her birth.'

The waitress looked at them both, clearly trying to place who was who and what was what. She nodded, like she'd worked it out and said, 'Well, congratulations to you both. What a lovely couple. I've got some water here for you. Are you ready to order?'

'I'd like the chicken peanut salad please and a green smoothie. And a side of fries please. Gotta keep my calories up!' Isabelle said, handing the menu back to the waitress, trying not to giggle at her mistake.

'I'll have the same please,' Louise said, too distracted to bother reading the menu She was too hungry to make a decision, she just needed to eat so that her brain would work properly. Now that she had realised she was hungry, it was proving difficult to think about anything else and she needed her brain on full alert.

Was anyone following them now? Was whoever broke into her flat still around? Were they being watched and by who and for what? Louise wished they'd gone inside instead of staying outside in the sunshine. It'd be easier to have her back against a wall inside where she could see everyone who could see her.

She'd been fine before, she could be what she decided was her real self with Isabelle. But now? Now she needed half a foot in her old life to keep herself safe, to keep Isabelle and Lottie from being pulled into it.

Suddenly, she was aware that Isabelle was talking to her.

'I'm sorry, what?' Louise said, her attention brought back to the table and her immediate surroundings.

'Are you OK? You're more dazed than I am and you slept all

night!' Isabelle laughed but with a concerned look on her face. 'Are you feeling all right?'

'I'm fine. Just hungry,' Louise deflected. 'What were you saying?'

Isabelle blushed and suddenly looked coy.

'I've something to ask you,' she said and then stopped, dramatically.

'Yes?'

Isabelle giggled.

'What?'

'Sorry, just after the waitress assuming we were, you know, together, this now feels too much like a proposal!'

'What does?' Louise was perplexed. She hadn't registered the waitress's comment and so was stumped as to what Isabelle meant.

'You've been so amazing in the time I've known you. You've absolutely rescued me in what has been the hardest time in my life. You've not done it for me but shown me that I can do it myself. I know I'm spoilt. I've been looked after my whole life. But you, in looking after me also showed me that I can look after myself. Thank you,' she said, reaching out to squeeze Louise's hand.

Louise welled up. She had not been expecting such a lovely speech. She was about to reply when it became clear that Isabelle wasn't done.

'You've been a proper friend when all my so-called friends abandoned me. You've not judged me or demanded anything and that is exactly the example I want for Lottie. I want her surrounded by good people, by kind people, and I want her to have a family she can rely on. So, I wondered...'

'Yes?' Louise tipped her head to the side, unsure of where Isabelle was going. It did sound like a proposal but what exactly she was proposing, Louise couldn't guess.

'Will you be Lottie's godmother?'

Louise gasped.

Isabelle took this as reluctance.

'I know it's a big ask and I know we've not known each other that long. I know you said you weren't religious! We're not really, I don't go to church, but it's always something I wanted to do for my children. Give them another set of grown-ups who are there for them, in case they don't necessarily want to talk to me about something. It's just... I can't imagine now, Lottie growing up without you.' She looked at her hands, embarrassed. Still looking down she said, 'You're family. We love you.'

Louise's heart soared. Family was what she never had. Family was all she'd ever really wanted. She got mixed up with Carl and the robberies because she felt like she belonged to something even though she knew what they were doing was wrong, deep down. She knew that Isabelle was grasping at something, just like she was herself. They were both lonely, both alone. All they had was each other. It wasn't taking advantage, it wasn't exploiting her weakness to accept. They were each other's life rafts.

'I don't know what to say,' Louise smiled at Isabelle. She was happy. And yet, at the back of her mind was a warning. An alarm saying that this couldn't go well.

'You could say yes?' Isabelle smiled, reaching into the pram to give Lottie's toes a gentle affectionate, just-checking-in squeeze.

Louise smiled but she couldn't focus on what Isabelle was asking of her. She couldn't shake the feeling that she was being watched. That all three of them were. The safest thing to do would be to leave, to break the lies that bound them. The problem was that Louise didn't want to. For the first time ever, she was actually happy. She'd found a job, doing part-time admin work from home. It didn't earn much but it didn't need to, not after how frugally she'd lived during her previous... employment.

'Yes, I'd be honoured.' Louise found herself saying before she could overthink it. 'I'm so pleased!' Isabelle replied, 'Do you think the café sells wine? This feel like it should be celebrated! Oh, is that inappropriate, do you think?'

'They have wine in church, don't they?' Louise smiled. 'Don't think God would smite you for having a glass now!' She laughed, wondering if God would smite you for agreeing to be a godparent whilst lying about being a criminal. Wouldn't she have to agree to reject the devil or something?

Isabelle called the waitress over and ordered two glasses of prosecco, and when they came over, she took one, handed it to Louise and then raised her own.

'To family – in whatever form it comes!'

'To family,' Louise said, squashing down the fear that had settled over her. She was allowed to be happy. She could let herself. She would let herself.

The question was, would Carl?

18

THREE YEARS AGO

'It's been a really lovely chat, my dear, thank you for calling round. I'll have to let the church know how much I appreciated it.'

'Oh, there's no need, Mr Hammersmith. We don't need thanks for doing the Lord's work after all?' Louise smiled as she stepped out of the house.

'I can't think when I've had such a good chinwag! Not since my Louise went, I know that much. Not found the enthusiasm for chit-chat.'

Louise jolted at the sound of her own name. Not that this was what Mr Hammersmith knew her as. She'd said her name was Chloe. She and Carl had a system, where each job was assigned a letter. So she'd been Alice, Bethany, now Chloe, next time she would be Dana.

'Like the hurricanes! 'Cept our little storm sweeps in unnoticed and sweeps out taking the crown jewels with it and they're none the wiser till we're long gone!' Carl had laughed. The whole thing was a joke to him. But three jobs in and it hadn't settled for Louise. She liked the people she'd met and had been genuinely interested in the stories they had to tell. Even the most mundane of lives lived had a collection of stories about love and tragedy and travel and home.

'It was a joy to chat with you, Mr Hammersmith. I hope your grandson can come and visit you soon. It must be hard, them all being so far away.'

His face darkened a little but then fell into an expression of resolution.

'Yes. It is hard. But they're happy. Australia sounds so glamorous, doesn't it? All sunshine and beaches. I wouldn't have had him miss all that just for me. I do miss him though.' He looked up at her, hopeful. 'Will you come again? I've just had a thought about a story I could tell you about this one time…' He shifted, needing to lean against the door frame as his elderly legs needed the rest.

'Are you OK?' Louise asked, concerned.

'Yes. Yes, I'm fine. Just old! Need a sit down. Will I see you then?'

Louise bit her lip on the inside and swallowed her guilt. She had to remain cold. Pretend to be all warmth and smiles but keep the core of her emotionless. Sympathy had no place here.

'Yes, yes, I'll pop back. We've a few more houses to visit but now I know you're happy to have visitors, I'll add your name to the repeat list. Is that OK?'

'Oh, absolutely. You sure I can't persuade you to take some cake with you? It'll only go off. I can't eat it before it does and those horrible individual slices are not as good as a whole cake. My doctor would have my guts for garters if I ate a whole cake to myself!'

'Thank you, but no. Maybe the birds will have it.' She smiled as she stepped away. She turned back and waved. 'Take care now, Mr H.!' He waved back before closing the door.

Back at Carl's workshop, he could barely conceal his glee.

'Bloody hell, Louise. You're a natural! He let you in after what? Two minutes chit-chat. You must have that sort of face! Trustworthy.

I've never looked trustworthy!' He chuckled. 'Even first day of secondary, teacher looked at me and said I'd be trouble. Not even said a word and I was trouble. He was right, to be fair.'

Carl was piling what he had taken on to the table, going through it to check.

'Found this in the cutlery drawer,' he said, chucking some rolled notes held together with a red elastic band of the type the postman often drops on the rounds. 'Very old fashioned, not many folk do that these days. Didn't take them all so he won't see straight away that some are missing. All this too...'

He scooped his hands into the deliberately large pockets of his jacket and took out two watches, one a Swiss brand so well known that Louise recognised it from those ads with the Hollywood actors – all tuxedos and teeth. There was also some women's jewellery, including a gold wedding band. Louise suddenly felt sick.

'We have to give that back,' she said quietly.

'You what?' Carl said, in disbelief. 'We ain't giving anything back, cos we didn't take anything, did we?' he said, aggressively eyeballing her. 'I was never there; you never left his side, did you? So if anything is missing, it can't have been you, can it? That's the Whole. Damn. Point!' He slammed his fist down on the table making the items on it, and Louise, jump.

Despite the rage that had sprung up so quickly in Carl, his teeth grinding as he tried to dampen it down, Louise was resolute. She wanted him to understand. That ring had to go back.

'He lost his wife years back but he said he sometimes looks through her things to make her feel closer. Her wedding ring will be an obvious thing that's missing. It could give up the whole game,' she said, trying to talk to Carl on a level that might get him to agree.

She swallowed hard, trying to feel more confident than she was, trying to assert herself as partner, not subordinate, in this business arrangement, even though Carl had just made it very clear where he stood on the matter. She had allowed her feelings for him, for what he offered her, to cloud her judgement. She had refused to admit that no one who steals from vulnerable people is a good person, no matter their motivation. He was not a good person. She was not a good person either. Her mum had been right.

'Well, we can't give it back. How would we do that?' he sneered at her.

'Post it through his door? Go back for another chat and I could just drop it in the house somewhere, like he'd done that himself?'

'Don't be stupid. The deal is we go in once, we never go back. Ever. Repeated visits increase the chances of being caught, you know that! Even like on the last job, when there was more than I could take in one go, it's not worth the risk. There are plenty more mugs out there!'

'Don't call them that.' Louise smarted. 'It's not their fault they're lonely.'

'Maybe not. But it's their fault for letting total strangers in. Even ones with pretty faces like yours.'

He ran his hand along her cheek. If it was meant to be a compliment, flattery, a way to bring her back on side, it hadn't worked. Not wholly. At first, her stomach had flipped. He thought she was pretty! But then his real meaning sunk it. It was a threat, like he could make her face not so pretty if she continued to fight him like this. It felt like he was saying, *Let it go, or I'll make you regret it*. Louise shuddered and he took his hand away, smiling like a cat who has got its prey exactly where it wants it.

'So. Are we taking it back?' he said, talking to her like she was a simple child who was having the lesson explained to them again.

'No,' she whispered.

'No,' he said, matter closed. He gathered up the things and his demeanour changed, like the clouds had cleared and the sun had come out again. He was cheery, all chirpy Londoner on a high of a job well done.

'First things first, eh? Cuppa, bit of lunch and then I'll get this lot down to Mike, see what deal he can do me and then we'll meet back here tomorrow, divvy it up and plan Hurricane D, yeah? I think I've found a good 'un. Woman, no kids, loads of flash clothes and I don't think her sparkles are paste.'

He chuckled again as he loaded up the spoils into a bag. Louise noticed that the money went somewhere different and she knew tomorrow's spoils would likely not be the fifty-fifty split they'd agreed. Nothing she could do about that though. All the contacts for selling the stuff on, no questions asked, they were all his. She would have no idea where to start and had no doubt she'd do the wrong thing.

And so Louise said nothing. She had come to a realisation. As much as she had felt trapped at home, trapped by the lack of love and the lack of any vision of a future, she was just as trapped now. She had sold her soul to the devil and now she needed Carl. He knew too much about her and she knew he'd drop her in it as soon as look at her. With Carl by her side, she could see her future clearly.

She just wasn't sure that she liked what she saw but it was too late now.

19

PRESENT DAY

It was only supposed to be a trip to the shops to get milk. The house ran on caffeine on some days and Isabelle had nearly burst into tears when, with a clingy, grumpy, Lottie in her arms, she had opened the fridge to find the milk bottle had barely a drop left in it.

'See?!' she had shouted, her face scrunching up as it did when tears were imminent, 'I can't even keep the basics in the house! How am I supposed to do this—' she gestured wildly, but Louise gathered she meant motherhood '—if I can't even keep enough milk in the house?!' Isabelle slumped onto one of the breakfast bar stools and kissed the top of Lottie's head, looking the picture of exhausted misery.

'It happens, I never have milk in. When I'm at home that is. And I have nothing like the excuse. I'll pop out. If you want, I can take Lottie, you can sleep or have a bath or do whatever you like. How does that sound?'

'It sounds like you're my guardian angel, that's what it sounds like!' Isabelle had said, her face lightening up at the prospect of half an hour to herself.

So Louise had loaded the pram with all Lottie's things, bundled her up into warm enough clothes and lifted the pram over the doorstep into the grey morning.

'Come on then, Lots, let's get your mummy some milk for her tea and maybe a nice treat or something to cheer her up. Something for you too, eh, little one? Got to make good use of the bad money, haven't we?' Louise murmured into the pram. She felt guilt whenever she spent any of the cash she had stashed away from before Carl's arrest. She hated spending it but knew that she was in no place to give it away. She had dreams of getting a job that would support her and allow her to go into a charity shop or somewhere and just hand over the cash. She couldn't do that, obviously. No decent job wanted someone with no qualifications, no references and a sketchy employment history. Even if she made up the gaps or fudged over leaving dates, there was no respectable person who could speak up for her. It's not like a call from Carl at HM Wandsworth was going to reassure employers. So she was stuck. A temp role, no questions asked, admin job was all she could find. Frugality had to replace penance for now.

Louise was just forcing herself to lighten up, pushing the pram across the main road at the traffic lights when someone – a man in a dark hoodie pulled down over his face, his shoulders hunched up – pushed into her, making her stumble.

'Watch it...' he hissed at her as he went past.

Something about it made her skin crawl but she reminded herself not to be silly. It was just someone in a bad mood.

'Some people are so rude, aren't they, Lots?' Louise trilled at Lottie, trying to hide the shake in her voice. Something about the interaction seemed... off. She couldn't place why. She knew the footprint at her flat had freaked her out and she'd not been able to tell Isabelle so hadn't spoken about it at all. It had just sat in the back of her mind.

Louise entered the supermarket and took an unnecessary

leisurely stroll around the aisles. She was only there for milk, but she did want to get something for Isabelle. She wasn't sure what, but the main thing was to be out long enough for Isabelle to have a break. She needed to be out for at least half an hour or more and so dawdling was required.

She was in the homeware aisle, smelling various candles to try to decide if they might be a nice gift for Isabelle, something that needed no effort but that might make her feel pampered. She had just reached for another candle when a girl, around seventeen or so, in black leggings and an oversized jumper, with pale splotchy skin, stepped next to her. Intimidatingly close in an entirely otherwise empty aisle.

'Nah. You don't want candles. Too easy to burn your flat down by accident. Or that's what they'd say anyway. You know what I mean? You need to be careful. You know what I'm saying.' She nodded at her meaningfully, almost with solidarity, and then turned and walked out of the shop, empty-handed.

Had she... Did she...? Had she just been threatened? Louise recognised a little of her former self in the girl. Young, trying to be more worldly than she felt, harder, more menacing than she really was, and Louise wondered. Was that a message? From Carl? She knew he had people everywhere, she knew he had likely been told that she was at Isabelle's and maybe that had freaked Carl out. He always assumed the worst first, in order not to be caught off guard later. Had he sent some people to scare her off?

Louise shook her head. No, no surely the girl was just winding her up for kicks. The man at the road just wasn't looking where he was going; and the footprint? Maybe she'd imagined it.

But then she realised how many people had cause to dislike her; how many people she had scammed. And then there was Carl. He was sitting in jail with all the time to think on how he'd got there.

She and Carl had argued after the bungled job. She had been

furious with him; he had been furious with her. Did he think she'd shopped him? And that was why she'd escaped detection when he hadn't? Had he convinced himself that she had bought her freedom with his? And now she had moved into his home. She was looking after Isabelle; she was the first person to hold Lottie. She'd seen Carl's temper first-hand and it wasn't pretty, but she never thought he'd aim it at her, at Isabelle, at Lottie. He wouldn't, would he? She hadn't shopped him. Not to the authorities and not to his wife. She was loyal, she was *being* loyal.

If the man, the girl and the unexplained footprint were messages to her, did she need to get a message to him in return? Isabelle's visit with Lottie was soon, maybe she could do something then? Before then? She knew she needed to visit but *how?* She felt sick to her stomach. A prison visit. She was too close to everything she was trying to get away from by trying to keep what she wanted. Honestly, if her grandpa could see her now. *Well, you have got yourself in a bit of a pickle here, haven't ya? You could make a sandwich outta that*, she could hear him say.

Buying the milk and a box of posh chocolate cookies, even though Isabelle would bewail her trying to lose the baby weight, Louise left the shop, feeling shaken. Lottie was fast asleep and Louise took the moment of calm to walk to the nearest green and take a seat on a bench under the trees. She'd not been sleeping well either, being woken when Lottie had woken the nights she stayed over, and sometimes getting up in moral support of Isabelle, even though that left them both tired. 'It's a waste of sleep, Lou. I appreciate it but you sleep and then at least one of us is with it during the day,' Isabelle had insisted.

Louise closed her eyes and let the gentle chill breeze float across her face. She could feel the bite in the air as the temperature flirted with the approaching autumn. She loved how even in the middle of a city as big as London, where humans had pushed nature to the edges, it still kept its cycle. Seasons made themselves known, concrete jungle or not. She could hear the gentle rumble of traffic from the nearby main road, and if she concentrated, she could separate out the cars from the diesel taxis from the large lorries delivering to the local shops. It was like a city-based meditation, to clear her mind from its tangle. As she took a deep breath she heard another noise, closer, much closer. A rustle, a brush of air that indicated movement very close to her. Aware of her responsibility to Lottie, she threw open her eyes to see what or who it was.

Nothing.

There was no one there. Despite the hairs on the back of her neck standing up, it was just as it was before. Her, Lottie, their shopping and people going about their own business. Louise let out a deep breath. Long and slow. She had got to keep it together. She couldn't start imagining things that weren't there.

Get a grip, woman! she told herself.

She pulled her jacket closer around her and started the walk back to Isabelle's. Her eyes flickered to every movement that she couldn't clearly see. The back of someone disappearing round the corner made her heart race. Standing at the crossing, waiting for the traffic to clear enough to cross, she could feel her breath stuttering and she had to force herself to breathe calmly. She moved her hands on the handles of Lottie's pram and could feel how clammy they were. She needed to get back, she needed to get Lottie back, safe with her mother. She'd promised Isabelle she'd look after her daughter and Louise was damned if any stooge of Carl's was going to make her break that promise. He could try and wind her up, try and spook her but he would not get to them. She would be sure of that.

Once they had reached one street away, Louise felt the urge to run. She felt exposed, like a mouse with nowhere to hide with an unseen bird of prey swooping. She looked around. She couldn't see anyone but she could sense them.

She was being watched. She knew it.

Louise was so jittery and on edge that she slammed the door when she got back and the noise woke both Isabelle and Lottie. The latter started screaming and the former came, groggy and sleep fogged into the hallway. She was rubbing her eyes and trying to come round from the deep sleep she had been in.

'Shit! I'm sorry, I'm sorry,' Louise stammered as she picked up the wailing baby and started shushing her and bouncing her up and down to try and quieten her cries.

'What happened? You're all sweaty and pale. Are you OK?'

'Yes. Yes, I...I think so. I...' Louise paused. What should she tell her? Should she tell her anything? What version could she tell that didn't have so much information missing as to make it utterly pointless? Should she just tell her everything? What if Louise wasn't being melodramatic? *Too easy to burn your flat down*, the girl at the supermarket said. *Watch it*, the man at the crossing. If they were from Carl then the message surely was to keep quiet?

'You sure? I'm not sure. You look terrible. Here, hand me Lottie.'

Louise did so and both women noticed her hands were shaking.

'I just. I think I got threatened.' Louise didn't have to say for what or by who. She could just see if there was any recognition from Isabelle as to whether in her world this was normal. The shocked expression that flooded Isabelle's face told her immediately that this was not the case.

'Oh my God! By who? What did they say? Are you all right?'

'Just. Oh, I don't know. Maybe I'm tired and imagining things.'

'Come and tell me all about it, she needs feeding and I can't do it stood up in the hall,' Isabelle said, trying to give Louise attention when Lottie was demanding it all.

Louise sat, jacket and shoes still on, and told Isabelle an edited version of what just happened.

'Oh, Louise! What are you like?!' Isabelle laughed. 'The lad at the lights was just being the usual cheeky bugger you get round here and the girl in the supermarket was probably just playing with you for laughs! You know what kids are like!'

Louise wasn't so sure it was just kids messing about but maybe Isabelle was right. Maybe her guilt was making her paranoid.

'I guess...'

'I thought someone had been right in your face and up front about it. I was about to try to get a message to Carl to have him sort it out!'

'How... could he do that?' Louise asked, her voice tremoring.

'Oh, he probably couldn't. But he's known round here as a community figure. If someone was messing about, and especially near Lottie, he'd have had a word. Maybe he could have asked his mates or something. But he uses all of his phone allocation to talk with me. I just... I just miss having the reassurance of him here sometimes, you know? Feels a little insecure with two women and a baby and no bloke. You know?'

'Yes. I get it,' Louise agreed. Suddenly this house, which had felt like their own little cocoon, felt exposed, dangerous.

She swallowed hard. It was suddenly crystal clear to her that she needed to talk with Carl, face to face. But how on earth was she going to manage that?

20

Louise's hands were shaking as she signed in. Her face was hot and her scalp was itching underneath the wig. She had to not show any nerves, not to give anything away as she stepped into the visitors' centre of the prison. The visit had taken all manner of dodgy deals to get set up and she wasn't about to blow it now.

Steve had been horrified when she called into the pub to suggest it.

'Are you off your 'ead?' he'd whispered at her, taking a large gulp of beer to calm him down. Louise couldn't tell if the shake in his body was due to the mother of all hangovers or his nerves. He looked in a bad way, far worse than when she'd stopped taking shifts at the pub once her work with Carl had taken off.

'No. No, I'm not, but I need to see him. It's important. I have to explain things and I can't exactly put it all in a letter now, can I? Same with calls, emails. There has to be no record of the conversation we need to have.'

Steve shook his head.

'So you wanna just waltz into the nick and have your chat right there?!'

'I can't rock up as me, can I? So. I need you, I need the network to get me a false identity. I know passports and stuff are part of the business. I remember Carl taking a phone call about it one day. I know they can help me and really by helping me, they're helping Carl, and by helping Carl, they're helping themselves so all's to the good. Isn't it?'

'It's a bad idea, darlin'. Don't mess. Don't...'

'Mess? I can show you mess, Steve. Like, when you do your finances, when you've passed cash through the tills for Carl. How, perhaps not 100 per cent of it always makes it through to him...' Louise let the accusation hang in the air whilst Steve worked out its implications.

His face went pale.

'I may not have done well with maths at school, Ste,' but I know when something doesn't quite add up.'

The thing was, Louise knew that Carl was aware of this already, but it was such a small amount, it was more useful to hold the information in case he needed it later, rather than call it out for what Carl called 'peanuts'. However, if Carl was *seen* to know and do nothing, well that would cause untold reputational damage and he wouldn't stand for that.

'Fine,' Steve said, looking defeated. 'I thought we was mates, that's all.'

'We are, Steve, we are. It's why I've not told him already and it's why you're helping me now. Cos we're friends.'

Louise felt sick but then reminded herself that she *was* being a good friend. Just not to Steve. To Isabelle.

It was by keeping Isabelle and Lottie in her mind's eye that Louise manged to get through the security protocol at the prison. She looked at her stained fingertips from the fingerprinting process at check-in. She had to believe that the network that had arranged her false ID had also managed to bribe the officer on duty to accidentally lose or damage her prints as promised. She couldn't be on the system in any recognisable way even if linked with a false name. She placed her hands down on the grey metal table in front of her, before tucking them underneath her as she sat on the brown plastic chair.

The door buzzed and the prisoners filed in, all looking near-identical in grey jogging bottoms and T-shirts. Louise had never seen Carl in anything other than a suit. She was shocked as she saw him shuffle in, his swagger only just about visible under more cowed shoulders. Her mouth went dry as her mind went blank. She had practised what she wanted to say, but, now, she seemed to have forgotten everything. Realising that hopefully he wouldn't recognise her, with the dark blonde bobbed wig and as much contouring as she could manage to alter her face shape, underneath a layer of thick make-up, she caught his eye and waved him over to her.

Carl sat down and pushed his shoulders back. He looked angry but Louise couldn't tell at who. Her, the prison or his situation. She swallowed.

Then, suddenly, Carl let out a laugh.

'Ha! All right, Lana! I'd not have recognised you, my own cousin. You've changed! It's good to see you!' he said theatrically, catching the eye of the guard who'd processed her fingerprinting. At this, assumed pre-assigned moment, the guard turned away from the table.

Carl leaned forward and said in a low, threatening voice,

'This better be good *Lana* cos the number of favours it's had to pull in...'

Louise glanced once again at the guard, still acting completely oblivious to their table, took a deep breath and began.

'It is. We need this talk and we need it now. I know you know where I've been. I know Isabelle and Lottie are about to visit you and—'

'How is she?' Carl interrupted, a flicker of worry briefly bothering his neutral expression.

'Uh, well, she's...' Louise flustered. She had prepared her speech, but not prepared herself for chit-chat. 'She's good, she's... happy. Though she misses you madly, obviously,' she added hastily.

The truth was that Isabelle was blossoming. She was starting to stand on her own two feet, starting to believe in her own instincts and was in her element as a mother despite questioning herself every day. Louise knew that her self-confidence was still low but it rose each time Lottie hit a milestone. Louise needed to tread a line between reassuring Carl and making him feel redundant.

'I'll be blunt. I don't know how you've managed it, but she doesn't know a thing. She truly thinks you're in antiques. I want you to know that I haven't said that I know you, or that I know... otherwise. She doesn't know about *me*. Her mum's been round, not happy with things, with you. But...'

Carl sneered. His mother-in-law clearly not one of his favourite people.

'That old bag? What did she say? What did she do?'

Louise needed Carl onside and fast. Divide and conquer was the best way to do that, even if it meant metaphorically throwing Sandra under the bus.

'She told Iz to divorce you and come home to her.'

Fury overtook Carl immediately.

'She did fucking what?!'

'Shhhh. No. Be quiet. No,' Louise hissed as a few people turned to look at them. 'Isabelle told her where to go and I showed the door. We kicked her out and comms have been frosty since. I can keep them that way. I can...'

Carl cracked his knuckles and Louise's stomach lurched. She could see the rage coursing through Carl and she needed him to be thinking straight. They didn't have much time here.

'Look. This is what I'm proposing, right? I've made friends with Isabelle.'

'I know. My people told me. You know that. I assumed that was why you wanted to come here. Why? Why? I wanna know what you're up to.' He picked at his nails, dismissively, but all Louise could see was the fist he was making with his hand. Those threats were real. She could see it now.

'I'll level with you, Carl. At first? I needed information on you, on us. To see what danger I was in. You'll understand that, I know you will. But then? Iz is great, a really good person and we got on. And now? Well, now we're friends and I figured we could *use* that, right?' She nodded at Carl encouragingly. 'I can keep her safe, keep the jackals from sniffing about, keep her family from asking too many awkward questions. Keep things as they were, for when you get out. So you know all's fine to come home to. Keep you innocent in her eyes. In Lottie's. No one need ever know different. No need to have people keep an eye as I'd be there every day doing just that. What do you say?'

Carl chewed his lip as he thought it through and Louise felt her heart racing so hard she could see it in the pulse point on her wrist. She looked at it, her life beating underneath her skin, just under the thin white scar there from the time when she'd had enough of it all. She'd survived. She would survive now. It was what she did. She looked up at Carl, defiantly almost.

'What other options do you have?'

'Is that a threat?!'

'No,' Louise said, 'it's the truth. If you let me stay, I can keep your family for you. If you force me to leave, who knows who might move in, what they might say, what they might persuade Isabelle to do. The house isn't in your name, is it? I assume not. She could sell up and move away. There'd be nothing you could do from in here.

When you get out, you could be homeless and alone. I don't want that for you. Do you?'

Louise meant it too. Her feelings towards Carl were a complicated mess that's for sure. He scared her. What he was capable of scared her. But Isabelle knew a good side to him. And he'd picked Louise out of the darkness she was in, he'd seen her potential, he'd trusted her, believed in her and she owed him. He wasn't all bad surely? Without him, there would be no her and Isabelle, no her and Lottie. Without him, she was nothing. She couldn't and wouldn't let his life crumble the way hers had before she met him. No – he could do his time, make his amends for what he did. She would make hers by being a better person for Isabelle and Lottie. Then, when he was out, they could all start again, together somehow. It would be fine. She knew it.

'Well?'

Carl shrugged. He was trying to look in control but Louise saw a hint of defeat at the edges of his expression.

'Deal. You keep it all sweet.' He nodded. 'You say nothing, I say nothing and we keep those who want to disrupt things out of the way. You make damn sure you do, you hear? No funny business. I got people. You know I do. In here and out there. Don't cross me. Don't make me change my mind.'

Louise nodded.

Deal done.

'Now, get out of here. It's too risky. If I need to talk to you, I'll find a way but do not come back. If they get wind of anything, of you, of any more evidence on me, then I'm done for. Go.' He made as if to leave but then, turned to her and added, 'Take care of my girls for me.' And Louise saw for the first time a softness to him, perhaps the Carl that Isabelle knew. A protector.

Carl called the guard for him to be taken back and Louise filed out through security as fast as she could, head down. If she'd thought she'd feel lighter, relieved, as she stepped away from the prison compound, having passed as Lana, at least for now, then she was wrong. Though the path ahead was now clearer, or so it seemed, she couldn't help feeling that she was trying to control the puppet master, to pull his own strings, to get her own way.

That just meant things were even more tangled than they'd ever been and that one day, those strings were going to snap.

21

Even before she opened her eyes to the darkness of the morning, barely pushed back by the weak glow of the street lights shining through her thin curtains, Louise knew that she felt sick. This was the day that things were either going to work or were going to fall apart spectacularly. The day that Isabelle and Lottie were going to visit Carl for the first time. Would he keep his side of the bargain and keep Isabelle in the dark about her? Or would he shop her, going back on what they had agreed? Lying looking at the ceiling, Louise felt her loyalties twisting as she tried to straighten them out in her mind. She was being a friend to Isabelle, keeping her innocent of the crimes Carl had committed, that they had committed. She was being loyal to Carl, keeping his secrets, smoothing over any worries Isabelle had, keeping distant those who might question things too much. Keeping everything as it was. So why did she feel so guilty?

It had taken a while to sort out the logistics of Isabelle visiting with Lottie. She had been frustrated by it all, at her recovery time, at the shock of the first weeks of parenthood and Carl's reticence at his baby girl being brought into prison. By the time it was all sorted,

Lottie was out of her newborn clothes. Carl had missed it. When Louise thought about the days she had spent with them, she felt happy. If it could be the three of them, and Carl be just... not even a consideration, then it would be wonderful. Louise had even asked herself if she had developed feelings for Isabelle. She had searched her soul to see if she had fallen in love with her, but no, that was not what it was. She loved her, she loved them both, but platonically, sisterly, nothing more. It would almost have been easier if she had fallen for her. At least that had a name, a recognisable relationship structure. What was this? What were they doing? Louise didn't know. But she knew it made her happy. That would have to do for now, despite the gossip that she was beginning to become aware of, the neighbours whispering as they saw the three of them. No wonder Carl had been worried enough to send someone to check on her.

Louise forced herself up and out of bed, trudging slowly to the bathroom, and looked at herself in the mirror. She could clearly see the anxiety in her face and she practised smiling but her eyes wouldn't light up. She could smile but it didn't reach them. She could only hope that Isabelle was far too happy herself to notice.

Today had to go well, for everyone's sake.

* * *

'Morning,' Louise said as she let herself in at Isabelle's house after throwing on whatever clothes first came to hand.

'Morning, sleepy head!' Isabelle trilled, already up, showered, dressed to the nines and in full make-up, as she turned to pour out Louise a cup from the cafetiere that was steaming on the kitchen table.

'Smells great. And you look amazing!' Louise said honestly as she took a sip. The strong, bitter taste hit her tongue and she could feel its energy zipping through her. Neither of them used to drink such strong coffee but then Lottie and her nocturnal ways had altered their need for more morning energy than the sleep they managed allowed.

'Thanks. I am *so* nervous! But I also can't wait!' Isabelle sat down, with Lottie in her bouncy chair beside her. On a plate on the table was a single piece of toast that had barely been nibbled at.

'Got mice?' Louise smiled, gesturing with her head to the toast, sounding for all the world like her own father on the rare mornings he graced her with his presence at breakfast time. He'd usually be still asleep, working off the night before. She rarely saw him before it was time for her to go to school.

'Ha!' Isabelle laughed. 'I'm just so nervous. My stomach is full of butterflies and any time I try to eat I feel a bit sick.'

'What are you nervous about? He'll be chuffed to see you both,' Louise said, trying to be supportive but feeling dread instead.

'Well. I guess.' Isabelle looked down at herself. 'The last time he saw me was just before I had Lottie. I was pregnant, glowing. Now?' She ran a hand over her stomach, which had reduced in size considerably since she'd given birth, but had not yet returned to its former tautness, if it ever would do. 'Now, I am a deflated balloon with bags under my eyes the size of... I don't know...' She looked up at Louise, worry on her face and with tears starting to brim in her eyes. 'What if he doesn't find me attractive any more? What if he sees a tired, frumpy waste of space? What if that's why he hasn't wanted me to visit?'

'Oh, Iz. Don't cry. Look, yes, you look different but not necessarily worse. You just had a baby! Of course your body is different, of course you're tired. If anything, Carl will probably feel bad that he can't be here to help.'

'I don't want him to feel bad though. And I know him, he won't just feel bad, he'll get angry and when he's angry...' She trailed off, not wanting to say.

'What?' Louise asked. 'When he gets angry, what?'

'I don't want you to think bad about him, OK?'

'OK,' Louise said, still concerned. She obviously knew that Carl had a temper, she'd very clearly seen that, but this was the first indication that Isabelle knew that too.

'He just gets a bit... erratic.'

'Erratic? What are you trying to say?'

'Well, he... He gets angry and he lashes out. And if he does that in prison, he's either going to get hurt, or bad marks against his name. Or both. He needs to stay absolutely squeaky clean otherwise it'll count against him. And I couldn't bear that. It'd be my fault!'

'What do you mean by lashing out? Has he ever hurt you?!' Louise demanded, suddenly worried that perhaps there was only one side to Carl. She'd convinced herself that the botched job was a one-off, a passing loss of control on Carl's part and that normally he wouldn't do such a thing. And that Isabelle knew a side of him that no one else saw, a softer, kinder man than the one he presented to the world. If that wasn't true, then...

'No! Well...' Isabelle said, as Louise looked at her, aghast. 'No. There was just one time when he lost his temper and he didn't mean to hit me. I was just in the way. He's never... done it again and he'd never done it before and he was so sorry. Immediately calmed down and apologised. He'd never meant to do it.' She looked at the floor.

Louise did the same. She couldn't allow Isabelle to see her face. Did this change things? Did this change what she'd agreed with Carl? Louise was trying to think at the same time as trying to reassure Isabelle. She didn't want her to think that she judged her for defending Carl and the silence grew louder the longer they were both silent. Louise couldn't deal with this now; she bookmarked it in her mind to go back to the topic, to find out just how sorry Carl had been and whether Isabelle was playing it down as much as Louise suspected she might be doing. She just needed to get through today. They both did. Then she would know if this could work, before working out if she still wanted it to, if she still trusted Carl as much she wanted to.

'I'm sure he wouldn't deliberately hurt a hair on your head,' Louise lied, reassured by the smile that returned to Isabelle's face. Just get today done and it'll all be OK, she told herself, knowing this to be another lie. They were stacking up fast.

'Exactly.'

'And he'll be over the moon to see you today. You look beautiful. You're more than you were before. You've given him his gorgeous little girl, his little princess. You two are what is keeping him going, I know it.'

'He says that every time he calls.' Isabelle nodded, patting her hair self-consciously. Louise knew that she didn't feel like her old self. But that's because she wasn't. Isabelle had changed, whether Carl or she liked it. That was just what happened when you become responsible for another human being. Being needed did that. Louise knew because she was the same. She was needed for the first time ever and, though it drained her to be looking after someone, it also made her stand taller. She had a purpose.

Isabelle went upstairs to change Lottie just as the phone rang.

'Will you get that?' she called downstairs to Louise.

'Sure,' Louise replied and picked up the landline in the hallway. 'Hello?'

'Oh. It's you,' the person on the line said.

'Is that Sandra?' Louise asked, fairly sure that she was talking to Isabelle's mum.

'Yeah. Is Iz there?'

'She is, she's just getting ready to take Lottie to see Carl.'

Louise knew that Isabelle been texting her mum. She looked at her phone when she was out of the room. She felt bad but she needed to know what she was thinking, who was in contact with her, so that she could keep her deal with Carl.

There was silence on the line. The disapproval was loud.

'Look, Sandra, I know you don't like Carl but I think you need to let it be. She loves him. He loves her. Give her some space, yeah? It's not like he can do much inside is it? Back off. You push too hard and Iz will push back. You know that. I know that. Best leave alone for a bit, OK?'

'Leave her to you, you mean. I don't know what your game is...'

'No game, Sandra.' Louise wasn't playing. She was serious. 'Leave her alone for a bit. She'll come round. Let her come to you.' She was forceful but not aggressive. She needed to be gentle here.

'I'll give Carl enough rope if that's what you mean.'

Louise could hear Isabelle at the top of the stairs. She had to get Sandra off the phone.

'Something like that. I have to go. Cab's here.' And she hung up. She didn't want to isolate Isabelle but she couldn't have Sandra asking the questions that Carl didn't want asked. So for now, Isabelle's mum would have to be kept at long range. That was all there was to it.

'Let's get going, shall we?' Louise said a little too brightly as Isabelle came downstairs. 'Better early and in time for a coffee at the station than late and stressed, eh?' The idea of spending more time than was strictly necessary in even the vaguest proximity to the prison was enough to make Louise beyond nervous, but like a sticking plaster being removed, it was going to happen and so now was better than a long, painful anticipation-filled wait. Get it done, get it over with. Louise just had to hope that she was going to be able to keep her shit together. It was getting harder every day. Lies within lies. Too messy to even know the truth any more.

'Who was on the phone?' Isabelle asked absent-mindedly.

'No one. Cold caller. Have you decided what to dress Lottie in?' Louise asked, knowing dressing her daughter was one of Isabelle's greatest joys and so would be a great deflection. 'You weren't sure whether to go pretty or practical?'

'I think pretty. I think it'll be what he's expecting. What do you think?' Isabelle was unsure of every decision about today. Her nerves were radiating off her and filling the room.

'I think that's a good idea. Show him his two gorgeous girls and he'll be the happiest man ever.'

Isabelle beamed back at her. She was so trusting. Trusting to a fault.

22

They'd arrived in Wandsworth far too early and Isabelle was jittery as hell. She could barely keep her hands still on the pushchair once they'd made their way out of the station. They had nearly an hour to kill before visiting time as they'd left time for delays and then there hadn't been any.

'Let's go to the pond on the common and then maybe to that little café that's nearby?' Louise suggested.

'Good idea. I should have thought about that.'

'You had other things to think about. You'd got yourself and Lottie and all the things you'll need for the visit.' Louise indicated the overflowing baby change bag and the gift she'd got for Carl. Isabelle wasn't sure what she was allowed to bring so she had printed a lot of photos of Lottie and made a book of them for him. It was sweet and heart-breaking all at the same time.

They killed time walking by the water pointing out the ducks to Lottie before going to the café to warm up. Lottie was a bit young to really get it but it felt like a wholesome thing to do before taking her into the grey walls of the prison. By the time they walked towards the prison visitors' centre, Louise pushing the pram as Isabelle was so nervous she was barely paying attention to traffic or people, Lottie was fast asleep and looking like an angel.

'I hope she naps for a bit and then wakes up,' Isabelle said fretfully, 'He'll want to see her awake and if he wakes her up then I just know she'll yell the place down. I don't want him to get upset or her to get upset either.' She put her hands either side of her temples. 'This is not how I wanted them to meet. It's not supposed to be like this!' Her voice wavered.

Louise knew that she had to take hold of things or else this was going to go badly. She stopped walking, put the brake on the pram and turned to Isabelle with a stern look on her face.

'Now look, Isabelle,' she said, using the voice she used on herself just before she did a job with Carl to stop her nerves from shattering her composure. 'You're introducing Carl to his baby. She will nap, you and he can chat and catch up and gaze adoringly at her. Then, you gently pick her up, we know that wakes her almost every time, but she'll be with you so she'll be calm. If she doesn't want him to hold her then he'll have to cope. It's not ideal but it's where we are. She...' Louise indicated at Lottie, blissfully unaware of her role to play this afternoon '...is your priority. He is a grown-up. She is innocent. Right?' Louise nodded to indicate that the point was made, no argument or deflection required.

'Right. She is my priority. He'll have to understand that.' Isabelle nodded, reassured by someone else taking the lead.

Louise noted that Isabelle did not insist on Carl's innocence too, as she had done every time beforehand when such a topic had been raised. She wondered if Isabelle had started to question things, started to see how things didn't quite add up. Louise was there to make sure that didn't happen, wasn't she? That was what she'd agreed with Carl. That was what she wanted too, wasn't it? Just, if Isabelle could see herself as separate to Carl, then maybe Louise could have one without the other and then she could really move on from her past.

Louise brought herself to her senses. Just because she wanted something, didn't mean it would happen. Her life had taught her that many times over already. She knew that this was likely to be the first of many visits and if she wanted to keep being a part of Isabelle and Lottie's life, she was going to have to stick with the plan she and Carl had agreed to. It was the only way that everyone got what they wanted. No, it wasn't perfect, but when had anything ever been perfect? Perfect was a sham.

At the prison visitor centre, a few people were gathering and milling about, readying for their appointments. Louise watched as Isabelle took out her mirror for the nth time since they'd left the café and checked her make-up again. A light mist of rain had been falling and Isabelle was convinced her hair had gone frizzy.

'But does it look OK? Do I look OK?' she gabbled. She looked as though she were on trial herself.

Louise felt sick standing here beside her. What if someone recognised her as 'Lana', what if she hadn't been as incognito as she had assumed last time she was here? What if this was all about to come crashing down? It would go badly for her, for Carl and therefore for Isabelle. Louise wished she'd agreed to wait for them at the café but that had seemed like a callous thing to suggest when Isabelle was so nervous.

Then, before either woman could get any more nervous, the door opened and it was time for them to go in.

'Good luck. He'll be so happy to see you. I know it.'

'Thanks! I hope Lottie behaves for her daddy!' Isabelle said, her smile barely hiding her concern.

Louise watched as Isabelle pushed the pram towards the door, turned back to wave at her. Once they were in the doorway, Louise walked away. She couldn't bear being there a moment longer than she had to. It felt too risky.

It was then that Louise realised exactly how much more she now had to lose, with Isabelle and Lottie, and the realisation made her feel cold to her core. Now someone, anyone, had a way that they could hurt her, a way that they did not have before. Now she understood all those songs that bands sing about love and pain being one and the same.

Louise realised that whatever happened from here, it was going to hurt.

23

By the time Isabelle and Lottie came out, the light mist had turned into pouring rain. Louise had spent the time that they were inside walking aimlessly around the leafy streets. She knew that she should not linger at pick up, or get involved in any idle chit-chat with others waiting to meet loved ones after their visiting slots. She had flagged down a black cab off the common and was waiting, parked up, meter running, opposite the visitor centre. It was times like these she was grateful that one good thing about her past behaviour and her refusal to live extravagantly was that money was no object when it really mattered. She could pay for the whole journey home, but would suggest just to the station. Isabelle may have questions about why Louise had so much cash on her. Louise never knew if she would need to get out of a tricky situation and she had learned from Carl that being able to flash the cash often helped smooth out more bumpy interactions. She always had cash with her, just in case. Even now, with Carl back on her side, Louise still had a feeling of constant misgiving hanging over her, never quite feeling free despite not being the one in jail.

'Over here!' Louise yelled to Isabelle, as she and the other visitors filed out. There was a noticeable difference in energy levels from the wait to go in. Before, there had been a buzz, an excitement, nerves. The adrenaline had been flowing. Now, they mostly all looked drained. Some happily, others exhaustingly so. Isabelle was the latter. She looked grey. Maybe they should get a cab all the way home. She looked fit to drop.

'Oh, a cab, that's a great idea,' Isabelle said weakly, as she looked up at the darkening sky. Lottie was fractious in her pram and was happy to be released into Louise's arms where she snuggled up on her chest, reassured by the familiar scent of her.

'I remembered everything but the rain cover, Lottie would've got soaked. Can we take this all the way home?' She told the driver the address and sat back, silent, looking blankly into the distance.

Louise didn't want to pry or ask questions and right now Isabelle clearly didn't want to talk either. Louise just wanted to get the hell out of there and back home, though she didn't know if home wasn't being watched still. She looked at Isabelle and wondered what Carl might have told her. What he might have told Isabelle about her. She felt ice run through her veins. What if Isabelle wasn't talking because she knew the truth? No. She'd handed her Lottie. She'd not have done that if she knew the truth about what had happened. And surely, Carl, still claiming innocence, wouldn't have confessed the truth in the middle of the prison.

Louise sighed out loud. She was tired, this double life, or half-life was exhausting. She hated withholding the truth from Isabelle. They would never be any closer if there was this lie between them. Maybe she should just tell her everything. Maybe she should just lay it all out there, and if Isabelle forgave her then great. If not? Well, then she had enough money to move far away and start over. Maybe that was what she should have done in the first place.

Moving to Carl's street had been a stupid thing to do. It further complicated an already complicated situation.

Just as she had decided to tell Isabelle everything as soon as they got home, two things happened. One, Lottie wriggled in her lap and then looked up at her and smiled. Smiled at her. Louise felt her heart melting inside her as she did. A warmth that spread from the very core of her, throughout her body, despite being chilled from the rain. And then, Isabelle reached out and took Louise's hand across the seat and squeezed it.

'I'm so glad you're here, Lou. I don't think I can do this without you. It's too hard. That visit was horrible. It was brilliant to see Carl but the visit was rough. I will tell you all about it, but right now, I just have to try not to cry. You know? But I'm glad you're here. You're like the sister I never had.' She looked at Louise with tears slowly and silently sliding down her face, and nodded, the whispering of a smile trying to raise itself on her lips, but her sorrow dragging it down again.

Louise knew then that she could never leave. She'd thought about it so many times but she had found a family and she was damned if she was going to give it all up because of a stupid mistake, her mistake and Carl's. He'd promised to keep his threats away, had agreed that she could be the one keeping a look out over Isabelle and Lottie. Carl and her wanted the same thing – for Isabelle and Lottie to be safe. She and Carl were working as a team again. And this time, she had the upper hand because she had the power to take it all away from him by telling Isabelle the truth – she could help her to join the dots to see the full picture. She wouldn't – that was what she'd agreed. But knowing that she could gave her a sense of power. Carl couldn't incriminate her – the police had no evidence on her, that much was clear now. And all Carl would have is a bunch of shady lowlifes who the police would very much like to talk to. They arrived back at their house and Isabelle paid the cab driver. Louise tipped him with some of the cash she had and the argument over payment was done. They stepped over the threshold with relief and Louise noted someone hovering near her front door across the road. She waited on the doorstep of Isabelle's, watching. The person struck a match, used it to light a cigarette, and blew smoke out into the rainy air. They didn't move until they had finished it, dropped it to the floor, ground it out, and with a glance across at Louise, turned to leave.

Was it a stranger taking refuge from the weather or was it another threat, a lit flame near her flat? Was it meant to tie in with the threat about the candle? She thought Carl had stopped all that.

'You coming in?' Isabelle called.

Louise looked back into the house, and when she looked towards her flat again, the person had disappeared. She peered out into the street but nothing. They'd vanished. Maybe someone new had moved in. It was a short-term lease place, so the tenants moved in and out like an airport departure lounge. Maybe they'd smoked and gone inside out of the rain. Maybe they weren't watching her at all. She had to believe that Carl meant it when they'd agreed to work together.

Louise followed Isabelle into the living room and sat down on the couch, tucking her legs underneath her, watching Lottie wriggle about on her brightly coloured play mat on the floor.

'So,' Isabelle said before sighing loudly.

'So,' Louise said, not wanting to ask questions but silently urging Isabelle to talk.

'Well, that was horrible,' Isabelle said, looking into her lap. 'It was weird and stilted and too short. It was like we didn't know each other or how to be with each other. He barely looked at Lottie. Like he hadn't registered she was his. He looked at her asleep and said she was gorgeous, but wasn't interested. He didn't seem interested at all. In anything.'

'Is he depressed?' Louise recognised that, the lethargy, the inability to feel anything at all, the impossibility of happiness. She had considered many things for Carl but depression wasn't one. He'd always got his own way in things before, maybe he couldn't cope in prison. Maybe he wasn't stalking her through his associates, maybe he was just trying to get through the days.

'I don't know. It was like he was trying not to say anything at all. He wouldn't talk about his case or the trial, said he wasn't allowed to. But he wouldn't talk about the birth and missing it, he wouldn't talk about anything much at all. I just jabbered on. Maybe he thinks I'm boring now I'm a mum? I mean, it is boring at times, isn't it? But, she's his daughter. It shouldn't be boring to him?' She took a deep breath. 'I don't know. Maybe I was expecting too much. Just, he always joked before about doing the whole *Lion King* 'Circle of Life' lift the first time he held his child. But when she woke up and he did hold her, he was really uncomfortable, really quick to give her back.'

'Maybe he's not good with babies. Every new dad is nervous. He just hasn't had the time to bond yet.' *I have to reassure her, keep this all on track.*

'When will he?! When he's out?! Let's be real. That could be years away and she won't know him. Maybe my mum was right...'

'Do you... do you think he's guilty?' She'd never asked this question before, but knowing what was going on inside Isabelle's head would be vital in playing out the situation.

Isabelle looked shocked. But she didn't say anything for a longer time than Louise might have guessed. She was twisting her wedding ring on her finger back and forth.

'No. No, I don't believe he is. I can't believe he is. I know why you're asking...' Isabelle's voice took on a hard edge, not threatening exactly but a warning all the same.

Louise's heart shot up into her throat. What had Carl told her?

'I know you're trying to be kind, to make me consider the possibility, but no. If we are going to be a family, I can't believe that he is capable of what they accused him of.'

Louise exhaled, her heart still going like the clappers. No, Carl hadn't said anything about her, about their shared guilt. She noted though that Isabelle didn't say she thought Carl was innocent, but that she couldn't believe he was guilty. Those two are not the same thing.

'What did he say? About his case? Anything?'

'He didn't. He wouldn't talk about it. Said his solicitor told him not to and then he got really angry when I kept asking.'

'Angry? With you?'

Isabelle shook her head, like it was nothing, like it was normal. How much of the same Carl did Isabelle really know? Did she always stick her head in the sand about things she didn't want to face? It would make her easier to manipulate sure, but Louise's heart dropped. She didn't want to have to. It felt wrong. She had to remind herself that it meant everyone got to keep what they wanted. It was for the best.

'It's fine. He's stressed. He's always hot tempered when he's stressed. Certain times of the year, he'd always be home late, worrying. Some antiques fair twice a year, the "major assignment" he'd called it. I always thought he'd want to chat it out, but if I pushed too far he'd lose his cool.' She gestured to the door, where if you looked closely, you could see the outline of a repaired dent in its solid hardwood. About the size of a fist.

'He did that? Over stress?' Louise asked, unable to keep the incredulity from her voice. Denting hardwood took some force.

'So I know when to stop. When he's ready to talk. He'll talk.' She crossed her arms over, almost hugging herself as if to indicate the matter closed.

Louise knew she shouldn't ask. She knew it wasn't wise and it wouldn't help her or Carl. But the question was out of her mouth before she'd had time to stop it.

'So you said he once hit you? Would he ever hurt Lottie?'

'No!' Isabelle looked at her, appalled. 'Why would you even ask such a thing? He loves us. He's just under a lot of stress. I expect he doesn't want to get too attached to her, to us, because it makes being in there harder. He'll win his case, they'll see they've made a mistake and he'll be out soon and then we can start again. Then we can pretend it never happened.' She sat, a look of thunder on her face, almost sulking. Louise knew she had crossed a line. This was the problem with the lie that sat between them, there was always a distance that one of them didn't know was there.

'Sorry. Sorry, that was rude of me. Insensitive,' Louise apologised and the three of them sat in almost silence, just the sounds of Lottie trying to grab something with her tiny fists and not getting very far.

'It must be hard for him. Inside,' Louise said, conciliatorily. 'Seeing the family he wants going on living their life without him. He's missing so much of Lottie's early months. It can't be easy. Especially as he's...' She couldn't bring herself to say it.

Because it wasn't true.

He was guilty as hell and deserved to be where he was. He had almost killed that man and for what? Trinkets. How much of his behaviour that day was normal for him? Louise hadn't been aware of violence from him before. Sure, he could get angry but he hadn't got a reputation for being busy with his fists; he ruled with respect more than fear as far as she knew. He'd been jittery that day. Maybe the stress of impending parenthood had got to him. Maybe it'd been a mistake, but even mistakes need paying for. That's how society worked, wasn't it? Her parents paid for the mistake that was her, didn't they? They did their time.

Louise sighed. She was so broken. She knew it. She was a

damaged human being. As much as she didn't want to be, and was trying hard not to be, she knew that she was. She was floundering and always had been. She had grabbed onto Carl to stop herself from drowning in the pointlessness of it all, and now she had grabbed onto Isabelle. Was any of it real or was she just trying not to sink? She wanted to be a good person. But she wasn't. She was actively lying to Isabelle, telling her what she wanted to hear in order that she, Louise, could keep what she wanted. That wasn't love. That was selfish. And yet, when Louise opened her mouth to speak, yet more lies poured out. She couldn't help herself.

'Especially as he's claiming innocence. I can't imagine that'll go down well with the other prisoners. It'll make him look weak. I don't know a lot about jail but I can't see that weak is an advantage. I just worry, that's all,' Louise said.

Isabelle frowned at her. 'He's not weak. He just isn't guilty. That's not the same thing.'

'Sorry. No, you're right. He's keeping his head down so he'll be out soon. Then you'll be able to be a proper family. Lottie can have a proper family.' She looked away.

Isabelle softened and she looked up at Louise, from underneath her eyelashes, trying to catch her eye.

'Lottie has a proper family, Lou. Us. You and me. And her daddy at a distance. Who has a proper family these days anyway? Did you? You've not said a lot about them. You had a mum and a dad, but was it all a bed of roses?'

Louise said nothing but shook her head. They'd talked a little about Louise's family and why they weren't about any more.

'No, it wasn't, was it?' Isabelle continued. 'But Lottie has two people who love her here and a father who does love her and will get to know her better when he can. She won't remember by the time he's out and we will make it all OK. I will make sure of that. For her. As her mother, that is what I promise I will do.'

'God, you're amazing, do you know that?' Louise said, floored by the strength that Isabelle showed, had been showing ever since Lottie arrived. When she was still pregnant, she seemed incapable, like she would never be able to do this without Carl. But now? She was a strong woman and parent, and she would do everything in her power for her child. No wonder the visit went badly, she was a different woman to the one Carl had left sobbing after him on the doorstep. Would he like it? Did he like it?

'You're amazing,' Isabelle countered. 'You've taken on all of this, helping me and you didn't need to.'

I did need to, Louise thought, it was this or the abyss.

'I told Carl about you; about how great you'd been. He said you sounded like the right sort.' She smiled, holding her hand out to Louise. 'We can be one big, weird, happy family and it's going to be great!'

She looked at Louise and insisted, 'Yes?'

Louise took all her doubts, her worries and her fears and squashed them away. 'Yes,' Louise replied, taking Isabelle's hand and squeezing it.

This was her family and she would fight for it.

24

FOUR AND A HALF YEARS LATER

Time passes quickly when you're trying to avoid a truth. Day after day disappears on the small things, pushing the big things to the outskirts of life. You get up, get dressed, go to work, come home, eat, relax, go to bed and repeat. If you do that again and again and again, then time passes by barely noticed. When she thought of him, Louise wondered if Carl carved up his time the same way. He'd got seven years, despite the best efforts of his legal team. It was a fraction of what he could have been facing, that was true enough, but Isabelle had been devastated when she learned that, even with good behaviour and an early release, Lottie would still likely be at school before her father would be home.

Lottie was growing up fast, crawling, walking, talking, running, turning from a demanding baby to a demanding toddler and then pre-schooler. It was a Sunday morning, around six, currently Lottie's favourite time to get up. Louise did Sundays, to let Isabelle lie in and recover a little from all the other wake-ups and the relentlessness of childcare. The early morning sunlight was peeking in from behind the slatted blinds across the window, the golden light that brings promise of a gloriously sunny day. It was flooding across the floor and making wonderful shadows in the room.

'What does that one look like, Lot?' Louise asked, nursing her cup of builder's tea, as Lottie had her breakfast. Louise had cut the bread into soldiers as Lottie liked to grab them and squash them into her mouth, spreading crumbs everywhere. It was messy but adorable.

'Does it look like a unicorn? Um, a frog?' Louise held up a squashed bit of toast as a prop.

Lottie giggled, encouraging Louise to keep going. 'A tractor? A budgie? A ladybird?!'

'No!'

'Ummm.' Louise's brain was struggling to wake up for the level of enthusiasm required. A calm quiet breakfast was never on the cards.

'Um, a fire truck? An ambulance? A cat?'

'It's a horse!' Lottie shouted happily. Horses were her favourites, Louise should have guessed.

The sound of the letterbox clattered in the empty hallway.

'Shall we see what the postman has brought today?' Louise said mindlessly to Lottie as she walked to the door. She was already in the hallway when the realisation hit. It was a Sunday. It wasn't the postman. Who would be up and working at this hour? It was practically the middle of the night. Even the milkman didn't usually deliver this early.

Louise bent down to pick up the letter that had fallen softly onto the front-door mat. It was a plain brown envelope. The type that the council tax letter comes in. Probably some local restaurant or garden services. That's what Louise told herself as she picked it up.

There had been a time when she was terrified every time the doorbell went or the post was delivered. Convinced that one of the network had decided they were unhappy with the set-up that she and Carl had agreed. He was one of the heads, but was he *the* head? Louise never knew. And besides, with Carl in jail, would someone try to step into his shoes? Eventually, what she chalked up to paranoia, faded.

They had their new life. Isabelle visited Carl twice a month, once with Lottie, once without. She was running around everywhere now and Isabelle found it hard. Carl had protested, but only lightly, Louise noted. She'd have wanted Lottie every time, chaos or not. Life had settled into a peaceful routine of denial: Isabelle's, that Carl would be home 'soon'; and Louise's, that the silence, the lack of contact or any more threats, meant that all was well. They were living their lives, but also waiting for Carl to get out, whilst never talking about how that would change things.

Denial was their normal.

Last week though, Isabelle had come home upset after Carl had mocked their home life set-up. Her living with her 'wife'. He'd teased her about sharing Louise when he got out. Isabelle had got angry and told him he was being a shit husband and Louise had been more of a partner to her than he had been. They'd rowed and Carl had chosen to end the visit early, which upset Isabelle further. Despite no one saying it out loud, it had reminded all three of them of how they hadn't worked out how things would be once Carl did get out, how this set-up could continue, or rather, how it couldn't.

Carl wouldn't have it.

He'd been on her mind since then in a way he hadn't been before. He'd been quiet in prison, his solicitor saying he'd been playing ball, keeping his head down, doing his time after his appeal failed, but something had shifted, Louise could sense it. That feeling of dread, of hyper-vigilance had returned.

She picked up the letter. In scrawled biro was just the name 'Rachel'.

Louise felt her stomach drop.

Rachel was her name from *that* job. Whoever wrote this knew who she was, what she'd done, and crucially, where she lived. She had thought it had gone away. It was never going to go away. She had not paid her price.

She jumped back as if scalded, letting the letter flutter innocently to the floor. Louise looked back towards the living room, Lottie was happily chattering away to herself. She felt dizzy and she had to hold onto the wall for balance.

'Loooou!' Lottie called from the other room.

Louise choked out a cough to clear her throat which had closed up.

'Coming, Lots, coming.'

Louise retrieved the letter, crumpled it in half and stuffed it into her pocket. She couldn't read it now. She was in sole charge of a rambunctious child. She couldn't focus on whatever the letter said and be present for Lottie, and Lottie came first, always. Louise walked back to the living room, trying to feel calm where she only felt dread. Lottie had abandoned her breakfast and had settled herself in the toy area, dragging out a puzzle, which she opened, dropping the pieces all over the floor in a loud clatter, just beneath where Isabelle was sleeping.

Isabelle. Thank goodness she was asleep. Louise felt a wave of ice creep over her as she wondered what would have happened if Isabelle had got the letter first. Louise could imagine.

'Rachel? Who's this for? I don't think there's even a Rachel in this stretch of houses, let alone here. Hand delivered at this time on a Sunday too.' She'd smile and think the best. 'I wonder if it's a love letter. A teenage boy trying to convince Rachel to go out with him! Though he'd do better to get her address right!' She'd laugh, tearing the letter open to see if she could let the writer know that they'd got the wrong house. She would never have guessed at the truth.

Louise looked up at the ceiling above where she would be, hopefully, still sleeping despite Lottie's best efforts. She didn't think Isabelle would ever guess the letter was for Louise, aka Rachel, aka the one who made it possible for Carl to break into that man's house. The one who made it possible for him to rifle through a stranger's things, their valuables, their sentimental items, to gauge them for resale value, to weigh up their worth to him before pocketing the best and rejecting the rest. Taking both the physical things and their owner's peace of mind with him.

Isabelle would never believe, would never accept that Carl, when surprised at this work, punched that man to the floor, kicked him when he was down and rained down blow after blow, bashing his elderly skull repeatedly into the cold kitchen floor. The same hands that she let hold Lottie, that she let hold her. The same hands that she was planning on welcoming back into this house. Louise felt sick to the stomach and she had to swallow back the saliva that was gathering, her body warning her that she was going to throw up.

Isabelle would never guess that she had shared her home all this time, left her precious daughter in the hands of another criminal – an aider and abetter of a terrible thing. Whatever was in this letter would have told her all that, Louise assumed, her mind in a panic. Whoever sent it, and Louise presumed it would be eventually traced back to Carl, was taking a hell of a risk that it would be her who found it. Not Isabelle. Maybe they didn't care.

Then the realisation hit. They had been watching. They knew that Sunday mornings were her time. They knew that Isabelle would be asleep. All those moments that Louise felt someone there in the corner of her eye but turned to find nobody. All those times when the hairs on the back of her neck stood up but never revealed why. Of course they could disappear into the crowd or the dark. She did, didn't she? She was hiding in plain sight, why couldn't they? Despite the arrangement that she had with Carl, that she had never reneged on, never in all this time given him cause not to believe that she was doing what she said, keeping things ticking over for him; despite all that, Carl didn't really trust her. Did he trust anyone? Louise felt stupid – she had taken Carl at his word. Why? When he had shown her who he was.

She knew.

It was because it was what she wanted to believe.

Louise was still on edge when, an hour or so later, Isabelle slowly made her way downstairs wrapped in a fluffy dressing gown and slippers, looking refreshed if sleep rumpled.

'Morning, my two favourite ladies.' She smiled at them both.

'Mama!' Lottie said as she ran over to Isabelle and hugged her. She held on as though she was relieved the relaxed parent was here. Louise had tried to be calm but her hammering heart rate and clammy hands had not gone unnoticed by Lottie who was playing up and behaving in an unsettled way with her. Louise knew that she'd picked up on the anxiety, but didn't know what to do with it.

'Tea?' Louise asked, desperate to get away and open the letter. She had gone through every scenario she could possibly think of in the past sixty minutes, from death threats to eviction demands, to threats of turning her into the authorities. All the things she had worried that Carl would do when he was found guilty, before she realised that she could confirm the guilt he was steadfastly denying, and before she realised the power that gave her. Had someone decided that it was time to take that power back?

'Please,' said Isabelle, as Lottie grabbed a handful of books and shoved them at her mother, a request for them to be read with her.

Louise looked at the scene and her heart ached. All that was precious to her was in this room. What was Carl threatening that would take this away from her?

Louise barely noticed anything as she went through the motions. She made tea and toast for Isabelle, forcing a slice down her own throat as she went. It tasted like cardboard and felt like she was swallowing rocks that then sat heavy in her stomach, threatening to be seen again and soon. She handed a breakfast tray to Isabelle and then announced,

'I think I'll go for a long bath, I've a headache coming on.'

'Oh.' Isabelle looked up, concerned. 'Thank you for this.' She nodded at the tray. 'Are you OK? Do you need anything?'

'No, I think it was just the early start, that's all. Monkey here wanted to see the dawn.' She laughed, forcedly. She knew what had caused the headache – the spikes of fear shooting through her. The adrenaline, the stress. Her body was going into fight or flight mode. Or possibly just total collapse. She wanted to sleep and not be conscious. She did not want to know what the letter said and yet she knew she had to find out.

Louise closed and locked the bathroom door and set the water running. She had no idea how she would react to the contents of the letter and privacy was difficult to be had in a shared house where usually there were no secrets. Other than one.

The room filled with steam and the letter started to go clammy in her sweaty hands. Slowly, she peeled the envelope open, the glue from the seal melting in the ambient heat of the room.

Louise unfolded the letter and read:

Rachel,
   This ain't working any more. It's weird. People are talking. I don't trust it, you, any more. Leave. I don't care how or where. Just go.
   Now.

K.

Louise lowered her shaking hands. K. Whoever wrote this thought they were being clever but it wasn't a huge jump from C to K. Was it even Carl who wrote this or had it written? Or was someone trying to play with her, with them both, to leave Isabelle isolated? Was someone trying to pull off a coup of the network?

Carl wasn't here. He'd likely not be here for a good few years still. Her vanishing into the ether was not good for his family. Not good for him. Why was he looking to mess up the plan now? Sure, what would happen once he was home was still up in the air, but had someone mocked him about Louise being Isabelle's wife? Is that why he'd said that to her – to gauge her reaction? To see if it was true? Was being inside chipping at his confidence, his belief in himself as the alpha male?

No. She wasn't having this. She would find a way of getting a message back to him like she had before She'd make him see that she threatened nothing, that it wasn't like that, in fact she was the one keeping his doubters at bay, reassuring Isabelle that her faith in him was well placed, even if she had to swallow her own guilt to do it. She was what Carl needed. They were on the same team still. She just had to make him see it. She would share them with him unless he forced her hand and then, well, then she would take them from him. Two could play at that game.

All he had to do was make his choice.

25

FIVE YEARS AGO

'Five, six, seven k. There,' Carl said, counting out the notes onto the table between them. He'd been able to sell on most of the things from the last job already. They'd been lucky. Their client had been a collector of silverware and they had liberated one or two key items from their cabinet, rearranging to hide the loss from immediate view.

'Is that £7k total?' Louise said, confused. 'You said we'd be able to sell just one of the pieces for several grand?' She picked up the notes and flicked through them, then looked up at Carl, trying her best to sound questioning rather than accusing. Carl didn't like either but he liked the latter less.

'Yes.'

'Yes... what?'

Louise could see the vein in his forehead starting to throb. She kind of liked it though. When he got angry he was also really authoritative. It suited him. She tried to unthink that. She knew it was inappropriate. They needed to be strictly business but there was something. The bond they had, the sheer rush they shared when a job went well, it felt like... something? Louise couldn't name it, but it felt good. It felt warm and happy. She wasn't going to risk that for nothing. Several grand wasn't nothing though.

'Yes, I said that.'

'So did you sell that one piece for a few grand? Or less?'

'Less, else there'd be more, wouldn't there?'

'So what about the other pieces then? I thought we were a fifty-fifty team, Carl?'

'Are you accusing me of ripping you off?!'

'No. Not that.' She had to tread carefully. After all, this was her only source of income now, having jacked in the terrible job at the pub so she needed to make this profit. And it's not like Carl couldn't replace her. But she would have no idea how to do this without him. Would she even want to? Each time they did a job she felt it should be their last but then his enthusiasm, his praise for how well she did, kept pulling her back in. And why not? She'd got precisely nothing given to her, everything she had, she had taken. That was just how it was. How it had to be.

'I just thought this was going to be a really profitable one, that's all. Nothing more.'

Carl at least had the decency to look ashamed as he scuffed his boot along the floor. It was clear to Louise now that he had taken a slice off the top.

'I know that you're taking the risk, selling on, so if there needs to be a cut for that, then let's work it out,' Louise said. Perhaps she could manage a better deal for her than this uncommunicated one. She couldn't live on six grand and didn't want to do more jobs than they were already doing. That would rush things and that could only lead to mistakes and mistakes were costly. Too costly.

'Well, yes, exactly. Maybe I should take a bigger cut. For the extra risk, yeah.' He finally looked up at her, eye to eye.

Her stomach flipped. As much as she wanted to deny it, there was something, an attraction there even if she didn't want it.

'So, what's the new deal then?'

He coughed and then laughed.

'You are a smart one, ain't ya? Guess that's why this works. Heh!' He took a wad of notes out of his inside jacket pocket, unrolled them and counted out some more without showing her and handed them over.

'Let's say I made sixteen grand, total, yeah?'

Louise knew this was likely to be an underestimation.

'And you get, say seven and a half. Not quite half. How's that?'

'Sure,' Louise said, flicking through the notes, 'but this is £7,450?' She practised looking stupid as she looked at him, like she didn't understand how it didn't add up, like she couldn't see he was still trying to scam her. It suited her to have him underestimate her. Then she held some power, even as she felt hers slipping.

'Ah, so you're right!' He added two more pristine £20 notes and a crumpled tenner to the pile. 'There you go.'

'Great. Thanks.'

'Cheers.' He folded up the rest of the money.

So she now knew she would be getting around 44 per cent of the official sale price, but likely less than the actual sale price of whatever they took. If things got harder, or she felt less inclined to keep going, she could renegotiate. She knew now how to play him a little at his own game and how far she could push before she knew the brick wall was coming up. She was sure that she knew how he ticked, what made him work. She had confidence in that.

Was that confidence misplaced?

26

PRESENT DAY

Walking from the Tube station, Louise tried to play out the conversation in her mind. She'd not visited Steve since that time she'd coerced him into helping her arrange the visit to Carl. She'd threatened him then so she was fairly sure she would not be welcomed with open arms this time. But she needed to get a message to Carl, to calm down whatever fears seemed to have caused him to change his mind so abruptly. She would just have to make Steve see that it was best for everyone. Isabelle was visiting Carl with Lottie so Louise took the opportunity not to have to explain where she was going.

Louise rounded the corner and stopped in shock. The pub was a blackened mess, with the roof collapsing in on itself, tarpaulin badly draped across the chasm where the top floors used to be. The whole place looked condemned and like it had been for some time. What on earth had happened? Steve couldn't have done some insurance job cos he never bothered with insurance in the first place. She walked closer to the pub out of morbid curiosity. Steve obviously wasn't there. She would need a new plan to get to Carl, though how, she had no idea.

The Silent Friend

"Orrible isn't it?'

Louise turned to see the lady who ran the corner shop across the road from the pub. She was stood outside, arranging the car-fume-covered fruit and vegetables on the outside display. She stopped, checked for traffic and then crossed to talk with Louise.

'I said, 'orrible isn't it? Wants a good pulling down that. Not that the council will listen. It's an eyesore. Makes my customers think we're in a bad area.'

Louise said nothing. It was a bad area.

'What happened?'

The woman suddenly looked suspicious despite it being her who initiated the conversation.

'Why you asking?'

'Oh, I used to work here. I came to see Steve. Do you know where he went?' Louise said innocently. 'I thought I'd pop over for a catch-up. It's been a while.'

The women's face relaxed as pity overtook it.

'So you've not heard then? Such an 'orrible situation. Lord knows what 'e'd got 'imself mixed up in, there.'

Louise's stomach turned.

'What do you mean?'

'Well, I don't like to gossip. But. Well. 'E's dead. The fire. 'E was in there. Trapped.'

Louise imagined Steve passed out stone drunk, unaware that his pub was burning around him. He'd not been the best of people, sure, but he didn't deserve that. The poor guy.

The woman's eyes narrowed as she continued. 'Proper nasty stuff it was. The place burned to the ground and when the fire brigade was able to get in, well, then they found him. Slumped over one of the tables, like he'd not even tried to get out. Some nasty bugger had tied him up and set the place on fire with 'im in it. One of the regulars who shops 'ere said there was a row with some rough blokes in fancy suits a couple of days before, but Steve hadn't gone to the police cos it was a bad idea. Next thing we knew, the pub was ash. And Steve with it. Like I said, proper nasty.' She sniffed and bunched up her sleeves like she was rolling them up for a fight. 'You all right, love? You've gone proper pale. Do you want to come into the shop for a sit down?'

Louise swallowed though her mouth was bone dry.

'Um. No. No thanks,' she managed to choke out. 'No. I'd best get home.'

'Suit yourself, love. You take care mind. They haven't caught who did it. Who knows who's still sniffing about the place. Makes you proper nervous I can tell you that. Well, ta-ta, love,' she said as she wandered back to her shop.

Louise could barely make one foot step in front of the other. Steve was dead. Killed in a horrible way by someone he'd crossed. She scanned her memory for conversations about Steve she'd had with Carl. He was mostly loyal but also a liability. He'd been taking a share of the money he ran through the pub's tills to clean it for Carl. His accountability with various authorities was questionable and he drank. Way too much. In fact, Louise recalled what Carl had once said:

'Bloody Steve. He drinks so much booze he's practically flammable.'

Louise scrunched her face up, trying not to panic. He wouldn't have. Carl liked Steve. He'd have had him roughed up maybe, he'd have taken the missing money and more to make up for it. He wouldn't have done... that. Would he?

He had a temper, sure. He lashed out when he felt cornered, yes. Had prison made him worse? Just how dangerous was he really?

27

'You OK? You've been very quiet since you got back. Did the visit not go well?' Louise asked. Isabelle had hardly said a word, which was unlike her. Usually she was chatting on about Carl this, Carl that, but her silence made Louise nervous. Things weren't right. She could feel it.

'Mmmhmm.' Isabelle nodded, playing with a strand of her hair, twisting it round her finger. Then suddenly, 'Ah!' She'd pulled her own hair out.

'What did you do that for?' Louise said, rather more tetchily than she'd have liked. She was on edge. Something had shifted, but Isabelle clearly didn't want to say what. It was like walking on a glass floor in a high up building, and not knowing if the glass would hold. You felt sort of safe, but you also just might plummet to your death.

'So. Carl's coming up for parole,' Isabelle spat out, like she had been trying to keep it in but it escaped her lips.

'Oh...' Louise was surprised by the sudden depth of the terror she felt. Everything was screaming at her that this was bad. Very bad. Like it was the missing piece of the puzzle and the picture was not one Louise wanted to see. She clammed up. Was this what had caused Carl to behave differently? It had to be, surely. What did that mean?

'He's fairly confident he'll get out. He's been good, made a point of getting the officers on side, kept his nose clean. No black marks against his name, no trouble. It's his first offence. He...' Her voice broke as she tried to keep composed.

'What is it?'

'Well. He's been really distant lately. Not talking, not sharing. And now he's saying that maybe he should lie to the board. Say that he did it and apologise. So he can show remorse, which might help. Only... only he can't look me in the eye when he talks. He can't look at me. He doesn't often lie to me, I know it, but when he does... he can't look at me. Because he knows I'll see it in his eyes.'

Louise bit her tongue. Carl had clearly lied to Isabelle about a lot of things and looked her in the eyes while he did so. It felt so wrong, knowing things about her husband that she didn't. It felt like betrayal. It felt like it because it was. She could never find out. She'd never forgive either of them. But, should she know? Did she deserve to know the truth?

'Do you think he should admit to doing it? Whether he did or not? If it gets him home, does it matter?'

'Yes, it matters! It matters what people think. How can I hold my head up if everyone thinks he's guilty? If he's admitted to it.'

'But people have walked away anyway. Why shoot yourself in the foot for people who don't care enough to believe you?'

Isabelle looked sick. Her face reddened as the truth of what Louise was saying sunk in.

'I guess. I just... I don't want a husband who is guilty of that sort of thing. He's better than that. I'm better than that.'

'That's not the only thing though, is it?' Louise knew there was more but that Isabelle was holding back. Something important.

'No... no, you're right.' She chewed her lip, trying to find the right words. Her nerves made Louise shaky. Was she about to ask her to go? It'd be strange for her to be here when Carl got out, she knew that. It was always the elephant in the room whenever they spoke about the future. How would it work?

'What if... what if...' Her breath was ragged. She cleared her throat.

Louise said nothing, but tipped her head to the side, listening.

'What if he comes home and doesn't like it? What if he's got the idea of us, of me and Lottie, in his head and the reality doesn't match? You know how he was when I stopped bleaching my hair blonde not long after Lottie was born? Too much maintenance to be doing with. He hated it. Remember? I was so upset. He was so mean about it. Said he didn't recognise his own wife. But it was the first time really that I felt like me rather than who people wanted me to be. I think he expected me to agree and go back to blonde because he wanted me to but I didn't, did I? I stood my ground on it and he didn't like it, did he?

'He's always had his head in the clouds when it suits him. I am not the person I am when he went in. I am stronger. I have opinions. I didn't always have them; I was happy for Carl to make the decisions, but now? Now I've had to make all of them and I like it. I like being in control of my life. When he went in, I didn't even know who our electricity was from, where the meter was. Nothing. Now? Now I know what goes out when. But I still don't know...'

'Where the money comes in from?'

'Exactly. He won't say. An amount appears in my savings account from an account with a random name and it changes from time to time. That's not good, is it?'

'I mean, companies have random names all the time. It's not necessarily a bad thing.' Louise tried to reassure her though she agreed with her. It was most likely Carl hiding the money from various deals from her, slowly dripping into her account from a range of places, to keep it from the police.

'But even money aside, how would this all work? Him home, getting to know Lottie, getting to know me. And how has he changed? Cos it would change you, wouldn't it? Prison. And you?' She looked at Louise, almost pained, and Louise knew that she was wondering what it would be like when Louise wasn't here. Because she couldn't be here, could she? That would be weird. Carl thought it was weird.

Louise got it. She didn't want to live with Isabelle and Carl either. But she could still be close, couldn't she? She'd left her flat across the road, but they came up all the time. She could get another.

'We'd work something out,' was all Louise could muster. Her platitudes sounded empty even to her own mind. They really hadn't thought this through.

'I know. I know we would but... Oh, I feel awful saying this, but right now, everything works. I see him, he sees us. You're here, you and Lottie are amazing...'

'Are you saying you don't want him back?' Louise said, surprised. Pleased yet terrified. How angry would Carl be if he knew?

'No! No. I don't think so. I don't know. I'm so tired and this just feels hard. We're all settled and this will unsettle us. But no, obviously I don't want him in prison forever. I just don't know how things will be and I am too anxious to work out how they might be and what I need to do in order to make it all work. But he's my husband, Lottie's daddy and obviously we want him home. But I want you here too. And that's...'

'That's weird?' Louise laughed, albeit morosely.

'Yeah! It is, isn't it?' Isabelle laughed. 'Like I want my village for

Lottie. You're like her live-in auntie and that's great. I want Lottie to be surrounded by people who love her. And you love her.'

'I do.' Louise nodded. 'So much.'

Isabelle sighed. 'Does it ever get easier?' she said, wrapping her arms around herself for support.

'Nope. Sorry. Don't think so,' Louise said, smiling.

She has no idea just how complicated this all is. What he's really like. It's never going to be easy. I don't even know if this can work, no idea what Carl is up to, she thought, as she went to Isabelle and hugged her.

'We'll work it out though, eh?'

Maybe. If Isabelle isn't sure he should come back, maybe he shouldn't. Maybe there is another way, Louise thought, a realisation starting to flicker inside her. Change was coming, whether they liked it or not.

28

FIVE YEARS AGO

The blood in her head was pounding, a loud, pulsing whoosh that drowned out most other sounds – traffic, birds, people. It pushed them all underwater, distorting them, making them feel distant. She tried gulping breaths to snatch some feeling of calm from somewhere, like she could swallow some from the air itself. She reached the end of the tree-lined avenue and turned left, back towards the meeting place that she and Carl had agreed upon.

When she got to the meeting place, the flat, he was already there, looking crazed, with blood that wasn't his, spattered on his shirt and hands. Louise felt sick. Carl was pale, shaking and wouldn't stop saying, 'Fuck! Fuuuuck. Fuck! FUCK!' as he jiggled up and down on the balls of his feet, energy pumping through his veins, making him look as though he'd taken way too many drugs. Looking at his sweaty face, his wide-eyed stare with dilated pupils and waxy looking skin, Louise wasn't sure that he hadn't. Was that why he'd lost it? Dammit! They were always supposed to be in full control of their minds. He'd insisted on that. 'I don't work with junkies,' he'd said, 'too unreliable.' Had he gone against his own rules and stuffed everything up?

She was furious, and when she spoke, she was cold. 'Did you do as I told you and get rid of the gardening tools?'

'The what?'

'I told you to pick up the tools. You could be his gardener. Did you? Did you just run off?!' His defiant look told her he had done. She suspected as much from what she had heard from inside.

'Fuck's sake, Carl,' she said under her breath. She rose her furious face to meet his.

'What did you do? Or rather, why? I saw what.'

'What?' Carl said, more a sulky teenager than anything else.

'Are you serious?!'

'OK, so it didn't go to plan. You didn't keep him talking. He was never supposed to see me. So don't look at me like this is my fault. OK?'

Louise couldn't believe it. She knew that Carl didn't respond well to criticism but was he really going to try to gaslight his way out of this?

'No, it didn't go to plan. But you didn't stick to the plan either. What part of the plan involved kicking an old man's skull in for Christ's sake?!' She was sickened even speaking about it. The image of the dark-red blood against the spotless white-tiled floor was one she knew would never leave her. She hoped he was OK. She hoped that the call she had made was enough.

'What did I do wrong? You tell me!' Carl was raging now. His eyes bloodshot, his hair crazed from him running his sweaty hands through it again and again.

'What the hell? I shouted. "There's NO ONE THERE." We agreed. That was the sign for you to get the hell out. He should have wandered through and found, at worst, a messy room, maybe a few things out of place. He was not supposed to find you, rummaging through his things. And, above all, you were not supposed to ATTACK HIM FOR FUCK'S SAKE. You were punching him and kicking him! What the hell?! We were not supposed to do any harm and that sure as hell looked harmful to me! I only hope the ambulance got to him in time otherwise he's a goner.'

'What ambulance?'

Louise hesitated.

'I called one.'

'You did what?!'

'He was going to die, Carl. He still might have or might do. You'd have murdered him. I am not going to let that happen. Not without trying.'

'Are you fucking insane?! You called the authorities to the scene of a crime. Your crime. You're the one he invited in. You're the one he spent fuckin' ages talking shit to. You. You're the face he'll remember.' He punched the table. How he didn't break his hand, Louise didn't know. He'd gone from defensive to furious in a millisecond. She needed to stand her ground. She would not be cowed by him.

'Oh, I don't know, Carl. You're the one who beat his face in. He might remember that.' She crossed her arms across her body. This was not the reaction she had expected. There was no remorse at all. None. She was still standing there, waiting for him to speak when.

Whack!

The blow came from nowhere. Or rather it came from Carl, punching the side of her head. The room spun and her ear was ringing where he had caught it with his fist. Confused, Louise brought her hand up to her face. DID HE ACTUALLY HIT HER? Her bottom lip was stinging, and when she brought her hand down, there was blood. *Is this my blood, or his? The old man's? How much blood does Carl have on his hands?* She ran her tongue slowly over her lip and found where the impact had split it open. It was her blood. That was better. Wasn't it? She couldn't think. Her brain was still recovering from the impact.

When she finally looked up at Carl, he was his old self. Confident, sure, a hint of menace, which Louise had previously misunderstood as flirtation. Or was it still that? Was he being cocksure? Louise knew her judgement when it came to Carl was skewed. She'd done one of those stupid questionnaires one time, from a magazine someone had left on the bus. It told her that she lacked a father figure in her life and would try to replicate this in her romantic relationships and that she should be aware of misreading controlling behaviour for affection. At the time she'd laughed it off. Just cos her dad didn't care about her, didn't mean she'd scrabble for affection elsewhere. But just now and again, with Carl, she wondered if that lightweight article might have had a point.

'Now,' he almost snarled at her, 'I didn't want to have to do that. But you were getting hysterical.' He nodded, affirming his own version of events. He had calmed now, as though the act of lashing out at her had alleviated his rage, the energy dispensed with.

Louise paused, then realising he required a response, nodded. 'Yes.'

'Right. So. Never call anyone. We don't do it. We get in, we get out. We do what it takes. Got it?'

She nodded mutely. He was rewriting their deal as he spoke and she didn't know how to respond. Do no harm was clearly what he told her to get her on board. Do whatever it takes was how he actually operated.

'This day never happened. I was at work, selling some old shit for someone. You? Well, make up what you were doing and make sure someone saw you doing it, do you know what I mean? Heads down, no work for a while, let the dust settle. Then we regroup and start again.'

Louise didn't know if she wanted to start again. But if she didn't, then she would have to start again in other parts of her life and she didn't know if she could or wanted to do that either. Was it so bad?

Maybe the man would be OK. Maybe Carl would calm down and this was a blip. Maybe, if she just did nothing, it would all work out. Lie low. She could do that. She could disappear. She was good at that. But. What about the man?

'Sure. Sure... but...'

'What?' Carl asked, his eyes narrowing with impatience.

'Will that man be OK?'

'What man? I don't know what you mean.'

He looked her dead in the eye and she could almost believe she'd invented the whole thing. The blow to her head was making her confused. The afternoon had happened. It wasn't some concussion related fiction was it? Why had Carl hit her? Her brain ached.

'The only thing you got to know, is this...' He looked at her, as serious as she had ever seen him. 'We work well as a team...'

Something in her shifted, a warmth, a good feeling at being part of something with him. God, her relationship to him was messed up, she knew.

'...but I've replaced you before and I can replace you again. Do you get what I mean?' He nodded at her, waiting for the penny to drop.

'You are disposable. You can be disposed of.'

Louise swallowed. She understood. She was not the first, and if necessary, would not be the last. If she wanted to stay, she needed to play along.

And if she didn't want to play any more? She wasn't sure if she wanted to find out what that involved. Instead, she just nodded.

'Got it,' she said.

'Good.'

29

PRESENT DAY

Louise sat at the dressing table mirror, with its white wood and gilt edges, and looked hard at her reflection. At her drawn, grey face. The spare room at Isabelle's house was theoretically perfect, decorated in greys and pale pinks with flecks of gold here and there. It was French chic apparently. It was ultra-feminine and as much as it was relaxing, it wasn't to Louise's taste. She had too much darkness for such a pretty room.

She ran her hands over the mirrored dressing table top, leaving fingerprints as she did so. Without thinking, she clocked them and used her sleeve to smear them so as not to leave them behind. *That's how my mind works, even now*, she admonished herself, untraceable, undetectable. Never existed. She laughed because she'd slept in this room, lived in this room, her DNA would be everywhere. Hair strands, skin cells, maybe blood samples from when she'd cut her leg shaving or caught her elbow on the sharp edge of the wardrobe door. That was the problem with mirrored everything. You could always be seen.

Carl's parole was on her mind. That letter was on her mind.

Steve and what had happened was on her mind. Looking at her reflection she caught sight of the small scar on her lip, from that day, when Carl had punched her, had 'brought her back to her senses' after the failed job. It was small and only she noticed it, and she only noticed it when she was looking properly. But it was a reminder of that day, of that old man. He'd made some sort of recovery so Carl hadn't been done for murder or manslaughter even. But Louise knew the man would never be the same as he was. His peace was gone. His home no longer a sanctuary. Louise wondered if he ever went back there. She wouldn't have wanted to if she were him. She'd never want to go back.

The night before, she and Isabelle had talked over what they could do if and when Carl got out. How could they bring him back in without pushing Louise out?

'Could you be, like, a live-in nanny? A home helper? Something like that? I mean I know Carl adores her but I can't see him helping with nightmares or the school run, can you?' Isabelle had suggested.

'Is he going to want someone else living here? He's missed you two as it is, he won't want me in his space.' Louise said.

She knew beyond question that he wouldn't want her here. He'd told her to go. His two worlds were deliberately and always kept separate. She'd tried to assure him of her loyalty, but truly, where did her loyalty lie? To him? To Isabelle? To herself? When push came to shove, wouldn't she throw him under a bus if she had to? And now? Now, he seemed angrier, more violent than the version she'd visited in jail that single time. She'd pushed thoughts of his temper, his outbursts to the back of her mind because, like Isabelle, she didn't want to face what that really meant.

'He's barely here in the day and he'll have his business to attend to. He said it's ticking over while he's been away but you can't leave a business for years and just step back into it surely? You'd need to build it up again. It used to keep him away overnight, it will again, no doubt.'

'Maybe I can move back across the road. Stay here when he isn't?' It wasn't ideal for anyone but it was all Louise could think of.

'But I don't want to throw you out. You've been amazing. You're more family to me than...' Isabelle stopped, her voice cracking. It hurt her daily, those who she had presumed she mattered to, who had stepped out of her life just when she needed them. Her relationship with her mum had been further strained when she'd moved permanently to her house in Spain. Louise had done a sterling job in keeping everyone away from Isabelle. Just like Carl had wanted.

'I know... it's OK,' Louise said, nodding.

Louise wanted to be the solid one. The friend who stayed. The one who helped when it was most needed. But, she was part of the problem, she knew that. She could see that now. She wanted the best for Isabelle as well as for herself, but she didn't know if that was the same thing. Isabelle thought she wanted Carl back, but really, she either didn't know who she was married to or what he was capable of. He was dangerous.

He'd hit Louise. Isabelle had said he'd hit her, at least once. He'd pulverised that man. Then there was Steve. And what had prison done to Carl? Shown him the error of his ways or taught him that he needed to be smarter, harder, to avoid going back? Would they get a better version of him back? Or a worse one? Was that risk worth taking, especially when you considered Lottie?

'These past years have been the making of me, 'Louise said. 'You and Lottie have made me who I am. I like who I am now.' If you don't think about the lies that is.

'So do we!' Isabelle laughed, before turning serious. 'You know that, right? And you have helped make me who I am now. I respect myself more than I did. I know I am more than my manicure and my blow-dry. Much more.' She smiled, a hint of sadness underneath. Louise wondered if the sadness was worry, concern that Carl would not be as pleased at Isabelle's personal growth as she was.

'Do you think Carl will still like me?' Isabelle said more timidly, as though she'd read Louise's mind and voiced her fear. 'The visits are so artificial and I find myself not being me, not really. I worry that he won't like who I have become. He was always the head of the family, the man. The alpha. I don't need him like I used to. I worry he won't like that.'

Louise saw the chance to ask what she wanted to ask but had held back from doing so before.

'Iz?'

'Yeah?'

'Are you scared of him?' She tensed, waiting for the explosion, for her annoyance at such a question. It didn't come.

'A little. If I'm honest,' Isabelle said quietly, as though she was ashamed.

'Oh.'

'He likes things his way. He likes things as they are. And now? This house isn't his. It's mine. It's ours. It's Lottie's. And I worry he won't like that. And I worry how he will react. I don't know how he will react. He can be...'

'Aggressive?' Louise suggested, trying to find a word like violent but without being so explicit about it. She was treading on delicate ground, ground that Isabelle could suddenly refuse to walk on.

'Yeh. Yes, he can be. The door... some plates he smashed, some of my stuff he... he destroyed cos I'd annoyed him.'

Running her lip over her scar, Louise asked the question she'd asked before, now suspecting the answer might be different.

'He ever hit you other than that one time?'

Silence. Isabelle chewed her bottom lip. She looked over at Lottie, peacefully asleep and blissfully unaware of the direction that the conversation was taking around her.

'Yeah.'

'Often?'

'Not often, no. But yes, more than once. A few times. I didn't want to say before, didn't want you to think bad of him. It was nothing serious, never more than a bruise. I never had to go to hospital...' Isabelle caught herself and the excuses she was making, she saw the look of pity and horror in Louise's eyes and she started to cry.

'Oh God, what am I going to do?'

What am I going to do? What am I doing here? Louise thought, looking at her best friend, her only friend, actively contemplating letting a violent, unpredictable man back into her life. As a friend, Louise knew she ought to tell her everything, tell her the truth about her husband, no matter how hard it was to say or how hard it would be to hear. That's what friends did, wasn't it? They made the hard choices when sometimes you didn't want to make them yourself. She couldn't be the silent friend, the one who says nothing. As Isabelle's friend, Louise should tell her to keep him away. She should tell her not to let him anywhere near Lottie, if he was even interested in his daughter. For her own safety. She could see that now.

Finally.

The blinkers had finally fallen. Louise could now see clearly past all her own baggage, her confused and conflicting feelings about Carl and what he did or didn't mean to her, what he did or didn't represent. Carl was bad news. He was bad news then and he was bad news now.

'You mean, what are we going to do?' Louise found herself saying.

In the end, she gave herself the answer. They would fix it, however that would be, they would fix it together. She and Isabelle were a team. That was all she could work with. It was all they had.

30

Louise was in the kitchen when she got the first phone call. Since moving in with Isabelle, she had discovered that she was good at baking. Baking was just following instructions and she had been doing that her whole life. Do what others tell you, keep your head down, pay attention to the details and don't lose focus. Same skills needed. It was relaxing and Louise needed to relax if she was going to work out what the hell she was going to do.

She had spent time trying not to jump to conclusions, trying to be rational about what she did and didn't know as opposed to what she suspected. There was too much at stake to throw things up in the air. She had to know what she was dealing with here. But there had been developments. She'd made a few enquiries, popped to another of the pubs that she knew had connections with Steve's and asked a few questions of punters whose lips had been loosened by booze but whose brains had yet to be drowned in it.

Steve had been taken in for questioning by the police. His fictional account-keeping had finally flagged down some unwanted attention and he had allegedly spilled names faster than Lottie could spill milk when helping in the kitchen. Rumour was that whoever he worked for had understandably not taken this well, and as soon as he was out, they had Steve dealt with. Was that Carl's doing? Was it the network? Had Steve worked for someone else as well? Louise had no facts. But no wonder Carl was spooked. She knew as least as much as Steve had done. Maybe more.

You're such a mess. A mess maker. A 'mess-take'.

Louise hadn't heard her mother's voice in her head for years. Her self-confidence had been buoyed by her relationship with Isabelle, by her bond with Lottie, and the monster on her shoulder constantly putting her down had been quietened. Now, with everything seemingly falling apart, she was back. Louise shut her eyes and tried to wish it away when the phone rang.

Isabelle and Lottie had gone out for a walk in the late-winter sunshine to the park while the rain held off. Louise had tried to convince her not to go, unsure of how safe it was. She knew things had shifted, but she hadn't had time to catch up. She'd been caught off guard. She'd got complacent. She'd got happy.

'Have to work off some of the calories you keep baking for us somewhere! I'll need my maternity jeans back at this rate!' Isabelle had laughed as she loaded Lottie into her coat and onto her bike. They'd barely been gone half an hour.

Louise wiped flour onto her jeans at the knees, the tea towel hiding in the chaos of the kitchen somewhere.

'Hey, Iz, what do you need?' She laughed as she answered.

There was just a shuddery breath at first, then stutters that sounded like Isabelle but also not.

'Iz? Are you OK? What's happening?'

Sounds filtered through Isabelle's heavy breathing, crowds of people, the clink of cutlery. Not the park.

Something wasn't right.

'Iz? Where are you? What's going on?'

'We've had a bit of a shake up,' Isabelle finally managed to say. 'We're OK. I think we're OK, but...'

'What happened? Where are you?'

'Um... I... I don't know. I...'

Sounds as Isabelle turned to talk to someone else nearby.

'We're in the Black Cat café, just across the road from the park. We... Some kids. Some local kids, probably just messing about but they put a lit firework in the basket of Lottie's bike.'

'They did what?! Is she OK? Are you?!'

'Yes. Yes, thank God she wasn't on it at the time. She was near the pond; you know how she is with looking for fish.'

Louise took a deep breath. They were OK. Thank goodness.

'But then...'

Louise closed her eyes. This couldn't be happening. It shouldn't be.

'Then?'

'Then one of the kids, doubled back and full on pushed Lottie into the pond! I was terrified and went straight in after her. By the time I'd got us both out, they were gone. I, I didn't get a good look at them, I was just trying to keep an eye on Lottie.'

What the actual...

'Are you sure you're both OK?'

'Yes. A very kind lady helped us over the road and the staff here have been wonderful. They've got towels and hot drinks and everything, but... I know it sounds ridiculous, but I'm scared to come home by myself. And Lottie won't go on her bike, I don't want to let her and I can't carry everything home by myself. Can you come and get us?'

'Of course, I'll be... about ten minutes. Faster if I can.' Louise said, turning off the oven, taking off her apron and heading to get her things together. 'You sure you're OK? No one is hurt? Lottie is safe?'

'Yes. Just shaken. Local twats messing about.'

'Sure. I'll be there as soon as I can. I'll bring some spare clothes and stuff. Sit tight.'

Louise ran upstairs to fling some things into a carryall and it was as she came downstairs that she saw it sitting on the doormat.

A firework. Unlit and with a little tag attached to it.

For Rachel.

Louise froze. What was going on? Was this all her fault? Asking too many questions? But Rachel? That job. This was all too much to process. She had thought she needed to get Isabelle and Lottie home and safe, but was now home no longer safe either. Was it all too late?

Louise's phone rang again. It was a number she did not recognise and she almost didn't answer in her panicked state.

'Hello? Who is this?'

'You know.'

At the sound of his voice, Louise's stomach lurched. It was unmistakable despite not having spoken to him in years. Carl. He sounded odd. Gruff. Like a darker version of himself.

'C—'

He cut her off. 'Go. Tell her nothing and go. Else you will regret it. You know I mean it, today shows that.'

'Today? That was you?! You put Lottie in danger? Your own daughter?! What are you playing at?'

'I ain't playing. I said to go. Now, go. Things have changed. People are talking. Too risky. Go. Before I have to make myself any clearer. Like I had to with Steve.'

Louise blanched.

'Look. Carl, just give me a little time, I need time to...'

The line went dead.

'Carl? Carl?!' Louise hissed, but he was gone. Louise pulled the screen down to look at it while her brain worked out the ramifications of the call.

Carl was dangerous and spiralling. She knew that for sure now. He had arranged the accident. He hadn't worried what could have happened. He would willingly put his own blood in harm's way to make his point. Who or what was he protecting if it wasn't his family?

Louise had always thought that the harm she posed to Carl was in her telling his family the truth about him. And she believed that her silence would counter that. That by staying silent on what she knew, she and Carl would keep Isabelle and Lottie cocooned in their innocence and everyone could just move on. That they could put their blip behind them and move on to something better. That she could start a new life with the people she cared about.

But now Louise realised for the first time that she did not really know Carl at all. What else was he caught up in? What bigger, more profitable but more dangerous job was he involved in? Either before prison or while he'd been away? Was that where all the money was still coming from? Did he think she knew more than she actually did? Who was he? A man who wanted to be right more than he wanted his child to be safe? A man who wanted the profits of his misdeeds more than he wanted his family?

Flashes of things Carl had said came to her, thick and fast as the realisation hit her.

I could replace you.

The one before, before I had to get rid of her...

Better you don't know. What you don't know can't hurt you. And we don't want you hurt now, do we, eh? Silent and safe, eh? That's what we want. Good girl.

The things that Louise now realised she had seen but refused to see. Carl had been her rescuer from the downward spiral she had been in. He had given her new purpose. He had told her it was the world's fault and set him and her up as rightful avengers of that fault. He had told her that she was making things right again.

All the things she knew. The threats against her, against others, him hitting her, him hitting Isabelle and more than once. The dent in the door. His lack of interest in or care for Lottie. The poor man who he beat to a pulp. Steve. The money, the unexplained money that just kept coming from somewhere. His agreement to let Louise isolate his wife in order to manipulate her into staying. These were not actions of kind man, of a remorseful man. But of a selfish, violent and unpleasant man.

Just how blind had she been? How hard did she have to not look to see the truth? How stupid was she? Suddenly, she saw him – an unpredictable and violent man who stopped at nothing to get his own way. She'd allowed her own desires to cloud her judgement and she'd allowed that for years. She swallowed hard to stop herself from being sick. Sick at her own stupidity, sick at her own selfishness.

She would not, she could not, leave Lottie and Isabelle to whatever fate Carl decided for them. All those niggling worries that she had pushed down and ignored, explained away and refused to listen to. She had gaslighted herself. She felt horrendous – her own behaviour had brought them here. If she had been brave enough to step away then he'd not have had anything to threaten them for.

No. No! If it hadn't been this, it would have been something else. The issue was not with her, the issue was with him. The issue was with the lies. All the lies. The lies had to stop.

It was time for the truth. Only the truth could keep them safe.

Even if it would mean the end for her.

31

The lights of the police station were bright and they made Louise's eyes hurt. Her head was pounding and she couldn't stop her hands from shaking no matter what she tried. She had told Isabelle she was just going for a walk after getting them safely home and Lottie tucked up in bed. She'd encouraged Isabelle to stay close to her and keep her phone on her at all times. Then Louise had walked to the nearest police station and asked to report a crime.

She'd been waiting in the reception area for a while now. Time she had spent working out exactly how she would explain why she was there and where she would start. Yes, the point was to corroborate Carl's guilt, in order that his parole hearing was cancelled and to get protection to Isabelle and Lottie and fast. That would buy everyone time. But she was also effectively handing herself in, admitting to handfuls of crimes; and she had no lawyer. She couldn't use her savings for one as they were both hidden and the proceeds of the crimes. She'd have to rely on a duty solicitor. She had no idea what was about to happen to her, but she knew she had to keep Carl away from Isabelle and Lottie and give them time to get as far away from him and his contacts as they could. Maybe they could go to her mum's? She'd moved again recently and Carl wouldn't know where to find her. She could get Isabelle to call her mum and tell her everything. Her mum would believe it. Her mum had seen the truth.

'Louise Warren?' a tired-looking police officer called, looking down at the clipboard and paperwork before looking up again and finding her the only one waiting. He tipped his head to the right, indicating she should follow.

'This way.'

They went into a small room with grey walls and a white plasterboard ceiling, strip lights flooding the room in an artificial yellow glow that made the police officer look as though he was going to be sick. She knew she looked the same except she actually did feel as though she was going to be sick. He left the door slightly ajar and sat down, beckoning her to do the same.

'So. You've something you want to report, is that right?' he said, clicking his pen and checking the sheet in front of him. He looked up at her, expectantly, but with a hint of impatience, like he had better things to do than listen to a hysterical-looking woman.

'I have. Yes. I want to...' She still didn't know where to start. 'I want to report a crime. Except it's one that has already been reported and there's been a trial and conviction.'

'So you want to add evidence to the case then, is that right? Do you know the case number?'

'No... no, I didn't think about that. I can give you the name of the man found guilty though?'

'If someone has already been found guilty then... I don't understand. Are you saying he is innocent? Do you want to report a miscarriage of justice as that's not really what we do here?'

Louise could see him mentally closing the file and moving onto the next thing to do on his list for the day.

'No. That's not it. No. He was found guilty but claims he is innocent. He's done years already. He is up for parole. I know he is guilty. Of that crime and of more. And of recently arranging an assault on his wife and child. That happened today. He called me. From prison, but not from prison. From a mobile. A burner phone, I assume. He's guilty. He's so guilty and he's dangerous and they're in danger and you have to help me. Please.'

'Wait, wait. OK, calm down,' he said, pulling his chair closer to the table, clearly paying more attention now. 'So how do you know all this? What proof are we looking at?'

'I have the call registered on my phone history.'

'Not from a withheld number?'

Louise thought about it. Maybe Carl was so convinced she'd never do anything like this he'd got sloppy, complacent. He'd underestimated her.

'No, I have the number. Can you trace it?'

'Possibly, yes. That could corroborate things.' He nodded.

'But the main reason I know all these things is...' Her heart was hammering inside her chest. She was convinced that the man could see it, could see what she was about to say, despite the still slightly bored and impatient expression on his face suggesting otherwise.

'Yes? Go on.' He indicated, waving his hand in a 'get on with it' gesture.

This was it. Now or never. Louise closed her eyes and pictured Isabelle and Lottie. It physically hurt her to realise that she would lose them. She would be separated from them and they would never forgive her. She faltered. Was this really the best thing to do? But then in her mind, bruises appeared on Isabelle's face, red marks on Lottie's arm and Louise swallowed. They had a right to know who Carl was, what he was capable of.

A right to have the chance to escape from him.

This was the right thing to do. She heard the police officer sigh. He probably thought she was wasting his time, keeping him from a stack of paperwork that never seemed to get any smaller, with accusations that would turn out to be false.

She flicked open her eyes and cleared her throat.

'I am also guilty,' she said. 'I was his accomplice. I committed the crimes too. I'm guilty too. I am here to hand myself in and to tell you all you need to know about Carl White.'

The police officer's mouth formed into a shocked 'oh' as he took in what he had thought was some wound-up silly girl, playing at cops and robbers, but who he could now see needed to be taken far more seriously.

'Right,' he said, 'stay here. I'm going to get a colleague.'

Louise noticed that this time he closed the door behind him as he went.

The next few hours passed in a blur. More police officers of increasing levels of seniority came and went. Louise repeated her testimony over and over for officers, for the tape record, outlining every detail that she could recall. Dates, locations, items taken, names of those she had helped steal from, where some of the things would be sold on, even if she didn't know where the money went from there. She was grateful that she didn't know exactly where Carl had stashed his share as she was aware that once that had been traced it would affect the money coming in for Lottie and Isabelle. As much as she'd like to return everything to its rightful owners, it had been things that had been taken and those would likely never be located. She didn't want to bankrupt Isabelle in the process of trying to get things right. She'd convinced Sandra to set up a savings account for Lottie and then she had paid some cash into it over the counter, hopefully making it untraceable back to her. Louise figured the elderly people she'd spoken with wouldn't mind that so much, helping a little girl start a life over without her dangerous father waiting in the wings.

Louise was tired, hungry and listless. The room she had been sat in for hours was airless and gave non-natural light so she had no idea what time of day it was by now. Isabelle would be out of her mind with worry. Louise felt awful. She loved Isabelle and Lottie more than her own family, more than herself, and here she was about to tear their life to shreds. For their own good, for their own safety, and yet Louise wasn't sure that they would thank her for it. She was 90 per cent sure that Isabelle was good, was honest and that she truly had no idea about the depths her husband went to. But there was a hint, a tiny part of her that worried that Isabelle was in on it all and had been stringing Louise along. After all, that was what she had been doing. Lies within lies within lies. If Louise had been able to lock that part of her life away from Isabelle, what's to say that Isabelle hadn't been doing the same? Both dancing around elements of truth they found too distasteful to share.

Too late now, she thought, as she looked up at the stern-faced woman who turned the tape recorder on, announcing her presence and the date.

'Louise Warren, I am charging you with the offence of burglary artifice, on the multiple dates as listed. You have admitted your involvement and guilt in these matters. You are eligible for legal representation should you not have a solicitor yourself. You do not have to say anything but it may harm your defence if you do not mention, when questioned, something that you later rely on in court. Do you have any questions? Would you like to call anyone?' the lady said, her face softening just a touch as she looked at her.

'I... I wondered if I might...' Louise paused, realising the ridiculousness of her request. 'I wanted to tell Isabelle face to face? Could I... Could you take me home and then bring me back? So I can explain?'

The woman was unable to hold back a laugh and the sound reverberated off the walls, mocking Louise as it surrounded her. She admonished herself and regained composure.

'Sorry, ahem, sorry,' she said, adjusting her suit so it sat just perfectly so. 'No, I'm afraid it doesn't work like that. The best we can do is inform her and ask if she would come to see you.'

Louise nodded. She had known that was the case really. She had considered telling Isabelle and then handing herself in, but had not because she knew the only way she could stick to her plan was to do this bit first. If Isabelle never spoke to her again, it would be better than Isabelle being in danger. No matter how much it hurt.

'Sure. I understand.'

The woman nodded back. Something in her had shifted. She was looking on Louise more kindly than she had done. Almost like Louise's atonement had already started. She was starting to pay for what she had done.

'I'll call her, explain the situation, see what she says. I'm not promising anything. The missus often knows more deep down than she's letting on. We need to talk with her anyway so we may bring her in for questioning.'

'Thanks. I appreciate it.'

'Any chats would be supervised though. So don't go getting any plans to cook up a scheme. We'll be listening.'

'No scheme. I just want to explain to her.'

'All right. I'll let you know. Now. We'll move you to a holding cell and get you something to eat. Hungry?'

Louise felt hollow, but she wasn't sure if that was hunger or the loss she was facing. She would be alone again. She'd done it before, but, somehow, this time it felt like she had lost herself in the process. She knew she needed to be strong to survive though, so she nodded.

'Thanks.'

She just hoped she wouldn't choke on it.

32

If there was one thing that Louise was thankful to her childhood for, it was the ability to shut herself down; to close in on herself and shut the world and all its painful shards out. She shut off her own senses. Sounds muffled until nothing coherent reached her brain. Her eyes lost focus so that all but her immediate surroundings were blurred. Tastes didn't reach her brain. She was cold, numb to the world.

Only her sense of smell remained untouched, and in her cell, Louise was assaulted by the stink of the cell toilet and the acidic bleach scent of cleaning. She was thankful the bleach cancelled out the stench of vomit or blood or whatever, which she had no doubt had decorated this room at some point. This was not a room of joy. No one who had spent time in here did so in celebration.

She had asked Isabelle to come. The senior officer had promised that she had offered Isabelle the chance to visit, chaperoned, when she had been brought in for questioning. Her legal aid solicitor confirmed as much. They both told her the same. Isabelle had said nothing, but shaken her head, her lips in a taut line. She had not said why or whether she would change her mind. She had simply refused.

The days had slipped away, one by one while she waited. She drew back into herself and waited, though once it became clear to Louise that Isabelle was not coming, she did not know what exactly she was waiting for. For it all to be over?

Her trial came around quickly, due to it being more of a tick box affair than anything else. She wore the clothes she had, no need to dress up smartly if all she was doing was confirming to a judge what she had already admitted to the police. It was to be open to the public and she hoped that none of those who she had wronged would be there. She was sorry for what she had done, but she didn't think that she had the strength to look at them and say that. Not yet. She had planned to write to them, but she realised that was more about her than them and so she had put the thought to one side.

'It's your time,' said her solicitor, who had been sat, silently scrolling through his phone while they waited, working on cases that were more interesting, more career-worthy than an open and shut admittance of guilt and sentencing. He gathered his papers, chuckled at something on his phone and packed everything away into his bag. He turned and looked at her.

'It's very straightforward, go in, answer the questions and submit your guilty plea. The judge may ask you if you want to say anything before they pass the sentence. I'd suggest either not say anything or keep it short. They want this open and shut in as short a time as possible. Be polite and hope for the best.' He nodded at her, not really seeing her, more just a guilty verdict that would do nothing for his chances of promotion.

'O—' She cleared her throat. It had been hours since she'd spoken more than yes or no and her voice had forgotten how to work. 'OK,' she croaked out. 'Actually, can I have a glass of water? I sound horrible.'

He rolled his eyes before stopping them by a water cooler in the hallway. The courthouse was not one of those gorgeous, classical old buildings you saw on TV, all creamy marble, sprawling staircases and beautifully decorated ceilings, meant to inspire and awe the criminal classes into acquiescence. This was a seventies nightmare of grey plasterboard walls and brown ridged carpets. It smelled like instant coffee and old trainers. Louise took a gulp from the lukewarm water that the water dispenser had dribbled into a paper cone. And another. She was suddenly nervous; terrified of what her future might hold and if she could hold on long enough through it. She didn't know if she could.

Because Louise had been on remand for her own safety, she had come from the prison to the court via police van and had mostly avoided the small crowd of journalists out front. At Carl's trial there had been swarms of them, calling out questions as people had gone into the court. The local rags had all wanted photos of the wife, the 'is she innocent or did she know wife', the photogenic wife – there to add colour to a grim and violent story and were disappointed not to see her there. Now, there was barely any interest in the case. It was old news. The people's outrage had moved on to some other topic, some other guilty person to scream at. But there was a court reporter there as she walked into the courtroom. They were the one taking notes. Louise looked around, to see if there was anyone she recognised, simultaneously wishing there was and hoping there was not. Then she saw her.

Isabelle.

Lottie was not with her and Louise was sad and grateful for that. She knew the little girl would be wondering where Louise had disappeared to, but if she had called out for her – 'Loooo' – in the court session, Louise knew she would not be able to hold it together. And she needed to because she needed this chance to make Isabelle understand.

Louise barely heard the proceedings. She could feel the sweat of the previous occupant of the dock on the shelf in front of her. Their fear leaking out of them. She wiped her own hands on the back of her waist, not wanting to add to it. The room was dusty, with high-up windows, criss-crossed with leading, letting in neither much light nor air. Even from this distance, Louise could see that the frames had been painted shut many layers ago. No wonder the air in the room was thick, it had been breathed in and out over and over, never really refreshing itself. It smelled fusty and you could see dust motes floating in the space, settling into nooks and crannies that would never get cleaned.

Other than these random details, the rest of the room that did not have Isabelle in it was unimportant and Louise couldn't see it. She did not hear the judge speak to her and the court guard had to tap her on her arm to bring her to her senses.

'Sorry, what?' she said, flustered by being brought so rapidly back into the room, into the bewildering situation. How the hell did she end up here?

'Can you confirm that you are Louise Warren, of 12 Robertson Avenue, London?'

'Yes. Yes, that's me.'

She was that person and yet she had never been that person. There were many people she had been and not been. Layers of self, layers of deception. No wonder it had been easy to slip into all her aliases, all her alter egos, living lives she'd never experienced, going places that Louise had only ever read about or seen on TV. There had been a joy in her work with Carl, in that she got to be whoever she wanted to be, without the restriction of who she really was or where she came from. She had been free despite being trapped.

'You have been charged with burglary artifice. How do you plead?'

Isabelle looked directly at her at this moment, but Louise

couldn't read her expression. Was it anger? Confusion? Or the worst, always the worst – disappointment. She had let her down. The one thing that she didn't want to do. She hung her head as she spoke.

'Guilty. I plead guilty.'

She scrunched her eyes up to stop the tears from coming. She had spent her life scrabbling to make sense of who she was, what she was capable of. She had been so lost, blindly following anyone who showed her any glimpse of hope. She had made so many mistakes. She had done some awful things. Her anger had overwhelmed her sense. This was the only thing she had ever done that was purely for someone else. She was doing this for them, to allow Isabelle to see the truth and get away, go somewhere safe. That she had to lose them for it was her punishment. One she deserved.

'I'm sorry,' she said quietly to the room.

'Pardon?' the judge said kindly, which surprised Louise. She had presumed that everyone thought her a vicious criminal. 'Was there anything you wanted to say before I pass sentence?'

Louise nodded. 'Yes. If that is OK?'

The judge nodded, raising her palm up, indicating the room. 'Go on.'

Louise took a deep breath. This was her chance, maybe her only chance to explain herself to Isabelle.

'Thank you.' She nodded at the judge before turning her attention to Isabelle, who had crossed her arms over her body. Her jaw was set in a hard line that Louise recognised. Stubborn.

'I want to say that I'm sorry. I'm sorry to everyone we hurt, everyone I hurt. I had convinced myself that no one was being harmed, but I can see now that I was fooling myself. I didn't mean to cause distress. There was certainly never meant to be any violence. That was never part of the plan. I didn't know C... my accomplice as I thought I did. I did not know his history of violence and how previous accomplices had disappeared as the police have now informed me. I did not know that he was dangerous. That he was a threat to everyone... even loved ones...'

'This is your trial, Ms Warren, please stick to talking about your own offences,' the judge reprimanded. 'And be quick about it.'

'Sorry, sorry, yes,' Louise said, looking to Isabelle to see if her message had got across. They had to get away from him, or he would come for them both. She knew it now.

'I am sorry that I lied about who I was. I did not like my past self. I did not want to be that person any more and I saw the chance not to be and I took it.'

The judge interrupted. 'Yes, we have heard your character assessment from your former teacher. About your difficult home life. That is no excuse, plenty have difficult starts and do not turn to crime.'

Isabelle started gathering her things. Louise was losing her before she lost her for good. She had to make her understand, and now. She was going to prison, the judge didn't seem particularly sympathetic, and why should she be? She took a chance and spoke directly.

'Isabelle. Listen, please. You made me the person I wanted to be, I want to be. You and Lottie showed me what it's like to be a family, to have a family. To care and be cared about. By the time I realised that, it was too complicated, too tangled. I should have told you, yes, but I was scared. I was scared of losing what I finally had.' She laughed ironically. 'Of course. Now I'm losing everything but this is worth it. You have to get away. You have to be safe. I am doing this to keep you safe, to give you time. Please listen to me, he's dangerous, please!'

'Enough now, that's enough,' the judge said, gathering her papers.

Isabelle wiped away a tear from her cheek, took one more look at Louise, and walked out of the room, the door banging behind her as she went, echoing around the mostly empty room.

'Ms Warren, you have pleaded guilty to the crime of burglary artifice. You have committed multiple offences, including one that resulted in significant physical harm being done to an elderly victim. You have stolen, cheated and lied. You did not come forward when the other offender was on trial, you withheld knowledge that could have given relief and comfort to your victims. These were not the actions of a remorseful woman,' the judge said, with ice in her voice.

Louise felt the world fall away around her. She would be going away for a long time. She knew it.

The judge's words hung heavy in the air.

'However.'

Louise blinked away tears, surprised by this unexpected 'however'.

'However,' the judge continued, 'you have come forward now, willingly, and have provided information that has resulted in a number of further convictions for your accomplice, and his parole being revoked, thus keeping a dangerous man in prison. There have also been other arrests made. This has all been taken into account when considering your sentence.'

The world slowed around Louise and she closed her eyes to hear the rest. It felt like a black bag was being draped over her head. The room went dark and it was hard to breathe. She knew that she deserved punishment – she had done some terrible things – and yet that didn't stop her being terrified of what was to come.

'In the light of your involvement in the crimes we have outlined, balanced with the good character references your counsel has provided to this court, along with your own remorse, albeit delayed, I sentence you to three years in custody, commuted to fourteen months, with time served on remand taken into account.' The judge turned to the guards. 'Take her down. Court adjourned for recess. Back at two thirty.' She got up and walked out of the courtroom.

The guards handcuffed Louise and led her back to the holding cell.

She looked around at the walls.

Fourteen months, minus the one she had already spent waiting for today. If Isabelle had really listened to what she had said, had read the letter she had sent, which had gone unanswered, and got away from here, away from Carl, then every single day would be worth it. She would give up every day twice over to keep them safe from him. They were what mattered now. She could crumble away in jail. She deserved no better.

She had done what needed to be done.

33

Louise's days had settled into a gentle rhythm once she had settled into prison life after the first few months. There was a structure to them that she could hang her time around. She guessed that was the point. Carl, Isabelle and Lottie were never far from her thoughts though. Had Isabelle believed her? Had she listened and got far, far away from him? Or had she refused to believe such things about her husband, even in the face of overwhelming evidence, and was still visiting him?

Louise had been assured that Carl would not know of her own whereabouts as it must have been clear to him who had suddenly revealed all of the information that had seen his parole revoked and his sentence extended. It was ironic really, how the threats he made because he feared she would grass on him, showed Louise who he really was and led her to inform on him and his network. Louise had been beyond fearful of what retribution he might try to wreak upon her or Isabelle and Lottie but had been reassured that the police had a system in place to protect them and her, though her own safety she worried less about. She did not know where they were, she was not allowed that information, but her solicitor said that Isabelle would be asked if she would receive communication from Louise, although she did not have to accept.

She had written letter after letter to Isabelle, begging her forgiveness, her understanding for why Louise had lied, why she had been drawn into her life in the first place and why she had waited so long to tell her the truth. She apologised for not talking to Isabelle first, for going straight to the authorities. For not being able to say goodbye. She wrote pages about how she loved them both like the family she never had. She wrote about all the goodness that they were and the light that they had brought to her. How they made her want to live a different life. How they made her want to live a life at all.

They went unanswered at first and then they were returned to sender, unopened. Eventually, Louise stopped. It was too painful to pour her soul into the letters, to tell Isabelle about the lack of care she had experienced growing up, surrounded by happy families that were not hers, then the lack of any safety net, the falling in with people who told her one thing whilst doing another, scarring her ability to judge others' characters, or even her own, and to have that met with silence. It was cruel. Maybe the love that she felt for what she had come to believe as her little family was one-sided. Maybe she was not loved. Maybe she had never been loved. Maybe she never would be. Perhaps that was truly her punishment. That and the continual fear that Carl would get to her, get to them somehow, and that everything she had done had been for nothing. That fear that she had missed her one opportunity to get away and to start again and that she had thrown it all away for someone who didn't really care about her.

She was working in the chapel, cleaning. Dusting, hoovering, polishing until the room gleamed and smelled like it was a piece of heaven. Clean. Renewed. It was the one place in the prison that had hope in its walls. In the rest of the prison the despair, the rage and the misery sank into the very fibre of the place. The shouts, the sobs and the crashes that were the soundtrack to most of the days here made the atmosphere heavy. Opening your eyes at first light and having the institutional smell of cleaning chemicals and metal hitting your brain before it is fully awake set the tone for the day. But not here. The chapel smelled like the flowers that the local florist donated weekly. Michelle, the chaplain, said that the florist had said 'nobody should be denied the joy of nature and the inspiration it provides' so she donated flowers to both prison and church alike. And she was right, today, the scent of what she had learned were freesias filled the room and lifted your heart as soon as it hit you.

'She said that she would consider it, doing some floristry training with you. She'd see if she had the time as it's busy running your own business,' Michelle said to Louise as she approached her, with a smile on her face that was always there. She didn't need flowers or the smell of furniture polish to bring her joy, she brought her own, within her, always. It shone from her every pore. To her, everyone in here was a soul in need of nurture, deserving of spiritual nourishment and Louise admired her more than she could put into words. She herself knew some of her fellow inmates and she did not necessarily believe that they were capable of rehabilitation.

'She did? That's ace. Will you thank her for me, even if she finds that she can't?' Louise responded. 'I think might like being a florist, and seeing the amazing displays she does for in here, I'd love to learn if she can be allowed in to teach me.'

'They might let you out to be taught at her shop. If you keep your nose clean and behave. Towards the end of your sentence. Day release. Temporary licence.' Michelle nodded at her.

'I'm going to need to be able to do something. I have no qualifications and it's not like I can ask for a reference from my previous job!' Louise said, initially thinking to be funny but the sadness of that hitting her. Being in prison was hard, but she had a feeling that being outside would be harder.

'There is a support system, don't worry, love. I can arrange all sorts if need be.'

Tears welled in Louise's eyes.

'What am I going to do? I have to leave London. I can't be there once I'm out.'

'Remember what I said, eh? One day at a time,' Michelle said, sitting down on the step before the altar and tapping the space next to her, indicating that Louise should join her.

Louise put down the yellow duster and can of polish on the altar, before worrying that it might be disrespectful to do so, and placed them on the old red carpet instead. She then sat down.

'Have you thought any more about what we talked about? Did you write to anyone else? To your parents perhaps?'

Louise shook her head.

'No. Isabelle didn't ever reply and it was too painful to keep going. Like banging my head on a brick wall. And my parents? What would I say? "I'm in jail and it's your fault for not loving me"? I worry that Carl and his gang will get to me somehow and I don't want anyone else dragged into this whole mess. I made my own choices, so did they. I can't blame anyone for it.'

Michelle tipped her head to the side, a kind and open expression on her face.

'Except you are, aren't you?'

'What do you mean?'

'You're blaming yourself. For all this.'

'Well, who else's fault is it?!' Louise raised her voice a little but the sound reverberated around the walls, built for the acoustics of hymn singing, making it feel like she was yelling, which she did not want to do. Not only because the weeks in here so far had taught her that someone was always listening, and often they wanted to use your weaknesses against you, but also she did not want to offend Michelle. She could see that Michelle genuinely forgave her and wanted to help.

'Well, the decisions you made, and your actions, yes. These are your fault. But you also did not reach where you are by yourself. You were helped, or rather not helped. You were neglected and abandoned, then manipulated. By people who also should have done better. The work of evil is rarely the work of one pair of hands alone. Influences – a lack of good ones, a ready stream of bad ones and here we are. There are very few prisoners that I have met in my many years here, who could not have avoided walking through those doors—' she gestured through the window, to where the double-shuttered main prison gates were, the imposing ceiling-high metal walls that opened to let the police cars drive in the new inmates '—had they only had a little more love, a little more support, a little more understanding from society as a whole. Not everyone gets the perfect family, every family has its own struggles and own crosses to bear. But there should be someone for everyone. A teacher, a friend, a chaplain—' she nudged Louise's side gently '—who sets someone back on the right path with encouragement and love. That's why I do the work here that I do. Because I want to be that person for those who have not yet found them. I believe in the goodness of people and I want others to see that goodness in themselves.'

Louise swallowed. She had found her person. Isabelle. And yet she had let her down and lied to her. She didn't deserve a second chance.

As though she could read Louise's mind, Michelle spoke again.

'Everyone deserves a second chance. Sometimes even a third or a fourth because people want to be good. We just have to let them. And forgive them. And sometimes, lovey, the person we need to forgive is ourselves.'

Louise laughed, a dry mocking laugh.

'What? You don't believe it?'

Louise sighed.

'It's not that I don't want to believe it. I don't think I can. There is so much bad in the world, and sadness and grief and rage. How can you get up each and every day and push against it? How can you not let it drown you, drown your joy? I don't know how you do it. Tell me, how do you do it?' Louise looked at Michelle, desperate to understand how she could be so positive when surrounded daily by so many examples of evil and wrong, people hurting people for their own gain.

'I'm not saying that it's easy. It's not. But it's a choice. You have to be the light yourself, you have to be the kindness, the gentleness, the care. Then you can see it in others, once you can see it in yourself.'

Louise nodded, though it was clear from her face that Michelle had yet to convince her. She got up and carried on with her work; she was due back in her cell soon and she wanted to finish her work here before she did so. It was her point of pride.

Michelle took her cue from Louise and got up too, gathering the papers she had carried with her when she came in, and headed for the door. At the threshold, the sounds of prison life echoing through the now open door, she turned to Louise.

'Just think of this. What would you say to yourself, if you were Lottie? How much kindness would you encourage her to give herself?' Michelle nodded, raising her eyebrows as she did so to emphasise her point. Then she went through the door, which thudded closed softly behind her. The only door in here, Louise noted, that didn't close with an intimidating clang.

What would I say to Lottie if she were me? Louise asked. *Forgive yourself. Forgive yourself, make amends, move on and be better.*

Lottie was innocent though. Louise was far from it.

Maybe she was beyond forgiveness.

34

Louise was lying on her bunk, staring at the cracks in the ceiling. The greying whitewash had breaks in its surface and she lay there, allowing her eyes to focus and defocus as she turned them into river deltas, tree branches, or blood vessels. Her mind both wandering and also thinking of nothing. It was less meditation and more zoning out, switching off from the relentless anxiety that she suffered from daily.

When she tried to imagine a future beyond this room, she couldn't do it. When she tried to imagine herself in a new life, new job, new friends, new home, she got nothing. Just the image of Isabelle turning and leaving the courtroom and the deafening silence from her since. Without Isabelle and Lottie in her life, Louise could see no way forward and the thought of leaving prison with nowhere to go nor anyone to go to was almost more than she could bear.

There was a gentle knock at the door which just about registered in Louise's consciousness. She pulled herself up to sit against the wall, tucking her knees against her chest, pulling her baggy sweatshirt over them, a poor attempt at hiding her dwindling frame. Food all tasted like cardboard to her. What was the point of eating?

'Louise? Are you awake?'

Michelle's kindly face peered around the door frame.

'Yes. Yes, come in.'

Michelle came in and sat herself down. She looked at Louise with concern but said nothing more. Like she was waiting for Louise to start a conversation, to see what Louise might want to talk about. Louise said nothing. Light chit-chat seemed pointless. Deep conversation was more than she had to give.

'Still having trouble sleeping?' Michelle finally asked.

Louise had dark bags under her eyes and her skin was sallow. Anyone who as much as looked at her could see that she was not well rested, her exhaustion was written all over her face. The irony being that Louise wanted to do nothing but sleep, its oblivion the only escape from the intrusive thoughts that plagued her.

'Yes.'

'Hmmm. Do you find it difficult to switch your mind off of a night-time?'

'Yes.'

'Do you catastrophise in your head?'

'Yes.'

Michelle nodded. It seemed that this was not uncommon.

'Well, I've got two bits of news and one bit of advice that might help. Firstly, Lorna, the florist, has agreed to give you some training. First, she said you can help her in the chapel, when she comes to arrange the flowers, help to choose what she brings in and then help her put them together here. Then, she said you could help her at the church when you're allowed out and then she said she'll see about maybe some shifts at her shop when you're out for good. She can't take anyone on full time as it's not a big enough shop for more staff but she'll try to get you started off.'

Michelle smiled, expecting, hoping for a positive reaction from Louise now that there was something to look forward to.

Louise struggled to raise a smile. She had loved the idea when it had first been mentioned but now it all seemed like it would take energy she did not have. Like it was a waste of everyone's time. She'd fail at it just like she'd failed at everything else.

'Thank you,' she whispered out of politeness.

'You're welcome. Now. The other thing. I know that you're struggling. I know you've lost sight of the point of everything... no, don't try to argue because I've seen it a million times before and I know what I'm looking at. You need a project, a point, a goal and I've found just the thing for you.'

'I'm fine, really, I...'

'No. You need something to strive for. Now, I did a little digging and it turns out your family history is really rather interesting.'

Louise wrinkled her face.

'My what is what? I don't really have a family. I'm an only child. No relatives. Nothing. Just me.'

'Now I don't think that's quite true.'

'Carl was my family. Then Isabelle and Lottie and now? Back to no one. I'm alone.'

Michelle shook her head.

'See, I love history and do you know why? It's because when you look at it, everyone is connected to everyone else. We're one big family. Religion tells us that if we go far enough back then we're all the same family and genealogy is similar. You look a little further back than immediate relatives, and suddenly, we're all part of a bigger family. Shared grandparents, great-grandparents, go back some more and our relatives include gentry, nobility, royalty. Or famous people. Or infamous people. It's all about lives lived, mistakes taken and amends made. We're all part of it. Every one of us. History teaches us lessons about compassion, rehabilitation and family. And that's what you need. You need connection and forgiveness. For yourself, from yourself.'

Michelle handed Louise a book, a folder and a notepad.

'There. I've got you started on a family tree. Your grandpa sounds like he was an interesting man. Lots of stuff on him!'

Louise sat up straighter. 'Really?'

'Yes.' Michelle nodded. 'Turns out he was part of a music group who used to meet up and listen to records and share stories. And one of the group members has a website that has some of the stories uploaded. There's lots out there to find if you look. And you have IT privileges and lots of time. Make use of it. Diane, another inmate, has been doing it for ages and knows lots of tips if you'd like?'

The idea that she could get back in touch with her grandpa and his life, from this tiny room or the library was one that appealed. She missed him. She missed belonging to him. Even though he was gone, maybe she could feel like she belonged to him still. Through his stories, which would be part of her story. She'd lost him, lost Isabelle, but maybe there was a way back somehow.

Louise smiled. 'Thanks. I appreciate it.'

'You're more than welcome. A smile is what I like to see. I'll talk with Lorna and see when she would like you to help out and shall I get Diane to pop into see you? She's a bit of a rough diamond but she's one of eleven children and her family tree is absolutely fascinating. A real dynasty!'

Louise nodded, 'And the advice?'

'Right. Well, I know you wrote to Isabelle and heard nothing back. But time has passed and sometimes people feel differently once they've had time to process things, to let things settle. People are also stubborn and might not want to make the first move. You did the wrong thing by lying to her, yes. But you also risked everything for her and Lottie. You're making amends. I have checked and she hasn't visited Carl since you turned yourself in. She is living somewhere new, though contactable through the right channels. Now, if you want to write to her again, I'd be happy to write a reference for you, outlining your rehabilitation. It doesn't always make a difference, but, on occasion, it does. Time is a great healer after all.'

'You think it's worth it?' Louise didn't know if she could take it if she still heard nothing back.

'You gave up your freedom for them. Doesn't that answer your own question?'

'Yes. I suppose it does.'

'Well then,' Michelle said, standing up to leave.

'Thank you,' Louise said, cradling the paperwork in her arms.

'Be kind to yourself, lovey,' Michelle said as she left.

Louise opened the folder to find a printed article, with a grainy photo looking out at her. There he was, front and centre, smiling out at her. Her grandpa. The only one who had loved her for her, always.

She had been loved. She could be loved.

She had been happy at times before, maybe she could be happy again. That thought lit a light inside her that Louise thought would never shine again. Belief in the possible.

A glimmer of a future.

Hope.

35

In the months that she had been inside, Louise had grown accustomed to almost constant noise. People – fellow prisoners, guards – all living and breathing and eating and shouting and laughing and walking around opening and closing doors, banging on staircases. The background noise was almost orchestral, with its deep booms and high-pitched squeaks, with rhythmic sentences that set out the day. But now? It was barely morning and the prison was quiet. Sleeping.

Louise had woken at the first shard of sunlight coming through the small window of her cell. She arched her back to let it fall across her face. Dawn on the day of her release. She wanted to feel it, see it, let it welcome her back into the outside world. She was jittery. Her stomach was in knots. Here, inside, she had boundaries, she knew what her day would hold and who would be in it. Outside? She had nothing. She knew that she should be feeling excited to be free, to have paid her debt to society, to be able to start again and yet... she was not. She was still terrified.

In less than twelve hours she would be free. But for what? To go where? To be with who? She had no home to return to, no family or friends who would put her up while she got back on her feet. The usual hostels would be too dangerous in case a contact of Carl's saw her there and let him know. She still had no idea where she would go.

All that freedom. Too much freedom. The prison counsellor had talked with her about maybe going back to college but the idea of being surrounded by so many people, all with aspirations and dreams and with clean slates all waiting for their opportunities to come to them, was too much. The idea of working in the florist's was the same. What Louise wanted was to crawl under a rock and stay there. Wait. For what? For it to be over? She had seriously considered doing something deliberately stupid, something disruptive in the last week, in order to have her release cancelled. But the idea that, somehow, this information would get back to Isabelle made it too shameful. Louise did not want Isabelle to think any less of her than she knew she already did.

Isabelle had not replied to a single letter that Louise had sent, not even the one that Michelle sent for her. She had refused every visiting request and not accepted a single phone call that Louise had tried to make to her before her phone number changed. Louise didn't know if she was angry, upset, or if she actually never cared at all and had just seen Louise as a temporary pair of hands to help out until Carl got home. Maybe Louise had made another terrible judgement call on her. She searched her soul but couldn't quite make that last one fit with the person she believed she knew. Isabelle was good. Louise literally bet her life on it.

She got up and made a cup of tea as quietly as possible. Now that she was more awake, Louise could hear the sounds of other people starting their day and yet as she boiled the kettle, the sound of the water bubbling and the noise of the teaspoon clinking against the cup still felt like the loudest sounds in the world, as if all her senses were on hyper mode. She sat back down on her bed and, somehow, watching the tendrils of steam rise and play in the air before disappearing into the ether, made Louise feel calmer. She held her hands around the warmth of the cup, keeping them there until the transferred heat was too much and she had to use the handle instead. It reminded her that she could feel. And if she could feel something then there had to be a way forward, even if she didn't know what it was. She wiggled her toes in order to feel them scratch against the sheets and blanket that she had slept her last night in. She placed one hand against the cool brick of the wall the bed was pushed against, knowing that she would never place her hand in that exact spot again. These small things, insignificant moments, reminded her that she was alive.

Then there was the sound of the key in the lock and a knock on the door as it swung open.

Michelle popped her head around the door. 'Morning. How are you?'

'Good. I'm good,' Louise said, standing up and playing down her rampant nerves. 'You?'

'Fine, thank you. Big day. I wondered if you might like a little company this morning?'

Louise didn't think she was quite ready for the full-on optimism of Michelle, despite appreciating all that she had done for her and had promised to continue to do. Luckily, as she nodded politely, Michelle widened the door to reveal Diane standing beside her.

'Diane's experienced release day before so I thought she might be of help this morning. Though obviously, she's back, which, as much as we love her, we're trying to avoid. But still.'

'Morning!' Diane drawled as she sloped in. Michelle nodded, and left them to it.

Diane had been great with the family research that Louise had done, which had made her feel part of something bigger than just her own bubble of one. It really had helped her feel like one part in a chain, and one that she owed her ancestors not to give up on. She'd found out about their lives, the troubles and struggles that they'd made it through to get to where she was. She owed them something. She owed herself.

'Nervous then?' Diane said as she took the chair and the cup of tea, leaving Louise to sit back down on her rumpled bedclothes. 'The outside world awaits, eh?'

'Yeah. I guess it does.'

'Don't sound too happy about it. I'd kill to get out of here.' A low throaty laugh followed. 'Not that I should say that in 'ere, should I? They might think I mean literally. Which I don't!' Diane said, as though the walls themselves were listening. 'Someone's always listening in here.'

'I know I should be. I am in a way.'

'Not gonna miss me then?' More cackles.

'No, I will. It's just...'

'The outside world a bit big, eh?' Diane said, her voice more kind than it had been before. Perhaps the tea was kicking in and she was less annoyed at being awake so early on a day that held very little significance for herself. Maybe she recognised the feelings.

'Yes. Exactly. When I step outside, I don't know where I'm going to go. Or what I'm going to do. I don't know for sure where I am gonna sleep tonight. My probation officer has got me a place in a hostel but I'm not convinced that I'll be safe there. I can't go back to Isabelle's house. I can't go back to my parents. I can't stay anywhere where Carl's lot might find me. I know that at least. I have to disappear. But to where?'

'Want my advice?'

Louise paused. She wasn't sure she wanted advice from someone who was in and out of here on a regular basis. She liked Diane but she clearly had no desire to change her life. Spells in the nick were just part of it and she seemed fine with it. Louise never wanted to be inside ever again. But in the absence of any other guidance, she figured she might as well listen to what Diane had to say.

'Sure. Thanks.'

'This is how I see it, right? You got three options.'

'I have options? Really?' Louise scoffed.

Diane sniffed. 'I don't have to tell you, if you don't want to know...' she said, put out.

'Sorry. Sarcasm is my defence, go on.'

'You have been listening to your counsellor. "Your defence", heh!' She hacked noisily, her morning cough loud and phlegmy. 'You got three options. One, you go back home. To your family, your parents. You give them and yourself the chance to start over. Fix things. Go back to college, you're not that old. Make the roots you didn't have, yeah? That's one. Two? You find Isabelle, you make her see your point of view and you keep going like before. Right?'

'But I can't do either of those. I don't want to go back. Not backwards. My parents didn't want me before, they're not going to want me now, older and with nothing to show for the years away but a criminal record. And even if they did, I don't want anything from them. Not now. And Isabelle? She's not replied. Ever. I don't know where she is. She doesn't want anything to do with me. Besides that, Carl might find me at my parents or I might lead him to Isabelle. And I know he wants me dead. If he'd nudge Isabelle and Lottie as a warning, I can only think he'd kill me. He had Steve killed, I know it. Literally. I can't.'

'So?'

'So what's the third option? It had better be good!' Louise laughed, despite the hollow feeling in her stomach. Fear? Despair?

'So, option three. You do whatever the hell you've always wanted to!' Diane said with a flourish.

'What?' Louise asked, confused. 'What do you mean?'

'You can literally go anywhere and *do* anything, can't ya? So long as you check in with your probation officer. Sure, you don't have a... whaddoya call it? A trust fund? Or wealthy parents to chuck money at you but you've um...' Diane stood up to face Louise, looking around the room as though checking for something or someone '... you've a little something tucked away, haven't you?' She tipped her head expectantly, as though it was clear that everyone in here who'd made money from their misdemeanours had been smart enough to hide some of it.

Diane was right. Louise closed her eyes and then nodded, barely perceptively, and Diane nodded back at her and sat back down. 'Right then, so. What do you want to do?'

'I don't know.'

'Yeah, you do. Everyone does. Me? If I had no ties, a little stash and all the time in the world? I'd go to Mexico, open a little beach bar and sell margaritas out of coconut shells. That's what I'd do. If I didn't have my family to go back to. So what about you?'

Louise thought and then an image came into her mind. It was Christmas morning and she and Isabelle, with a faint echo perhaps of future partners hovering, unfocused and smudgy, at the edge, were watching an excited Lottie tear open carefully chosen presents. She winced at her own cliché. It looked like an advert for a supermarket – a blended family brought together by modern circumstances and enjoying each other's company. She couldn't tell Diane this. She couldn't tell anyone this.

She opened her mouth to describe some desert island with palm trees and lush turquoise seas. Then she stalled. This was just as much a cliché, only this wasn't true. What was paradise with no one to share it with?

'I want to be loved.'

'Oosh, that's a hard one to pin down. I can't tell you where to go for that. But I can tell you that you won't find it festering away somewhere. Where have you always wanted to go? The world's a big old place. You could either wait till you're not on licence, or persuade 'em it's the best way to avoid Carl. What have you always wanted to do? Before grown-ups and jobs and rent got in the way. They don't half 'ave a way of stomping on ya dreams. But dreams are all we have, aren't they?'

'What's your dream? What about you?'

'Told you, di'n't I? Beach cabana. Maybe that's what I'll do when I get out next time.' She laughed in a way that suggested she knew that she wouldn't. Her life was set. 'But we're talking about you. You're the one stepping out into the big bad world today, after all.' She got up and started making another cup of tea, the sounds of the prison waking up all around them now. 'Another?' She raised the cup at Louise, who shook her head in reply.

'See, the way I see it is this. You're like a newborn baby. Fresh, clean, world at your feet. You get to go wherever, do whatever.'

'Babies are born into families who look after them. Babies belong to someone.'

'Ach, belonging to someone can just as well be seen as being tied down. Belong to yourself and the rest'll sort itself out. Too many in here care what people think of them and it makes you make bad choices. Choices that don't sit right with you. I know. I can tell who's gonna come back and who this is gonna turn around. I know.'

'Well, what do you think about me?'

'I know that I'm never gonna clap eyes on you again. You're done with this.' She nodded, self-satisfied and sat back down with her next cup of tea.

'Italy. I've always wanted to go to Italy. Maybe I could sell flowers in Italy...'

'There you go! Italy is the perfect place to be loved, i'n't it? All that romance swilling about. Brilliant. Do that. Just don't fall for any Mafia blokes, OK? You're done with this life, right? Don't make me wrong!'

'I'll try,' Louise said, smiling. If Diane believed in her, then maybe she could. Maybe she would haul herself off to Italy as soon as she could. She didn't speak the language but if she went somewhere touristy she'd be OK and she could pick it up. She could find a cheap hotel or somewhere to rent at first. It's not like she wasn't used to basic. Even cheap hotels didn't tend to have a toilet right there next to the bed. Maybe she could make a whole new life, be a whole new person. Maybe the mistake she made last time was not getting far enough away. How often had she berated herself for moving into Carl's street? What a stupid move that was. But then, she'd not have met Isabelle. Not have seen Lottie born. Not got to hold her while she slept on her chest. Louise felt her insides tear apart as the pain of losing them hit her all over again. Could she forget about them in Italy? Would she ever? Those years were the absolute best of her life. She didn't regret them. She couldn't.

'Time to pack up, love!' Diane said, as she handed her the daily uniform of jogging bottoms and a T-shirt.

Louise did as she was told and slowly she put her small number of things – her notebook, her book, pens, into a small bag. She then waited for Michelle to come back and for the first day of the rest of her life to begin.

Her nerves built as she sat on alongside Diane on her bunk. Her knees started to bounce up and down of their own accord until Diane silently placed her hands on them and pushed them down to the floor to stop them jumping.

'Italy. Just remember Italy, yeah?'

'Italy,' Louise whispered, trying to swallow but finding her throat too dry to do so.

The keys jangled outside then the handle turned as the door

opened for Louise for the last time. Light flooded into the room as the guard stood in the opened doorway, silhouetted against it.

'Today's the day, eh?' the guard said.

'I guess so,' Louise replied.

But what the day was for, what it would bring, she couldn't guess.

36

The holding room was dark and dingy and Louise's bottom had gone numb from sitting on the metal bench for so long. She sat, upper body forward, as though she was feeling sick. In fact, she was struck by how she felt... nothing. The only indicator that this was not a normal, uninteresting, unremarkable day was the fact that despite the room being cold, with a dank feeling clinging to its dark grey walls, barely illuminated by the harsh strip lighting on the ceiling, when she moved her hands from beside her on the bench, her sweaty palm prints remained. There was the briefest moment when her hand was outlined, and then, it evaporated into thin air.

Louise felt she herself had evaporated. Despite her final farewells to Diane and Michelle, both providing pep talks of the wonderful new and fulfilling life they believed Louise was stepping into, Louise felt numb.

Alone in the room now, the rest of the prisoners moved on to other prisons or out to court. Only those being released were left and she was the only one getting out today. Louise knew that the cameras were on her but she also knew that she had a reputation of being a goody-two-shoes and they'd barely bother to look in on her.

'What am I gonna do now, Grandpa, eh?' Louise whispered to herself. 'I can't go to Rome and sell flowers. This isn't some fifties Hollywood film! That doesn't happen for people like me? I know it, Diane knows it, no matter how much she likes the idea. You'd have liked her, you know. Apart from the drug dealing, don't think you'd have approved of that bit.'

Louise chewed her lip.

'I'm lost. I've been lost for so long. What do I do? Where am I gonna go? I'm so scared,' she whimpered to the floor.

She waited for some celestial advice to rain down on her, suddenly looking up in expectation.

It did not come.

There was just silence, with the muffled clatter of life going on inside the prison, several closed doors away. Her old life, fading into the background already. Her new life, whatever it was, awaiting her through more closed doors in the opposite direction.

She rocked gently back and forth as silent tears rolled down her face. She felt something now. Fear. She felt like she was being dropped into the ocean with no life jacket and with rocks in her shoes. No rudder, no lifeboat, just being told to swim. She knew the only thing she would do, the only thing she could do, was to sink. She had thought that she had reached the bottom when she was in here. Only now had she realised that there was further down she could go.

There was a small hole in the cuff of her jacket and she poked her index finger through it, twisting until the material tightened, starting to cut off the blood supply to her fingertip. She watched it drain of blood and go pale, before releasing it and watching the blood rush back, flushing the skin pink again. She did this over and over and over. By making her movements small, by proving to herself that she existed, that her actions had consequences and that she had choice, Louise kept the rising panic from overwhelming her. A small part of her brain wanted to stay inside. If she showed enough distress, would they keep her? But she knew that this moment would be the same if it happened now, or if it happened in another year. She had to face the outside world. She had to accept that it offered her nothing, but that could be OK. She had to realise that she had messed up every life she had tried to live, but she had to not mess it up again.

Suddenly, there was the familiar rattle of a door being unlocked and the warden walked through into the room.

'Ready?'

'As I'll ever be.' Louise laughed, trying to find some levity.

'Let's go. And I don't want to see you back in here, do you understand?' the warden smiled at her.

Louise nodded.

'Right then.' The warden led Louise through the corridors that she vaguely remembered from when she arrived. She had been in such a state of panic and distress then that it was difficult to pin down any memory at all.

They reached the final door. A mundane looking door. More like one you'd find at a garden centre, or at the back of a library. with that toughened glass with the threads running through it so that the light fractures into tiny diamonds as it shines through it. Louise thought the doormat on the inside was an odd touch. At least it didn't say 'Welcome'. Maybe there ought to be one outdoors.

'Good luck!' the warden said as she watched Louise step through into the car park.

The air outside tasted different somehow, despite it being the same air that drifted over the walls and into the exercise area. Maybe air tasted sweeter when you could follow it wherever you wanted. Louise found herself wondering if the air in Italy tasted sweeter. This air had a definite tang of dual carriageway about it.

'Right,' Louise said, to no one. She was stuck to the ground. Where was she going to go?

She ran through her options, glancing warily about her in case some contact of Carl's was already aware of her release date. She was miles from Wandsworth – practically the whole country away. He'd not have contacts this far north, would he?

'Back to my parents,' she said out loud, trying it out on her tongue. The most practical option. Her 'home' as it was supposed to be. But it would be too depressing. Too humiliating. As much as this was the most sensible plan, she could not bring herself to do it.

'To Isabelle then,' she tried next. The emotional option. The place Louise's heart most wanted to be. But she did not know where she should start to look or even if she would be allowed to.

'Somewhere else. But where?'

All of the options, none of them good.

Louise ran them through her mind once more, rejecting each one in turn a second time before picking up her small bag of stuff and walking aimlessly out of the front courtyard and onto the street, no idea where she was heading or where she planned to sleep that night.

She had barely got a few metres down the road when she became aware of a van accelerating down the street before screeching to a halt just outside the prison. The driver got out, stood on the door footplate, peering over towards the prison building. They then sat back down and honked the horn once. Then, after a period, sounded the horn again, several short blasts.

Louise stopped, turned and walked back. She didn't know who they were waiting for but she could at least tell them that she was the only person being released today so perhaps they had got the day wrong. Start her new life with a good deed done before she'd even been out ten minutes. It was only as she approached the van that her pulse quickened. Had Carl sent someone already? Surely he'd not do something right outside the prison gate?

Her feet suddenly felt as though they were cased in lead as she took one step and then another closer to the van. Her breathing turned ragged and her head felt as though it was lifting from her shoulders when she saw who it was and she would have sworn that in that moment, her heart stopped.

It was Isabelle.

Louise's heart leaped and then immediately sank again. *Why was she here? Why, when she'd refused all of my attempts to contact her, to explain? Why now?* Louise stopped and doubled over when she realised. *Maybe she is who Carl has sent. Maybe I locked myself up, got myself a criminal record and for nothing. For worse than nothing.*

From where she stood, hunched over, defeated, staring at the tarmacked road and the pocked white lines in its centre Louise heard the van door open again and someone get out. She willed herself to stand up, to face her, but she couldn't. Shame and fear and soul exhaustion kept her welded to the spot, in the middle of the road, where, if any oncoming traffic approached, she would be in danger of being hit. She didn't care. She couldn't find any single ounce of effort to care.

'Lou!' Isabelle called. 'You OK?' She sounded genuinely concerned. Still looking at her feet, Louise tried to find any trace of menace in the Isabelle's tone, any small thing to suggest that she should turn and walk away. She didn't want to. Every fibre of her being wanted to go towards her, run towards her and pour out her apology, her explanation, again and again. Something held her back. She'd practised the skill of self-preservation in jail. When to shut up. Silence was often the safest course of action and she decided to use it here. She'd say nothing, and see what Isabelle had to say instead.

Louise stood up. She pulled in a lungful of air, and slowly

walked towards the van and Isabelle, and as she got closer, she could see Lottie too, sleeping peacefully despite the unfolding drama, in her seat in the back. Her breath caught in her throat. If Isabelle was going to tear into her, if she had been sent all the way here by Carl for some awful reason, she wouldn't have brought Lottie with her surely? Was it... could it be that she genuinely wanted to see her? Hope flared in her heart before the cynic in her pushed it down again. Let's just see, she told herself.

'Hi,' Isabelle said, almost shyly as Louise approached. She started to smile but then stopped, as if she had to remind herself to be angry.

'Hey,' Louise replied, trying to keep the joy at seeing them both under control. She could not let joy, or love or hope take over. She could not survive having them snatched away again. That would end her.

Isabelle stood in front of her, not saying anything. She didn't look angry. But she didn't look happy either. Before they had been fine not to fill all the time with talk. Words were not always needed. But now? Now there was so much to say. Louise didn't want to bombard her, to push her away if there was any chance that she was here as a friend. Eventually, she cracked and spoke first.

'It's so good to see you. But. Why are you here? Miles from anywhere, miles from home?' Louise said, having to literally stand one foot on top of the other to stop herself from going to her.

'Honestly?' Isabelle said, her face hardening in a way that made Louise's heart sink. 'I'm not really sure.' She looked at her feet and then back to the van to check on Lottie, still sleeping, blissfully unaware of the tense conversation unfolding metres away.

'You didn't visit. Or reply to my letters. I thought... I assumed...'

'Assumed what?' Isabelle crossed her arms in front of her, eyebrows raised.

'That you...' Louise needed to choose her words carefully.

Isabelle seemed poised for a fight and Louise didn't want that. She didn't have the strength left for that and she still didn't know where the hell she was going to go from where she was stood. Italy, she told herself, think of Italy.

'That I what?'

'That you didn't want to see me again. That you hated me for what I had done. For the lies. For my not being honest with you from the start. Or that...' Louise looked up to Isabelle's face for some guidance, any clue as to how this was coming across, but her face was a blank. Had Louise not really known her at all? *Fuck it*, she thought, *what's the worst that can happen?* As she decided to just let it all out. 'Or that you knew already. That you knew about Carl, what he had done, what he was in prison for and all your naivety about it all, your surprise and your belief in his innocence was all a sham.' She spat the last word out, surprised at her own anger, for being abandoned the way that she was. She didn't care if she upset her now, she deserved it. At least a little.

'You what?! You thought I knew and I was OK with it all? That I was just playing along?! What the hell do you take me for?!' Isabelle had gone red with fury, her hands clenching at her sides.

'You didn't reply! I sent you letter after letter. Sent visiting request after visiting request. I called, you never accepted it. What was I supposed to think?'

'Um, that I was angry?! You lied to me, Louise. You lied to me about who you were, what you had done, where you were from. You came into my life at my lowest point. My life was falling apart, and suddenly, there you were, like some heaven-sent angel, to help me pick it all up again. I was lonely and scared. And you were there. Perhaps I was being naive but about you as well as Carl. I knew almost nothing about you and I let you into my life, into Lottie's, with barely a question! And you took advantage of that! Mum was worried but what could she do?'

'How is she? Your mum?' Louise felt awful about her role in keeping them apart. She should never have done that. Never have done any of it.

The question threw Isabelle off course. She screwed her face up and shook her head.

'She's fine now. We talked. We're good. Thanks. She's good.'

'I'm glad.'

'That's not the point. Yes, I was angry. I didn't know who you were. Who you are! And I felt stupid, if you must know. I felt like a raging idiot. I fell for all of Carl's shit and then I fell for yours.' She breathed in, raggedly, and she bit her lip, trying to keep the tears away. She nodded. 'I'm an idiot. And here. So I really must be!' Her face screwed up and she started to cry. She moved away, as though she was going to leave.

'Wait!' Louise shouted, suddenly petrified that this was her final chance at something, at being happy, at being her real self. 'You're not stupid. Not at all. You're kind, and open and trusting. You're all the good that I am not. Was not. You and how you are, how Lottie is, made me want to be a better person. You made me a better person.'

Isabelle stopped, turned back. Her expression was mellowing, Louise knew that this was going to be her only chance.

'Did you read my letters? Any of them?' Louise asked gently, looking up from underneath her eyelashes, trying not to come across as aggressive or accusing.

Isabelle shook her head.

'No. I was too angry. I ripped them up.' She pursed her lips and then added, 'Sorry.'

Louise nodded. 'I understand, I thought you would be. You deserve to be. I lied. I'm sorry.'

'I'm still angry if I'm honest. You took advantage of me, of us both. You lied every day you were in my house. And you got my husband sent to prison for longer. Though, clearly, it seems, he deserves it.'

Louise's stomach dropped. Carl.

'Have you... been in touch with him?'

'Carl? No. No, I won't see him either. Now I really am an idiot where he's concerned.' Her face turned stony; the colour drained away from her face. 'I don't think he ever didn't lie to me. Not since the day we met. I married a man who made his money from screwing over other people and I really believed he dealt in house sales and antiques!' she laughed bitterly. 'The worst thing is that I was young, we both were when we met, and don't think I ever grew up. I went from my parents looking after me to Carl looking after me and I didn't ever ask any questions. I should have asked questions! He lied about everything.'

'I do think he loves you, in his own way, if that's any help?' Louise proffered, unable to take seeing Isabelle so upset.

'Really?! He deliberately sent someone to terrorise me to make a point! He could have maimed Lottie – his own daughter.' She sneered. 'That's not love.'

'No. But I think it was his own version of it. He sent them to make a point to me in order to keep you. He wanted to keep you and Lottie, he wanted me to step aside to make sure that happened. To stop me from telling you the truth about him.' Louise's voice cracked as she said this. It was true but it was still awful.

'Didn't work, did it?' Isabelle laughed.

'No. No, it showed me just how blind I had been. I thought that if I kept quiet for his sake, for my sake, then we could all move on together and forget it had ever happened. I thought he loved you, I loved you, we could be a weird little family together. But...'

Louise took the opportunity to step a little close to Isabelle. She wanted to look her straight in the eyes to show her the truth in her words. She knew that she had to make Isabelle trust her again.

Whatever happened from now, whatever life Louise was going to have, she could only do it if she knew that Isabelle understood why she had done what she did, and how important she and Lottie were to her.

'But then he hurt Lottie. And then I admitted to myself that he was dangerous. Cruel and violent. I couldn't let you go on not knowing the truth and I realised I'd been holding on to a false hope, a tiny thread that somehow I could make things all right and keep what I'd always wanted.'

'And what was that?' Isabelle uncrossed her arms.

Was she really going to unburden her soul on the road beside a grey tarmacked car park, outside a dour prison building, her only possessions by her side in a holdall? It seemed she was.

Louise opened her mouth to speak but only a squeak came out. She took a deep breath, sniffed back the tears that were forming and tried again. 'To belong to someone. To be part of a family. To have someone who cared if I was there or not.' She sniffed again but the tears came all the same.

Isabelle looked at her with pity, but a kind pity, a sympathetic one.

'You never really mentioned your family. I... I should have asked more.'

'I didn't have one. As you know, I had a mum and a dad who didn't want me and a grandad who died. I left as soon as I could and as far as I know they have never tried to find me. I know my case was in the papers. They don't live far away. Someone they know or they would have seen it. They could have contacted me. They didn't. I don't have a family. I have no one.'

Louise's throat closed up, she couldn't swallow the lump that was sitting there, making it hard to breathe. Her last sentence was part statement, part question. Did she really have nobody?

Isabelle was silent.

Louise was tired now. Too many emotions were coursing through her and she was exhausted.

'Isabelle, why are you here? What do you want?' It came out colder than Louise had planned.

'I wanted you to tell me this to my face. To work out if I could trust it. Trust you and your words.'

'You can,' Louise urged. 'That's why I gave myself up to the police. To keep Carl in prison, to keep you safe. To keep Lottie safe. And me? I needed to do my time, to make amends, to finally put all that behind me. I couldn't keep lying to you. You know that you can trust me because I have admitted what I did wrong, I have paid for it. I gave up my freedom to keep you safe. To let you get away from him. I gave you time by losing my own. Can't you see that? I did this —' she threw her arms back towards the prison walls, '—for you. To show you that I'm sorry and to tell you the truth. All of it.'

Isabelle looked cautious. She sighed.

'All of this made me question my judgement. How could it not?! I had no idea who to believe, what to think. It's why I stayed away. From you and Carl.' She cleared her throat before pausing. 'I finally had to rely on just myself. You wanted to belong? Well, I wanted to stand on my own two feet. I wanted to be my own person. And you know what? It's going really well. Lottie and I are doing really well.'

Louise smiled though her heart had just cracked. They didn't need her. They didn't want her. She was just here to rub salt into her wounds. She swallowed the pain, clear in her eyes for anyone who cared to look.

'That's great,' she whispered. 'I'm pleased. I'm really proud of you.' Louise paused, letting her thoughts settle before her face darkened and she turned back to Isabelle. 'What about Carl though? We know he's dangerous and I have no doubt he's angry. My warden practically told me to disappear now I'm out. Inside, they can keep an eye on me, but I don't get any protection now I'm out. If he finds me, he will kill me. I know. What about you two? Are you staying in London? Are you going to be OK? Will you be safe? Will you be safe from him? Are you... are you going back to him? He is Lottie's father...' Louise's heart rate rocketed as she thought about this and all Carl might feel pushed to do, even from within the limitations that extra time in jail would have given him.

'Nooo. Oh no. Carl and I are done. He doesn't deserve me and he certainly doesn't deserve her.' She looked back to Lottie who was starting to stir in the car. When she turned back to Louise, the glow of love was shining on her face. 'No. We're leaving.'

'That's good. That's good,' Louise said, though her heart was breaking. So this was it then. This was goodbye. At least she got to say goodbye.

'We've moving to stay with my mum for a while. That's why we're here actually. I thought, once we'd left, you'd not know how to find us. That's the point. We need not to be found. Mum's moved. I don't even know where to. We're meeting at a specific place at a specific time and she will take us to where she is. Carl won't find us. He doesn't know anyone who will know where we are. He never bothered with my family. It used to annoy me, but now it's finally worked in my favour.'

Louise felt herself shutting down. She couldn't bring herself to talk.

Isabelle waited for Louise to speak and when she didn't, she continued. 'You'd not be able to find us. And then... then I thought that once you were out of here, I'd not know where to find you. I mean, I presume you won't go back to your old flat. Cos, well, Carl knows where it is. So. So we might not have ever seen each other again. Ever.'

Louise chewed her lip. Her knees were starting to shake. This was harder than she could have imagined.

'We'd not ever see you again,' Isabelle repeated. 'And I felt panic. Utter panic. You'd... sacrificed yourself for us. I mean, yes, you lied, but then you threw yourself under a bus for us. For me and Lottie. To tell us the truth. The police told me that you'd asked to be able to see me before they locked you up, that you wanted to tell me everything to my face. To make me understand. And then you tried in court. And I didn't let you.'

Louise drew in a breath.

'I'm still angry, but I am trying to understand.'

'I'm sorry,' was all Louise could muster.

'We're leaving. As soon as we can. Here's our van and I'm all packed at the house we're in. Just got to put the little stuff we need in the van and go. I sold the London house. Carl put it in my name, I thought for generosity, but I suspect now for fraud reasons. But the police can't trace it apparently, so it's mine. I've got the money, it'll keep us going for a while.'

'That's good.'

'So...' Isabelle paused, biting her tongue.

Louise closed her eyes, not wanting to look at Isabelle as she said goodbye.

'Are you coming?'

Louise snapped her eyes open. 'What?'

'Are you coming? Are you going to come with us? Do you have a plan or...'

'I don't have a plan, no,' Louise said, shell-shocked. 'Other than my mate's idea, which was to move to Italy and be a street florist!' Louise laughed at how ridiculous that sounded.

'Why not?' Isabelle was sincere. 'We could work that into a plan.' She shrugged.

Louise looked at her, confused, before realising that she meant it. Isabelle really meant it. She was letting her back in.

'You, you mean it?' Louise said, scared to ask but sure that she had to be clear on what was being offered. Terrified that Isabelle was playing with her.

'Yes. I mean it. We were a good, "weird" family as you said. Lottie adores you. She hasn't stopped asking where you are. Every day, every single day. "Where is Loo? When is Loo coming home?" We can be a good, weird family again. I just needed to see you face to face, to know if I could trust you. I know now that I can. You said that you lied to me all the time before but I don't think so. I think you showed me who you really are. You're good, Louise, you just need to believe it.'

Louise burst into tears and ran to Isabelle who wrapped her in a tight embrace.

'You're good, I know it. I will make you believe it,' Isabelle said again.

Louise let herself relax and realised that she had not done so since that day when she had worked out what it was that she had to do.

Now she was free.

EPILOGUE

Louise sat in the driving seat, parked up overlooking the port and the sea behind it, watching as the sun rose over the water. The early morning light was dancing over the waves as they lapped towards the boats nestled at the shoreline. Just on land were the multi-coloured sand-toned houses that Louise had only ever seen in photos. The combination of the orangey-yellow sun, the azure-coloured sea and the rainbow of houses made Louise's heart soar. Never in a million years would she have imagined that she would be here, looking at such a wonderful scene with her own eyes.

Even so early in the morning, dawn barely having broken, the port was busy with people bustling onto vessels, boats and their inhabitants waking up to sail across the sea to Corsica and onwards, all around the Mediterranean. Louise wondered how many millionaires were waking up to the same sight as her and she felt lucky. So lucky. She felt lighter than she could ever remember being.

Tired from driving overnight, she stretched her arms and rubbed her gritty-feeling eyes. The past few months had been an exhausting whirlwind. Outside the prison, once she and Isabelle had stopped crying on each other, they wiped their tears and got into the van. The closing doors woke up Lottie, who had been napping after such a long drive, and who was beyond excited to see who their passenger was.

'Loo!!!!!' she had yelled and immediately demanded to be released from her seatbelt and when she had been, ignoring her mother's cries to be calm, had thrown herself into Louise's arms. Louise breathed her in and held her close. So happy to have her back, having been so convinced that she had lost her forever.

'Lottie love. I've missed you,' she said as she kissed the top of her head. 'I'm sorry I went away.'

'Mum said you'd been bad.'

Louise nodded. 'Yes. I lied. And I took things that weren't mine.'

'That is bad,' Lottie said, a serious expression on her face.

'It is. But I owned up, I said sorry and I did my time. I know not to do it again. It hurt people and I don't want to hurt people,' she said, aware of the truths that we tell children often turn out to be truer than we imagine.

'You're back now? You won't go again?' Lottie asked, looking fearful.

'I won't. I'm here for good.' Louise smiled.

'We're going on an adventure! Mum said! To go see Granny and sunshine and the seeeeeea!'

'We are.'

'You're coming too?!' Lottie looked as though she would explode with happiness.

Louise looked at Isabelle, not wanting to speak in case she had misunderstood.

'She is coming too, lovey. We're all going on an adventure together!'

And it had been an adventure. They had found somewhere to be while Louise was still on licence. Her probation office had been happy with the fixed address and with her being back in touch with

Isabelle. And then, as soon as Louise was free to leave the country, they had loaded the new mini van with the little that they needed, Lottie insisting on every soft toy that now surrounded her as she slept soundly in the back. They had driven to the coast and through the tunnel under the sea to Calais. Lottie had been in awe that they were under the sea, though disappointed that you couldn't see the fish. She had still insisted that she could be a mermaid though, just one in a van.

They had driven through France and over the Alps into Italy. Isabelle had said it felt like being a Von Trapp, after all they were running away from Carl. She had meant it to be funny but it hammered home that they were on the run. Yet Louise could feel nothing but gratitude. She was here, with Isabelle, with Lottie and they were safe. She looked at Isabelle, bedraggled from two nights sleeping in the van without a proper bathroom, and to Lottie, innocent of all they were running from. She'd never really known Carl and Isabelle had said she would explain it all when she was older. For now, what she knew was that she was loved and safe and that was what mattered.

Louise knew that they would be looking over their shoulders forever, hoping that Carl would leave them be. They may never be able to stay in any one place for too long but Louise knew that wherever they were together it would be all right.

They would be home.

ACKNOWLEDGMENTS

There is always such a long list of people to thank for getting a book out into the world, onto bookshelves and into people's hands and minds and I am grateful for each and every person.

Thank you for the practical, emotional and creative support from my amazing agent, Marianne Gunn O'Connor, who is nothing short of wonderful. To my brilliant editors, Tara Loder and Emily Yau, who helped me shape *The Silent Friend* from the initial draft into the final book, working as part of a team with you both is always a joy.

To the brilliant team at Boldwood, who couldn't be more supportive and to my fellow Boldwood writers who are a cheer-leading team in itself, thank you for welcoming me into the Boldwood family.

To my copy editor, Sandra Ferguson, and my proof reader, Rose Fox, thank you for finding all my errors,-one day I hope not to make any but apparently not this time! To Aaron Munday for the fantastic cover. I don't know how you do it but I'm glad that you do!

The book was inspired by the lyrics of the song *Winter* by Tori Amos. I have been a huge fan since I was a teenager and regularly listen to your music for a creative boost-thank you.

To Neil Lancaster, who talked through the legal complexities of the plot with me to ensure plausibility, thank you.

To my fellow 2023 debutantes, who have been therapists, marketeers, reviewers and friends, thank you for being so kind and talented and I am loving watching your books fly!

To my writer friends, who have helped to bring the niggle of an idea to a fully formed book with plot wrangling and the reading of early drafts, Julia Laite, Gytha Lodge, Laura Morley, thank you for making the process so much fun!

To Book Twitter and wonderful book bloggers, it is fantastic to be part of a brilliant community of people who love books as much as I do!

The support from my Cambridge Literary Festival colleagues and the CLF team in general has been fantastic, from encouragement to advice and general wonderfulness. Thank you.

To the brilliant booksellers in my local bookshops-I appreciate your support. Having my books in your shops means the world to me so thank you, in particular to David Robinson, Sarah Whyley and the wonderful booksellers at Heffers, Cambridge.

This book is about the power of friendship and I have certainly felt that during its writing. I am incredibly lucky to have the best friends in the world, and to those who have been excited with me, nervous with me and celebrated with me, thank you. In particular, Michelle Perrott, Heather Bell, Mark Wood, Clare Cordell and the Wonder Women. There are more of you but I feel that the musicians are starting to play the get off the stage music...

To my parents, my family both here and in Australia, thank you for listening to all the highs and lows and excitement and nerves and always making me feel like a real writer. Your support is everything.

To the readers who make the whole enterprise worth it, with your feedback and positive words, thank you for trusting me with your time. I appreciate it more than I can say.

And finally, as always, to Beatrice, Madeleine and Malcolm. I couldn't do this without you, thank you for being here with me. x

MORE FROM ALISON STOCKHAM

We hope you enjoyed reading *The Silent Friend*. If you did, please leave a review.

If you'd like to gift a copy, this book is also available as an ebook, large print, hardback, digital audio download and audiobook CD.

Sign up to Alison Stockham's mailing list for news, competitions and updates on future books.

https://bit.ly/AlisonStockhamNews

The Cuckoo Sister, another totally absorbing psychological thriller by Alison Stockham, is available to buy now...

You want the best for your sister...
But what if she wants your children?
THE CUCKOO SISTER
ALISON STOCKHAM

ABOUT THE AUTHOR

Alison Stockham has worked in TV documentary production for the BBC and Channel 4, and is now the Events Coordinator for the Cambridge Literary Festival. Her debut novel The Cuckoo Sister, was longlisted for the 2020 Lucy Cavendish Fiction Prize.

Follow Alison on social media:

twitter.com/AlisonStockham
instagram.com/astockhamauthor
facebook.com/AlisonStockham-Author

THE *Murder* LIST

THE MURDER LIST IS A NEWSLETTER DEDICATED TO SPINE-CHILLING FICTION AND GRIPPING PAGE-TURNERS!

SIGN UP TO MAKE SURE YOU'RE ON OUR HIT LIST FOR EXCLUSIVE DEALS, AUTHOR CONTENT, AND COMPETITIONS.

SIGN UP TO OUR NEWSLETTER

BIT.LY/THEMURDERLISTNEWS

Boldwood

Boldwood Books is an award-winning fiction publishing company seeking out the best stories from around the world.

Find out more at www.boldwoodbooks.com

Join our reader community for brilliant books, competitions and offers!

Follow us
@BoldwoodBooks
@BookandTonic

Sign up to our weekly deals newsletter

https://bit.ly/BoldwoodBNewsletter

Ingram Content Group UK Ltd.
Milton Keynes UK
UKHW041846110723
424908UK00003B/81